Grab

Bag

2

FOR LITERARY HEAT

www.barbarianspy.com

This book is copyright © habu 2013
Published by BarbarianSpy in 2013
Cover design © S Bush 2013
Cover image: © Wrangel | Dreamstime.com
ISBN paperback: 978-1-922187-26-0
All rights reserved

Published by BarbarianSpy
Jindalee St
Toronto, NSW 2283
AUSTRALIA

Grab Bag

2

by

habu

Table of Contents

Introduction

    Grab Bag 2 follows along behind habu's Grab Bag 1 story collection as a gay male anthology that is totally unstructured other than the twenty-one stories in the collection being offered in the order written. It also follows no coordinating theme other than the stories being designed to evoke arousal and the pleasant surprise of some new gay-male twists to some classic plotlines.

    The inspiration for the locales, characters, and themes of habu's stories are complex and varied: they flow from his travels; his early careers; flashes of arousing images and circumstances emerging in that early-morning state between sleep and full awareness; his search in writing for ultimate satisfaction in male-to-male encounters; and experiences, observations, and "cautionary" tales that burble up into his memory from the past during conversations with friends and past—and current—lovers. As has become the hallmark of habu, this is a collection of tales (and tails) that are guaranteed to excite and stimulate—not just the mind. A true grab bag of surprises and pleasures that are sure to be savored more than once.

    It took no more than the flash of an image while habu was picking someone up for a day trip out of town—a predawn runner seen passing a lit-up house on a quiet, wealthy residential street with the jarring incongruity of a beat-up old red Ford pickup parked in front of the house—to conjure up the first story in this anthology, "The Second Man." The "out-of-place" presence of the pickup truck gave habu an ominous twinge, and his imagination turned this into a story of the dangers of running alone at that time of the morning.

The "Swift Sword of Justice" story idea came to habu as he was visiting Natchez, Mississippi, and remarking on the wide discrepancy between the gingerbread plantation houses on the edge of the town and the much deteriorating downtown area. As he passed the police station, he saw a young man dressed in worn clothes leaning into the window of a big, black Lincoln Town Car and talking with a snappy-dressed middle-aged man. Out of those combined images emerged a story of power, privilege, and corruption played upon the less fortunate.

While living in Bangkok, habu encountered the fetish of double penetration, or DP, and it was while he was living there for the first time, that an Indian doctor expertly initiated him into the pleasures one man could have from another. The story "Double Trouble," a story of a young man bought from a bordello in Mumbai, India, by a wealthy businessman to service a Belgian client in Bangkok who shared a fetish for DP, was written to capture the essence of this Bangkok period.

As far as habu can remember, the short "stroker" "After the Game," providing a no-plot sex scene in a football locker room, was written immediately after he'd viewed a Jeremy Hall video, although neither the characters nor the plotline relate to the film—only the use of a sports locker room and the sense of arousal immediately and totally satisfied.

The story "The Bonus," about a businessman taking a work bonus he hasn't told his wife about to finance a gay male vacation to Key West was extracted from habu's encounter with just such a businessman in a Key West bar. The businessman was quite open about renting a Jaguar convertible in Key West rather than the usual Mustang convertible (once it was Sebring convertibles that were seen everywhere in Key West) to enhance his cruising capabilities. Habu took a ride in his Jaguar. Key West is a favorite "hair letting down" locale of habu's (and apparently many more randy young men), so it features frequently in his memories and his stories. The club basement playpen, The Pile, mentioned in this story is a favorite group-grope device of habu's, which is more fully described in one or two of his other stories. He experienced and enjoyed The Pile in a club, but not a club in Key West. Nonetheless, it's featured in a few of his Key West stories. Both The Pile and a Jaguar in Key West will pop up in another story in this anthology.

Habu conceived the story "Coaching Change," about the lengths a pro tennis player will go to land a good coach, while hunkering under the Fitzgerald tennis stadium stands and waiting for a rainstorm to pass at the Legg-Mason tennis tournament in Washington, D.C., at the most recent men's final he attended.

"Made to Fit" is an unusual story for habu. He doesn't write much horror or Sci-Fi, but he does have a fetish for hugely endowed men and a wish that the stories in this anthology range widely. Although just a bit nasty, this story of experimentation with "the fit" in some future century allowed him to feed that fetish.

A week on a writing retreat, at a house at the top of the Blue Ridge Mountains, with the Appalachian Trail in its front yard, to wrap up a mainstream novel also resulted in the short story, "Appalachian Trail," about a writer on retreat bringing home a hiker met on the trail for some mountaintop fun and games.

"Trawler Initiation" is a short ditty habu whipped up after his lover showed him photographs of scantily clad seamen from a stint on a fishing trawler where, isolated at sea, senior trawler hands were in a position to initiate newer deckhands.

A discussion of people's favorite guitarists surfaced memories in habu of a Cypriot classical guitarist who briefly was a lover of his when habu lived on the island. Habu's particular liking of young Cypriot men—Greeks almost, but not quite, as much as Turks, led him to a hedonist lifestyle on Cyprus that was only rivaled by the years he spent in free-for-all Bangkok. "Guitar Me" is the result of reminiscing about habu's guitarist lover. Both Cyprus and the Tree of Idleness restaurant crop up occasionally in habu's stories and books—he even coauthored a book with that name—and it indeed is a favorite restaurant of his—in both Turkish and Greek versions, both located where he places them in his stories.

Beyond having recently, before writing "Bound to Bait," priced a vacation to the Lake Como region of Italy, there was no strong inspiration for habu's story of a pair of hustlers using twink sex in striking business deals in Europe and Africa. Habu wanted to do a story with a twist about bondage and blackmail, and the plotline and hook of this story popped in his head while he was sleeping one night. Many of his stories are just basically "there" when he wakes up in the morning.

Habu likes to include one or two sports locker room stories in his anthologies, because, like the videos with the same theme, they have an attentive audience, especially among the "stroker" set. Some of his sports stories, like the earlier "After the Game," are primarily strokers. "Doing College," like "Coaching Change," adds a theme and a fuller plotline. In this story, the protagonist, Stud, wants to be on the college football team first string, but his football skills don't quite make the grade. So, he has to find other ways to make the grade.

Habu's "Free Pottery" was inspired by a house guest who asked about the wall of shelves in his den housing art pottery. Some of it is from Japan, Korea, and Thailand—and a bit is inherited American antique pottery—but most of it is from a small pottery on the northern Cypriot coast between Kyrenia and Karavas. The guest reminded habu of how he had acquired so much of the Cypriot pottery, and as habu quite openly has a fetish about young Turkish men, and because the pottery near Kyrenia was owned by a randy Turkish man and his equally randy twin sons when habu lived on Cyprus, this story just sort of flowed out of habu's memory. The gay-friendly beach cottages described in the story are above Kyrenia on the way to Bellapais, a favorite story scene of habu's. As habu had a rented house in Bellapais, though, he never was checked into one of those cottages (although he admits he slept there more than once). Habu still uses the half-glazed coffee mug he describes in the story.

The tongue-in-cheek story, "Hey, Good Buddy," of Yellowstone Park rangers accosting a young man caught relieving himself in a stream, was written for an Earth Day story contest. Similarly, "Uh-Oh," a story mixing mixed up candy store orders with a flexibility fetish, was written for a winter holidays contest.

Erotica involving incest is both very popular and controversial. Habu doesn't write much in this genre and what he does write clearly depicts adults making adult decisions and something less than nuclear family relationships. But this being a wide-ranging anthology, he wanted to include a taste of what he does write on incest themes, most of which focuses on something other than the incestuous relationship and uses that more as a foil than a centerpiece. In "Uncle Carl," he includes both his research into a future trip to Italy with another story element he likes to use: the image of coupling that mirrors the artwork on the walls of the chamber. In the case of "Uncle Carl," it is photographs of young men's faces right after they have been masterfully taken.

Habu comes from an intelligence background, and spying is a frequent theme of his stories, as is working with an "everything is not as it seems" plot theme. "Nuclear Meltdown," which deals with the coaxing of a nuclear physicist to defect, is habu's spy story for this anthology.

A common theme for erotica is the loosening of a protagonist's inhibitions through hypnosis therapy. "Into the Dark" is such a story about happily married Brandon who has had trouble performing in bed because of a childhood trauma of being afraid of the dark.

The bittersweet story "Remembering Miles" was inspired by a family reunion habu went to where he encountered an ailing, older cousin. Earlier in life, habu had worshiped this cousin without realizing at that time that the worship was couched in physical desire and the sexual preferences that both were eventually to form—nor that the childhood attraction had been a mutual response. Although the bond was not consummated in a physical sense, the story tries to capture the "almost too late" emotional closure reached by the two cousins.

The wanting of gay male cruising can cause a man to toss all reason and thoughts of self-protection out of the window. Habu thinks that stories reflecting this are rather scarce. His

"The Compassionate Reporter" explores this concept with a well-meaning newspaper reporter.

One of the most scary "inevitabilities" for a young man desired by men is that one day he will grow older and less toned and will become a hunter rather than the hunted—if he stays in the hunt at all. While dreading when that day will come, many men fail to see it arrive and have at least one embarrassing moment of recognizing this inevitability. It is perhaps fitting that this anthology conclude with a story, "Back Where . . . ," that explores that moment of revelation.

Grab Bag 2 exhibits the breadth and depth of habu's overarching inspiration and his ability to always be exploring some new facet of locale, theme, character, or circumstance of being unapologetically gay, and attracting and seeking, in the real world—while often striving to bend that world into one more accommodating to the seekers' desires.

In this "bag" are twenty-one stories that adhere to no uniformity of theme in time, space, locale, or message and that have never been published anywhere before.

Enjoy!

The Second Man

I woke to a nudge at my side and a hand snaking over my waist and down my belly.

"I wanna. OK?"

Oh, Lord, I thought. This was why I didn't normally let them spend the night—even for an extra $25. They'd want it again. And they'd want it without paying for it. I guess letting them stay the night signaled to them that I wanted them to marry me.

"Frank," I murmured. "You used up what you paid for. You know the rules."

"I know you want it again. You know you want it again. Your dick don't lie."

My dick was trained to go full staff at a touch. This was how I made most of my money. But Frank wasn't all wrong. He was well built, not much into his forties, and kept fit in construction work. His cock wasn't phenomenal, but he knew what to do with it. And he was one of my regulars. Still, give it away for free once, and that's the end of getting paid for it.

"You're married, Frank. You gonna move in and pay my bills?"

"It's just a morning fuck, Danny. Just to get the day off right for both of us." He had his hands on my waist and turned me on my side, him wedged close in behind me. His cock was between my thighs, and he was already dry fucking me, with his cock head pushing against the base of my balls.

I was weakening. Maybe if I just let him get off this way, it would be OK. It felt good having his strong arms wrapped around me.

"I'll be good to you. You know I will. You can't get it any better than me."

That snapped me back. When they started getting possessive like this, we'd gone too far over the edge. I pulled away from him and, with effort, got back onto my back. His mouth went to my cock and his fingers snaked under me and went to my hole.

"No freebies," I said, trying to make my voice stern and dominating. I knew if I was going to hold the line, I needed to keep the upper hand. He could take me if he wanted to. I'm sure we both knew that. "You want another fuck, it will be another $50."

"How about $25? We're already here; it's not something completely new. It's just an extension?"

"Thirty," I said with a sigh. The one thing I knew for sure was that I wasn't going to let him spend the night again. He'd said his wife was visiting her mother and he'd told her he'd work the night shift then at the construction site. He had whined that he couldn't sleep alone. He'd been such a big teddy bear about it.

I didn't know for sure until later, after he was gone, that he'd even heard my counteroffer. In the end it was just a game, though, because when he left, he left $125 on the dresser. Regardless, before we could haggle more, he'd rolled onto his back and, in the same motion, had lifted me, facing away from him, with strong hands at both sides of my waist and had my channel wedged on the glans of his hard cock.

It was unfair; he knew I liked it this way.

"Frank. Oh, Frank!" I cried out, as my channel slid down on his cock. He encased my chest with one arm, latching onto one of my nipples with a thumb and finger; reached for my cock with his other fist; and bent his knees, digging his heels into the mattress to leverage off of while he got deep penetration with my butt wedged into his lap.

"Oh, god, Frank, oh, god!" I wrapped my legs around his bent ones and hooked the tops of my feet under his ankles—trying for all of the penetration of his cock that I could get. I locked my wrists around the back of his neck and we kissed until he nudged my torso to one side so that, with my arms still raised, he could bury his nose and mouth into one of my pits.

I groaned, knowing why I'd let him stay the night. He had some of the most arousing ways of fucking a man. And he was all man. Hard, solid, muscle—the experience of an older guy and the stamina of a much younger man.

* * * *

Frank was gone and it was still dark outside my apartment window. I had to do my run. I groaned and turned over, fully fucked and wanting to do nothing more than go back to sleep. But I had to be at the advertising agency at 9:00 a.m., and if I passed on the run this morning, the next thing I knew was that I'd be passing on it occasionally—and then often.

I rolled out of bed, smiled at seeing how much Frank had left on the dresser, opened the dresser drawer, and took out a jock strap and a pair of running shorts.

I stopped in the kitchen only long enough to eat an energy bar and drink several swallows of milk from a carton from the refrigerator and then I was off down the stairs, across the parking lot, and plunging into the trees on the path that led to the nature trail that wound itself through town.

It was still dark, but dawn was less than an hour away and I wanted to get the run in and be back in the shower before the sun came up.

I didn't stay on the main trail. There was a place where a small path veered off and over a wooden footbridge over a creek and then the railroad tracks and into a wooded subdivision, where the houses were pretty snazzy and set on large lots. By going down one street here, I could hook up to another trail running through this subdivision that was more private. These well-heeled folks didn't get up with the rest of us.

I was surprised, though, when I passed one French Provincial rambler, where there was a light on inside and a vehicle, an old Ford pickup, in the driveway. I hadn't ever remembered having seen a light on it this house this early, and the Ford pickup was completely out of character with the neighborhood. Thinking about it, I couldn't remember seeing any car parked there for weeks.

These were just observations that skidded across my mind as I loped down the street, my eyes concentrating on where there'd be a small break in the trees between two lots that would mark the woodland trail I sought.

Not long after passing the driveway of the French Provincial house, I sensed—and could hear—that I wasn't alone. I turned my head to see that there was another runner in my wake now. This was unusual; I'd never picked up a runner on the mornings I'd used this trail.

He looked all right, though. A big, blond crew cut, well-muscled guy. A good six inches taller than I was, and he had me by a good fifty pounds. A strongly chiseled face, with a prize fighter's bent nose. Maybe a soldier returned from Iraq. He looked too much like a gym guy and too young to live in this neighborhood. But he was running easy, obviously enjoying not having to do it alone.

I thought maybe he'd keep on down the street when I veered off on the woodland trail, but he didn't. He turned with me. He stayed behind me, but I could feel him close.

I didn't even think of the possibility of any personal danger, regardless of how strange it was to have someone running with me. If I had, I must assume I wouldn't have taken the woodland trail. In hindsight I wondered what I was thinking—or not thinking.

Thus, I was completely taken by surprise when, as we reached a small clearing with a picnic table in it, I felt my arm being gripped, and my body was snapped around and slammed down on my back on the picnic table.

The wind was knocked out of me, and what was happening was such a surprise, that before I could do or say

16

anything—or react in any way—he was crouched close over me, breathing heavily, and had a hand stuffed down the front of my running shorts and wrapped around my balls.

"Get off me!" I then mustered enough energy to cry out. "What? Oh, God!" I melted into pain and my eyes began to water as he crushed my balls in his fist.

"Shut up!" he commanded. "I've seen you go into Chester's, haven't I?"

The pressure was released long enough for me to whimper a "Yes." Chester's was a gay bar not far from my apartment. It was where I hooked up with most of the men who paid me for sex.

"Fuckin' queer," the guy muttered. Then I lost interest in anything other than the pressure on my balls and what he now was doing with his other hand, which was grabbing my throat and squeezing so that he had me seeing stars and blacking out.

When I came to, I was on my belly on the table, with my hands tied over my head, attached to something underneath the table I couldn't figure out. I could see my running shoes on the ground, without their laces, so I could figure out easily enough what he'd used to tie my wrists. I figured I could get out of those restraints fast enough if the big guy wasn't there, but he *was* there, with his mouth on my dick, which he'd pulled back through my legs.

His mouth went to my channel, and then I heard him curse. "Somebody's already been up here today, hasn't he?"

I didn't answer, upon which he put a fist in my hair and arched my back toward him. He put his lips next to my ear and whispered, menacingly, "Hasn't he?"

"Yes," I moaned.

"Fuckin' queer. Tell me, did he have one this big?"

I yelped as he thrust his cock inside my channel. He was as big and thick as I'd ever had.

"No. Oh, god no."

The next several minutes were taken up with his grunts and groans in taking me in a deep pistoning action and my moans and cries at being taken so brutally and fully. He had his hands around my throat again—and again I blacked out.

17

When I recovered, I was no long tied and he was dragging me into the underbrush beyond the rim of the clearing. He found a mossy area under a tree and dropped me onto my back and knelt down between my spread legs and thrust his cock inside me again.

This time—I don't know if it was the instinct to survive or the want for what he was giving me—I wrapped my arms around his neck and my legs around his hips and gave him nipple play with my mouth as I counterthrust against him, taking him deep, and using my channel muscles to give him a ride he wouldn't soon forget. I moaned for him and whispered to him how good he was being to me—using everything I'd learned to please a man and make him want me. Wanting him to believe that I'd given in to him willingly; trying to calm him down and to be satisfied enough not to hurt me any more than was necessary.

He seemed to enjoy it immensely—and I wasn't exactly unhappy with it either once I'd decided to stop resisting him.

When he came—which was after me—he knelt up, away from me, and looked down and smiled at me through his heavy breathing.

"That was good for you, wasn't it?" he said—almost with a sense of wonder in his voice.

"The best," I murmured. "Fuck me again." I tried to keep my voice from showing how badly I was trembling—not just out of fear but also because it had been one of the best fucks I'd ever had. But there was also the fear that he wouldn't let me leave here alive. I certainly was trying to work his vanity and calm his anger by telling him I wanted it again. But if he'd knelt back down into the moss, I would have gladly opened my legs to him again. If he'd laid on his back, I would have happily mounted him and ridden his cock again under my own power.

He gave me the strangest look then, and stood and muttered. "I'll be back."

And then he was gone.

* * * *

I was out running the next day before dawn too. I had already decided that I would stick to the main nature trail, but

18

when I came to the small path leading off across the brook and railroad tracks, my feet turned in that direction under their own power.

I didn't even think about why I was doing it—what I wanted to happen. I just ran my own route, like an automaton.

This day was as unusual as the previous one, though—in a different way. As I came up level with the French Provincial house that had had the light on the previous day, I saw today that it was lit up like a Christmas tree and that there was an ambulance and a police car in the drive.

I put my head down and ran right on by, although my mind was going lickety-split on possibilities of what was happening at that house in the predawn hours.

So engrossed with that was I that, although I heard the engine start up, I only half realized that I was passing a dark sedan parked across the street from the house.

It didn't take me long, though, to realize that the car was riding beside me, keeping pace with me. I turned, and a lone man driving the car rolled down his window and said, "Hold on for a few minutes. I'd like to talk to you."

This had happened to me before—even when I was out running. It's one reason I ran at this time of the morning now and took this route. If I ran on the other side of the apartment complex and during the day, I'd be stopped every few minutes by men who wanted a blow job or a quickie fuck.

I walked over to the side of the car.

"Can I help you with something."

"Maybe. Just a few questions. Come on around and sit in the car with me for a few minutes."

"Won't get in the car without some up-front money," I said. "BJ's go for $25, me do you, or $20, you do me. Anything beyond that is $50, assuming I want to do what you want me to do."

The man gave me a hard look. He wasn't all that hard to look at. Maybe a bit on the chunky side, but it looked like it was mostly muscle. Pushing forty hard, or maybe a bit older. Craggy-looking face, but not bad looking. A crew cut, but dark, not blond like the guy yesterday. Remembering the guy yesterday made me shudder, and I almost just pulled away from the car

19

and went back to running. I never really was comfortable getting into a guy's car.

He must have seen that I was about ready to brush him off, because he suddenly had his wallet out and was producing a $50 bill. "Here. OK? Come around and sit with me for a couple of minutes. Just some information."

"Sure," I said, but I couldn't help myself from making it sound a bit sarcastic. He didn't pull the bill away when I reached for it, though, so I walked around to the passenger side of the car and got in. He pulled right over to the curb, which surprised me. I thought we'd be driving to someplace more private.

"Here? We're gonna do it here?" I asked.

"Just talk. That's what I said," he answered. And then he launched right into talk. "Do you run here at this time every morning."

"Most mornings, when the weather permits, yes."

"Did you run here yesterday?"

"Yes," I said. I suddenly was thinking vice cop. I realized I'd half thought "cop" the moment I'd seen him.

"Notice anything back around that one-story house yesterday?"

"No, not really."

"Nothing at all unusual?"

"Well, now that I think about it, there was a light on inside, which I found surprising for this time of day. I don't remember that happening before. And there was a truck in the driveway that seemed out of place."

"A truck?"

"Yeah, an old beat-up Ford pickup. That's not the kind of car the folks in this neighborhood drive."

"I know it was dark, but could you tell the color?"

"Yeah, that was part of it being out of place. It was red. Fire-engine red. Again, a little flashy for this neighborhood."

"Well, could you look at these photos and tell me if you saw any of these guys around here yesterday."

The guy who had furious-fucked me was in the middle photo. I pretended I didn't know any of them. I had no wish to be caught up in a vice sting if I could afford it.

"Nope, sorry, I don't recognize any of these guys."

"You sure? You hesitated over one of them. I could tell."

"Yeah, I'm sure. They do something wrong?"

"That's helpful. The truck. Thanks, that's all the information I need. Have a good run."

I wasn't sure what to do next; just open the door and walk away? Would he let me get three yards before busting me for solicitation?

"That's it? That's all?"

"Yes, thanks, you've been very helpful."

"So, I guess you want the fifty back . . . ?"

"Keep it. Keep it on tab, if you want. It's not that I'm not interested. But we're pretty busy. As I said, have a good run." Then, as I was getting out of the car, he said. "Warren Copely."

"Excuse me?"

"His name's Warren Copely. The guy in the center picture. The one you did a double take over. If I'm right, you'll want to stay very clear of him. Just a friendly piece of advice."

I stood on the pavement, dazed, holding the fifty, while he did a U-turn and headed back to the house with the ambulance and police car in the driveway.

* * * *

It was a week to the day that the guy—Warren Copely, I'd been told—had assaulted me in the park. And I was out, running again, in the same park. I still hadn't resolved what I wanted. But above all else, I didn't want my life limited by where I could and could not go.

And then there was the fucking Copely had given me. Yes, it was rough. But it brought me to heights I'd never gone to before. That was what was wrong with this selling of my body. With each paid fuck, I was becoming less sensitive to arousal, more needing to control myself, to pretend. With Copely it had been pure animal. He'd surprised me, and he'd handled me—took all control out of my hands. For some reason I found that arousing—and liberating. And the size of him. Overuse was making me slack. He filled me to where I knew I was being

21

fucked. Even the choking was exhilarating. The lack of oxygen gave me a rush, hardened and lengthened me, made me gush.

All of these thoughts were going through my brain as my feet took me on the path across the brook and railroad tracks even though each and every morning for the last week, I had resolved that I would stay to the main nature trail.

He popped out from behind a tree as I entered the narrow woodland trail. I saw him in my peripheral vision. He was wild eyed, grinning. He reached out for me as I passed him, but I struggled away and began to run in earnest.

Another dozen yards and I veered off the path and started crashing through the underbrush.

I was panting, and so was he. His panting was getting nearer and nearer. It was like we were in a jungle and he was a lion bringing me to ground. He leaped onto my back as he caught up with me, sending us both crashing into a bed of ferns.

He flipped me and backhanded me twice, once in each direction across the cheeks. Still I tried to struggle up from him, tried to break away. He made a fist and reared back and socked me in the cheek, under my eye. My head snapped back and I sprawled back on the ground, surprised and in pain. Dazed. This couldn't be happening. I'd made the sex good for him. I'd give him good sex. he didn't have to do this.

I lay there whimpering, totally cowed. He was straddling me, knees on either side of my waist, me putting up zero resistance. He pulled my head up with a fist in my hair and backhanded me again with his hand. Then, as I just fell back into the ferns, he went up in a crouch beside me and jerked off my running shorts and jock strap.

He stood over me and removed his own shorts and jock. He was hung like a horse. Even in half erection he had the biggest equipment I can remember ever seeing.

He came down again with knees straddling my chest and grabbed my head by the hair and pounded in up and down on the ground a couple of times.

Why was he doing this? I wasn't putting up any resistance. I could show him a good time—I had already shown him a good time.

I gagged as he forced his cock beyond my lips and face fucked me. He was saying something, but, with the ringing in my ears from the beating, I could barely . . . just barely make it out.

"I said I'd be back for you. The second man."

His knees pushed up under my buttocks and his cock pushed inside me. He bottomed and then started fucking me hard and deep. I was too far gone to go with the fuck—to do any of those things I'd done before to give him pleasure and to want have me going with him. I just lay there, moaning and whimpering at his full, cruel possession of my channel. His hand went to my throat, and I was fighting for breath and consciousness.

When he came, he let out a victory yodel.

That, undoubtedly, was what saved me.

The next thing I knew, we were surrounded by blue uniforms, and Copely was being pulled away from me and being dragged off.

The guy who had been in the dark sedan the other day was there, and he was pulling me up, and helping me put my running shorts back on. The waistband of the jock strap had been snapped in Copely's run to get it off me, so it was of no use.

The guy helped me over to the picnic table and had his handkerchief out, dabbing at the blood at the corners of my nose and mouth.

"I'm Detective Madison. Henry Madison. Sorry we didn't get to you sooner. If he hadn't pulled you off the trail—"

"Sorry. That was me," I said. "I left the trail. You from Vice?"

"No, Homicide."

I moaned at the recognition of what that meant.

"We had planned to take him before he did this to you. Sorry about that. If you'd ID'd him the other day . . . but your description of the truck helped us narrow it to Warren Copely."

"You've been watching for him?"

"Every day. Every day you were running. You were the second man. We figured he'd come back for you."

"The second man? That's what he said too . . . while . . . while he was taking me."

23

"That's was what linked the crimes. This guy had it out for homosexuals and targeted them. But, go figure, his way of punishing them was through sexual assault. So, you can figure what that said about him. Well, he had a pattern. He'd murder one man and then find a second man to have sex with."

"So, that first day, when the light was on in that house and the red truck was outside."

"Yes, we found the body of a young man inside. Copely killed him there. Those folks are on an around-the-world trip. The young guy was house sitting for them. Their neighbors called in the light being on and the truck in the driveway. It was gone by the time anyone responded, though."

"So, I was—"

"The second man that day, yes. I can understand you not telling me when I asked you about him. But if I'd known he'd attacked you that day, we would have been faster in pulling him off you today."

"And this second man?"

"On a subsequent day, the second man became the first man. That's what was happening today."

"Oh."

"Let's get you home now, if you live nearby."

"In the apartment complex across the railroad tracks beyond this development."

"Good. We'll get you cleaned up and when you feel like it, I can take your statement. We can see what we can put together that will keep you as much out of this as possible."

"You'd . . . you'd do that . . . for me?"

He went on, as if I hadn't spoken. "Then, when you felt well enough for it, we could see about working off that $50-tab I'm running with you."

Swift Sword of Justice

Judge Thomas Oakley slowed the car as he crossed Martin Luther Key Street on St. Catherine where it turned into Jefferson. He often slowed down here, in passing the King's Tavern Lounge—although he'd never gotten up the gumption to go in there. It was too close to home and he was too well known. When he wanted that scene, he didn't go anywhere here in Natchez. There were some private men's clubs up in Vicksburg where he could scratch that itch.

He wasn't slowing down outside the King's Tavern Lounge today to see what trade was out and prancing about but because he couldn't quite figure out where in town that boutique, Claire's, was that Peggy Ann had dropped hints about. He was at a total loss about what to get his wife for her birthday that was coming up in less than a week. There wasn't anything that he knew of that she might want that she didn't buy for herself—with a vengeance—holding over his head what she suspected and what had sent them into separate bedrooms five years earlier.

The judge was still a young man, though. He had needs. And he had preferences too. It wasn't really his fault that they were inconvenient preferences for a sleepy Southern town like Natchez, Mississippi.

He pulled the Lincoln Town Car over to the curb while he rummaged around in his wallet for an address for the Claire's place. He assumed they had a list for him of things Peggy Ann wanted—or else she wouldn't have wasted all that time dropping hints about the place to him.

It was a hot day, and the air conditioner in the Town Car needed Freon. It put out cold air well enough once it got going, but it took a long time to kick in, and he'd left the car out on the hot asphalt. So, he'd rolled the windows down when he'd started off for town.

"Anything I can do for you, mister?"

Judge Oakley looked up smartly, surprised at the interruption and by the smooth, insinuating voice. He looked over to the passenger side of the car and saw a young man, his elbows almost inside, and his head, with its mop of blond hair, filling the space where the open window was.

"Excuse me?"

"Anything you might want?" the young man repeated. He had a knowing smile plastered on his face.

How could he possibly know? Judge Oakley wondered. He'd never known them to come right out on the street and proposition someone just passing through. But then he realized that he wasn't really "just passing through." He'd pulled over to the curb right outside the tavern. And he had his window rolled down.

"No, of course not," he replied, his voice full of "what do you take me for?" huff.

"Nice lookin' car," the young man said. "And you look buff too," he added. He retained that smile, and the way he was hanging in the car, it seemed like he was going to take up residence.

"I . . . I . . . I just pulled over to get my bearings. I'm down here buying a birthday present for my wife." It was the

26

first thing he could think of—something defensive to put him in an entirely different world from his young man. This young man with his handsome, ready smile and that endearing mop of blond hair. And soft, milky blue eyes. He couldn't be more than nineteen.

"I thought you looked like, you know, you'd like some company," the young man persisted. "Look like you might want to buy a present for yourself. If there's anything you're interested in—"

Judge Oakley put a right fast end to that, though. He hit the passenger window button, and the young man barely had time to move out of the way of that and step back before Oakley pulled back out into traffic—to the sound of the horn of a woman in a car that had been on the road coming up behind him and had to slam on her brakes.

The judge dipped his head almost as if he feared she'd recognize him and get the wrong impression of what he was doing at the curb outside a gay bar with a fine-looking young man hanging in his window.

He muttered to himself as he drove on. He was shaking badly, upset by the encounter. But also aroused by it, his mind going lickety-split over the conversation that had transpired between him and the young man—and then racing on to the implications. Followed by the possibilities. It had been nearly two months since his court schedule had allowed him to travel up to Vicksburg.

In two more streets, he turned left and then left again on E. Franklin. He was driving on autopilot. Two more lefts and he found himself turning off of MLK onto Jefferson again. And driving slowly past the tavern a second time.

The blond smiled and waved to him.

Judge snapped his head away and applied pressure on the gas pedal. He was almost to the Mississippi River when he managed to pull over to the curb again to get control of his shakes. He took a handkerchief out of his pocket and mopped his brow. He sat there for a couple of minutes, thinking, and then he took out his cell phone and made a call to the police department down in Sibley, a small town to the south of

Natchez, where he was restoring an old plantation house on the Mississippi.

* * * *

The door on the Sibley police department—just a one-man operation, really—was locked when Judge Oakley arrived there later in the evening. That didn't stop him from getting in, though. He had a key. Judge Oakley was probably the most important person who had settled in Sibley since before the War of Northern Aggression, and he held the key to any business or government building he was interested in in the small, dying town.

And he'd made a point to make really, really good friends with the town's one policeman, Dooley Lumpkin. Part of how he had ingratiated himself so well with Dooley was that he usually took Dooley with him when he made his trips to Vicksburg.

It was this special relationship with Dooley that had prompted Judge Oakley to call him in Sibley rather than the Natchez city police.

Oakley looked up and down the sidewalk before letting himself in the jail's door. No one was out and about, though, which didn't surprise him a bit. He closed and locked the door behind him. And then he just followed the sounds.

He could hear Dooley grunting and another man moaning. They were in one of the only two cells in the room off the back of the office. The other cell was empty.

Judge Oakley stood there for several minutes, watching Dooley work on the young man—the young blond man who had asked Oakley if there was anything he wanted out in front of the King's Tavern Lounge in Natchez.

Dooley certainly had a way with that nightstick of his, the judge thought. Both of the men had their trousers and briefs off, and the young man was handcuffed to the bars above the cot in the cell by his wrists. He was laying on his back, with his legs splayed out, and Dooley was hunched over him and working the tip of the night stick at the rim of the young blond's asshole.

After a few minutes, when it looked like Dooley was going to change nightsticks, Judge Oakley cleared his throat.

Dooley jumped away from the young man and turned in a crouch, ready to spring. His eyes were those of a wild animal. When he saw it was the judge, though, he relaxed.

"Oh, it's you, judge. I didn't hear you come in."

"I can see why not," Judge Oakley said, followed by a low laugh. "Hate to interrupt you, but don't you think it would be good to keep this all in order? The trial first and then the punishment?"

"Um, sorry, Judge. Where do you want him?"

"I think we can do this out in your office," the judge answered.

"Uh, OK. I'll get him up and dressed and—"

"Oh, I don't think we need to set anything into reverse. Just bring him on into the other room."

The young man looked like a scared rabbit as he was dragged into the outer office. While Dooley was uncuffing him, the judge was going to the front of the room and pulling down the shades. Then he went and sat behind the desk.

Dooley pulled the prisoner to the front of the desk and made him stand there.

"What's your name, young man?" the judge asked.

"Bart. Bart Smith," the young man squeaked.

"You got a wallet from him, Dooley?"

"Yeah. Uhh, yes judge," he said as he saw Judge Oakley purse his lips. "That's the name on his driver's license. It's from Maryland."

"You're a long way from home, Mr. Smith. Visiting relatives in Natchez?"

"No, sir, just passing through," the young man murmured.

"How old are you, young man?"

"Uh. Nineteen."

Judge Oakley turned his eyes on Dooley, who smiled and nodded his head.

"Do you know what you're doing here, Mr. Smith?"

"Getting fucked," the young man said, and quite acidly too.

"That will be enough of that. This is a court of law, young man. You will have respect for the court."

"What in the shit—?"

The young man didn't get any more out than that, because Dooley backhanded him across the cheek. It wasn't enough to send the young man toppling, but it got his attention.

"You heard the judge. Respect."

"You are here on a charge of solicitation and vagrancy."

"I'm not homeless or nothing, and all I asked you was if you needed anything."

"I'll take that as an admission of guilt. I hereby find you guilty of solicitation and vagrancy. You have three options. Jail time—thirty days, here in this jail, under the supervision of Officer Lumpkin here. Or a $300 fine, or community service. Which is it to be?"

"I ain't got that much money. What would the community service be?"

"Twenty-four hours here, servicing Officer Lumpkin and me."

"Christ almighty, you could have had that back in—"

Another backhand across the face shut him up.

Judge Oakley took him first, back on the cot in the cell, Bart's wrists handcuffed above his head on the bars of the cell and Judge Oakley gripping his ankles and fucking him deep and slow.

Oakley was a relatively young, handsome man in good shape, and Bart went with the fuck, moving his pelvis with Oakley and making all of the noises of satisfaction that egged Oakley on.

Dooley's turn wasn't quite as welcome. There was that nightstick he wanted to use again and then the sounds he wanted to hear out of Bart were more on the pain than the pleasure side—and he worked hard at getting the sounds he wanted.

The judge and Officer Lumpkin played a game of checkers and killed off a couple of beers out in the front office while they were building up desire and need again, and then they had another round, much like the first, with Bart, who wasn't nearly as happy to see Oakley the second time as he had been the first. But he had agreed to the community service option, so the judge and policemen were feeling just fine about how justice was working out. The young man had been soliciting sex up there in Natchez.

Judge Oakley went home for his supper and a quiet evening alone with his wife while Dooley was setting up for a new round with Bart. There would be time for Oakley to come back to help Bart Smith some more with his community service the next afternoon. The sentence had been for twenty-four hours from the time of sentencing.

* * * *

Early the next afternoon, Judge Oakley was stopping in at Claire's boutique—finally having located where it was—before his drive south to Sibley, when Detective Grimes of the Natchez police opened the door and walked in. As he did so, two Natchez policemen stationed themselves outside on either side of the door.

"Judge Oakley?"

"Why good afternoon, Jack. What brings you in a place like this? Your wife drop hints about what she wants for her birthday too? We got a conspiracy going on in this town?"

"Not of that nature," the detective said. Then he cleared his throat. "I'm afraid I'm here to ask you to come over to the station."

"I've got kind of a busy schedule today, Jack. What do they need me over at the station for? Some warrants to sign or something? I could—"

"Umm, no, I'm sorry, but—"

"Here, let me do it." The voice was from another man altogether.

Judge Oakley looked around toward the door and his jaw dropped. There, standing inside the door, his police shield out, was . . . Bart Smith.

"I'm not Bart Smith and I'm not nineteen, and although I'm new around here, I'm not from Maryland," the young man was saying. "I'm from the Natchez vice squad, and, Thomas Oakley, I'm arresting you on the charges of assault and corruption. I wish to inform you that you have the right to . . ."

Double Trouble

I knew where this was going.

I was sitting in Kamrod Tikka's lap, both of us naked, me facing him, and with my heels resting on the headrests of the adjacent seats in his business jet high over India en route to Bangkok.

He already had his fat cock up inside me and I felt his hands go under my buttocks from each side, and my buttocks spread and a finger from each hand enter me as well. I was grabbing the headrest on both sides of his head for dear life to stay in place as his hands no longer were encircling my waist.

I moaned as a second finger from each hand penetrated me as well.

"You liked the copilot, didn't you?" he murmured to me. "I can have him back here in a minute. I know he'd like it."

"No, Kam, not now, please. Maybe someday, but . . . oh god, oh god!"

A third finger from each hand had entered me, and he had grasped his shaft with his fingers and was moving it back and forth inside me.

I panted and gasped . . . and came up his hard, dark belly in the rivulet of black, curly hair that descended from his chest into his pubes.

Kamrod wasn't done, though. He was only beginning. He had superb control. The fingers came out of my channel and he was grasping my buttocks and pulling them apart, and with the strength of his strong arm muscles, raising and lowering me on his shaft too, until, finally, as the jet started its descent into Bangkok and I nuzzled my face into the hollow of his neck and gasped and moaned, he gave me his seed in three prodigious jerky bursts.

I lay against him, panting, while he ran his hands up and down my back and went tumescent inside me. I whimpered for him, letting him know he had mastered me. I knew it was what he wanted. India putting America in its place.

I even asked him to do it again in a low whisper of longing, knowing there wasn't time before we landed, but also knowing it excited him to have that control over me and that well into his fifties, he could still have a twenty-two-year old blond beg for it from him. I felt him stiffening again at the thought, but then there was a ding, the red light went on over our bank of chairs, and he muttered with regret that I'd just have to wait—that we were descending into the Thai capital.

I took his face in my hands, kissed him, and wiggled my butt on his shrinking cock, as if I wouldn't listen to reason. And I knew that this excited him as well. I needed to keep him excited.

I knew he wanted to double me. He'd been building up to it for some time. But I had fended that off. I didn't know how much longer I could do that. If I truly didn't want to give in to it, I'd have to find another daddy. And it would be hard to find another man in Mumbai as hard bodied, hard cocked, and rich as the international entrepreneur, Kamrod Tikka. And not having my passport in my possession, Mumbai was pretty much my selection pool.

He had picked me up in a male bordello in Mumbai after I'd been there less than a weak, abandoned by the American businessman who had brought me there and suddenly decided he preferred dark-skinned Indian boys to American beach bum blonds.

I had gone with Kamrod willingly, because after a week in the bordello, and discovering that young blond men were in high demand in India, I didn't know if I could survive another week in that place. On the whole, I'd found Indian men small cocked, but they had some peculiar notions of what to do with their cocks. And the Western businessmen who visited the brothel wanted their money's worth and generally wanted rough sex that they didn't think they could get away with in their home environments.

Kamrod had been both the hunkiest and most refined of technique of the Indian men who had bought my time, and he took his time with me. I found the fingers plus cock routine he liked painful at first, but I'd been with him a full month now, and one night I'd even managed most of his hand buried and gripping and rotating his cock inside me. He took it slow and gave me plenty of time to adjust.

He was tall and burly for an Indian. A handsome face and an assured manner. He was dark skinned, telling me that he was from south India, where that was normal. And I liked the black, curly body hair he had on his forearms and thighs and cascading down from his Adam's apple to his cock.

His mouth was sweet and persistent on my cock, and he could play me for nearly an hour at a time, bringing me to the brink and then holding me off. Then suddenly entering my channel with three or four fingers and spreading them and making me cum in a flood as the pad of a thumb thumbed on my prostate. Sometimes that was the end, but more often, he'd move between my legs then, and I'd feel his thick cock entering me between the fingers and he'd work me for another eternity, showing that he knew how to control himself as well.

And, as I said, he took his time and made love to me with his voice as he fucked me. He had a mesmerizing tone to his voice and he could speak in the rhythm of the fuck.

I was never quite sure how long he would want me. He seemed the type who could keep in thrall a young man of his own choosing from his own business world and who didn't need to go to a brothel.

35

I actually saw that in the first week I was with him in his home. A young German man, who obviously didn't like Indians and who visibly pulled away from them and showed distaste at their touching manner, came—reluctantly, I'm sure—to Kamrod's house for a business meeting and no more than two hours later was coming on a toilet stool, his ankles on Kamrod's shoulders, and melting at the love Kamrod was making with his voice in the young man's ear and with his cock in the German's channel.

I asked, apprehensively, why he had brought me from the brothel—and then not just discarded me when he'd done all he wanted to do to me. He told me that he had heard about me from a colleague and that I was just the kind who turned him on. He also smiled and said he hadn't done everything he wanted to do with me yet, causing me to shudder as much from the way he'd said it as from the touch of the backs of his fingers gliding up the inside of my thighs.

He more than hinted that he liked threesomes and double penetrations, but I didn't hop on that suggestion. Increasingly, though, I figured I'd either have to show interest in that or find another way home from India.

I was in India illegally now. I had no papers. Whatever man I was with could pretty much do anything he wanted with me. I felt lucky that Kamrod, hunky, not too old—maybe early fifties—refined, and filthy rich was the man who had me.

When he said he had to go to Bangkok on business and he wanted me to go with him, there wasn't much I could—or wanted to—say other than yes. I started to mention the problem of leaving the country, but he produced my passport, which he somehow had managed to acquire.

He didn't give it to me, though, and I didn't ask him to.

We were booked at the Oriental Hotel, Bangkok's most prestigious hotel.

That night, in a tenth-floor suite, Kamrod was all about my needs rather than his. Although he was a good lover, everything we'd done before was because he wanted to do it. On this night, though, he wanted to know what I wanted. He said we could just sleep too, if that was my wish.

I would have liked the "just sleep" suggestion—Kamrod was quite virile and had fucked me at least once a day since he had, essentially, bought me from the bordello. But knowing his appetites, I didn't want to do anything that lessened his ardor for me.

So, I asked him to take me out onto the balcony overlooking the Chao Phya river, with the Wat Arun temple lit up across the water, and lay back on the chaise lounge out there, while I mounted him and fucked him slowly and gazed out over the exotic river scene, the water still alive with small long-tail boats even in the night.

He seemed pleased with my choice and came twice for me.

The next day, he was in meetings until the evening. I sat by the pool, where I got several propositions—from men and women alike. But it was nice not to have to say yes.

Except for a young, small Thai pool boy, who assured me that he was in his twenties and who I fucked down in a patch of bougainvillea near the river's edge, happy to be the top for once in a very long while, I politely turned aside all other offers.

Near sunset, Kamrod came back to the room and told me we'd be dressing formally for dinner and that we'd be eating with the Belgium businessman he had come to Bangkok to strike a deal with. I didn't ask what sort of businesses Kamrod was in—and he didn't tell me. I surmised there was more than one business, though, and I could tell they were lucrative.

As we were leaving our suite for the hotel's Le Normandie restaurant, Kamrod leaned in to me and said, "I believe I have the deal I wanted, but he has expressed an interest in you. I need for you to be pleasant to him—despite whatever impression he makes."

Of course, I thought. Why wouldn't I be pleasant? But then I met the man. Kamrod introduced him as Hugo Jaguerman. I would have thought that Pig would be a more fitting name.

He was a massive man, even bulkier than Kamrod. But I could tell by the way that he filled out his tux shirt that it was mostly muscle, not fat. His jacket must have been specially tailored for him to accommodate the girth of his upper arms.

His head, a pig's head, complete with snout, seemed to lay directly on his shoulders. What little I could see of his neck was as thick as his head.

He was bald, with folds of fat at the base of his neck, and his ears looked like those of a pig too. His eyes were small, buried in puffy cheeks, but as he squinted at me, I could see the same expression of lust that I'd seen in men's eyes most of my life.

He ate like a pig too, his eyes rarely leaving mine, as he chewed noisily on all of the artistically prepared dishes that were wasted on him.

He and Kamrod talked—although Jaguerman looked at me rather than Kamrod. But they spoke in French, which I didn't understand. I was disgusted with how the pig would stuff his mouth and then talk. He left the impression of a coarse man with huge appetites that were almost impossible to satiate. I shuddered at the thought of what I assumed I was there for.

Hearing French coming out of such a hoggish face was a surprise. But he was Belgian, so I suppose it was natural that he'd speak French. It was more of a surprise that Kamrod spoke it—and when he spoke it, it sounded like music. A little chill went up my spine at the thought of him speaking soft French in his mesmerizing voice while he fucked me.

When the coffee was served, Kamrod stood up from the table and walked away without a word to me, although he leaned down and spoke softly in Jaguerman's ear, which was answered by a leer.

And Kamrod didn't come back to the table.

"We go now," Jaguerman said in heavily accented English when he'd finished his coffee.

"Mr. Tikka?" I answered in a surprised voice.

"We will meet him at apartment."

I started to object, but a burly man in a black suit was at the side of our table. He had a chauffeur's hat tucked under his arm and seemed to be well known to Jaguerman. I got that he was Jaguerman's driver and that I indeed was going someplace with Jaguerman. The Belgian alone was muscle enough to manage that even if I didn't want to, but here in the best restaurant in Thailand, his bulky chauffeur made clear that I shouldn't make a scene.

I knew for sure now what Kamrod meant by being pleasant to the Belgian businessman. And I probably knew exactly why I'd been brought along for the jet ride. I would not be surprised to find out that the Belgian had specified what type of young man he wanted Kamrod to bring with him from Mumbai and that this was what prompted Kamrod to take me from the brothel.

The thought struck me that I would not be flying back to India with Kamrod. But this was quickly replaced with the fear that I would not be leaving wherever I was going now alive.

In the back of the Mercedes limousine, where I half assumed I would be thoroughly fucked, I wasn't.

I sat in the middle of the back seat, and Jaguerman, taking up much of the width of the seat, sat across from me and stared at me and picked at his teeth with a toothpick.

"Let me see it," he said in a low growl.

"See it? See what? Oh." He was motioning with his hands what he wanted to see.

I spread my legs and unzipped my trousers and fished my cock out.

I cupped my balls in the palm of my hand, and we sat there for several moments, Jaguerman picking his teeth with a toothpick with one hand, his legs now spread too, and his other hand holding himself through the fabric of his tux trousers.

I assumed this was the start of rough sex. But it wasn't.

"Enough," he said, and I folded my goods back into my trousers and zipped up. He kept his hand on his crotch, though, and it was obvious he was aroused.

We didn't have long to drive after that—to yet another high-rise building on the banks of the Chao Phya.

Jaguerman lived in the penthouse, which, although large, was surrounded on all four sides by terracing that dwarfed the apartment.

I held back a gasp when we entered the apartment and he flipped on the light switch.

The lounge room we entered, with an S-shaped sofa winding its way through the center of the room, lit up in a soft glow—but not from any lights overhead or on floors or tables. Instead, track lighting in the ceiling spotlighted onto paintings on the walls.

My almost gasp was caused by seeing that all of the paintings were male nudes—or, more precisely, male torsos. An impossibly muscled—almost cartoonish in its muscle definition—highly erotic torso and legs, bringing to mind that of a muscle-bound satyr.

"Sit on couch. You want drink?"

"Umm, yes," I answered. "A beer is fine, if you have it."

"Bottle or can?"

"A Bottle's fine, thanks."

He laughed. "You choose wisely. But, then again, maybe not."

On that strange note, he left the room and went into another one overlooking the terrace, which looked like it was a bar.

When he came back, he was swinging four bottles of beer—two in each hand—but I hardly noticed them, as shocked as I was.

He was naked. And what immediately dawned on me was that he obviously was the model for the paintings lit up on the walls. And the paintings no longer looked like exaggeration. His body was horrible and magnificent all in one sweeping impression. All of the muscles were where they should be, but they were almost grotesquely overbuilt. His waist was thick, but with plates of muscle rather than fat—his abs looked like those of a Roman breastplate. His chest muscles overpowered his torso so that his waist looked tiny in contrast. And his arms were as thick as telephone poles, with bulging muscles.

And his cock was as thick as a telephone pole too, with two baseball-sized balls hanging behind it. He was already in full arousal.

I moaned as he set three of the beer bottles down and, sitting down close beside me, took a big swallow from the bottle still in his hand. Then, encasing me in one arm, he pulled me to him and took my mouth in his.

I almost gagged as the beer swished into my mouth, and then I did gag as his tongue followed.

I closed my eyes, not able to look at his piggish face, and let him hold my mouth captive with his as his hands moved across my body, unbuttoning, unzipping, pulling clothes off my arms and legs.

I was trapped in the embrace of one of his arms while the hand of the other encased my cock and he started a slow pump.

My nerves were standing on end. His technique of tease in the car leading directly into this no-preliminary assault had me on edge and confused. It would have been useless to resist him anyway, but I was completely disarmed, yielding to him. The reflex was involuntary, but my hips were going with the motion of his hand on my cock. He loosened the grip, while keeping my cock encased, and I found myself slow-fucking his fist.

He released my mouth and then, thankfully, all I could see of his head was the bald top as his mouth was going down onto my chest.

The hand on my cock was crushing now and was beginning a faster, more demanding cadence.

My eyes went to the paintings on the wall. His body really was a wonder. And none of the paintings showed his face. I could take the body. I looked back down at him and could see—and appreciate—the bulge of the shoulder and muscles on either side of his shiny, billiard-ball-smooth head. He was pulling me over into his lap, and I could feel his hard cock at the small of my back and those thunderous thighs under my naked ones.

I panted hard to the rhythm of his jacking, and I cried out in little huffs of breath in response to what he was doing with his mouth on my nipples.

I shouldn't just be giving it to him. He was a gross pig. I should let him know I didn't want it—or that I'd give it to him but not because I wanted it. Because I didn't have any other choice. Make him demand it and take it by force and then not be able to fully enjoy it, as I couldn't enjoy sex from a beast like this.

If I just didn't have to . . . look . . . at his face.

I brought my hands up to glide over the lines of his fantastically defined muscles.

It was OK, in the almost dark, with the lights just highlighting the paintings. I could let him have it and enjoy it.

I wanted to reach back and grab his cock—to get the measure of it. Both thrilling and moaning to the thought of it inside me. Had I ever taken something that thick and long? Would I have a sense of triumph when I had?

God, I wanted it. I moaned and involuntarily whined, "Please . . . please."

I heard him laugh, a low, rumbling chuckle. I couldn't be doing this. I couldn't want it. Not from a coarse pig. As if in evidence, he bit my nipple and I cried out and stiffened.

Fight him, fight him, I screamed inside to myself. Stay stiff. Make him take it. Don't let him know . . . God, I wanted it. I relaxed, all of my senses going to the rising seed in my cock. My butt twitching. My channel crying out for attention.

Fuck me, fuck me, fuck me. I was surprised that I wasn't saying it—that I was only thinking it. It was the fear of the size of him, though—and the fear of having to look into his piggish face while he plowed me that held back what my aroused body wanted me to cry out to him.

That cock. How much of it could I take? Oh, god, give me that cock. Once more I tried reaching around him for it— but his waist was just too thick.

"Come for me," he said in a low, guttural voice. "Come for me."

I realized that I was on the brink of doing just that. And, shockingly I was overcome with a sense of loss and disappointment. No, fuck me, fuck me, fuck me, my mind was screaming.

And then I came for him.

He laughed and released me. He pushed me over to the side, and I just toppled over on my side on the curving sofa.

He stood over me, in magnificent erection. If my eyes just rose up his body as far as his nipples, I could remain in full arousal myself. I knew I could. Just don't look into the face.

He picked one of the beer bottles up from the coffee table set a couple of feet in front of the sofa and handed it to me.

"Drink," he said. "Drink. Then we fuck. No, I fuck; you scream."

He laughed at his little joke. I shuddered. A few seconds before—before I'd exploded—I'd wanted the cock. Not now. Now I was scared of it again. I could see his evil, piggish face again.

He had already finished off one of the other bottles. I took the bottle, keeping my eyes at the level of his navel, although they kept moving down to his cock and balls and causing little shivers to go up my spine.

I took several swigs, and so did he.

But then he took the bottle from me and put it back on the coffee table.

He turned and sat on the sofa and ran an arm under me and lifted me up and pulled me over to his lap, facing him. I turned my eyes to one of the paintings on the wall.

Here we go, I said to myself. Remember not to hold your breath. Breathe easily, don't tense your channel, be loose, very loose. Eyes on the paintings. It's the body. You're being taken by that magnificent body. That monstrous cock. Not the face.

But then, rather than setting me down on his cock, he pushed my head toward the carpet in front of the sofa. I felt his thighs go over mine on each side as my shoulders and neck hit the carpet. My thighs were trapped between his and the edge of the sofa. My legs were spread in the air. His feet were on my shoulders at the arm pits, holding my shoulders to the floor.

I shuddered as I saw his face above mine and then, again, when he reached over and took the fourth bottle of beer from the coffee table.

I lurched and gasped and he laughed as I felt the cold beer stream into my channel. And then the neck of the beer bottle.

"Good choice, maybe, the bottle not the can. But when I fuck you will wish you had been prepared by the can."

I whimpered and moaned as he fucked me with the beer bottle, my channel sloshing with beer.

He took my dick in both hands and started to work it again. "You come for me."

43

I was overcome for several moments, but then I got angry. No, you come for me god dammit. Fuck me. Fuck me.

Again it was an internal cry.

But I managed to reach up with both of my hands and grasp his cock and start driving him as hard as he was driving me.

He let out an animalistic yell, and the first thing I knew, I was dangling from his side with his arm around my waist and we were moving across the room.

Into another room we went, dark, but for only a brief moment. When the lights went on, it was another room with lighting spotting on paintings. Three of them. The same grotesquely gorgeous torso. But fucking a small, dark-skinned youth—a Thai I presumed—in three different positions.

It was a bedroom, with a gigantic king-sized bed in the center of it.

I was dumped on the bed, on my belly. The hand under me, palming my waist, pulled me up onto my knees, while the fist of Jaguerman's other hand grabbed me by the back of my neck and smashed my face into the thick material of the bedspread.

I managed to turn my head and found myself facing a painting of just this fuck position. The cock of the top in the painting was gigantic.

I cried out as Jaguerman's cock head fought for entry in my channel. But only with the bulb of the cock. Pressing in but holding there.

Again the tease, the hint o preliminaries as briefly the bulb moved back and forth just inside my entrance—and then the long plunge, with no further preliminaries.

Yes, fuck me, fuck me. Don't hold your breath, reach back and pull your buttocks apart, relax, relax, relax your channel, relax your . . . oh god, oh GOD. Oh, Holy SHIT! Oh, yesss!

Fuck me, fuck me, fuuccckk me. Moooannn.

Oh, shit, I've got it all. Can feel his pubes on my buttocks. Breathe, breathe. Oh, holy shit. But I've done it. I could do it.

And then, as I felt his balls begin to slap on the tender skin of my inner thighs, the screaming started. It was mine. Giving me no quarter, he was pistoning me to beat the band.

The second painting had me lapped, facing away from him and making love to his cock with my channel. Slower, more sensuous this time. Lovers finding each other's arousal points.

Now he had lost control too. Now he was moaning and groaning.

And it was OK. No, it was great—as long as I wasn't facing him.

But in the third painting position, I *was* facing him. Laying on my back on the bed, with him standing between my legs.

But I was beyond caring what he looked like. Every fiber of my senses was concentrated on the gigantic staff inside me. Deeper, deeper, thicker. Moan. Faster, deeper, deeper. Oh god, oh shit!

He didn't come. I came. He said, "You come for me," and I came. But then he stopped.

I looked up into his face. Just barely being able to do so now. Any man who could fuck me like that deserved to be looked in the face.

With him stopped, inside me, like that, I could get the measure of him as never before. No, I'd never had it like that before. Never as deep, never as thick. And it was pulsating inside me.

I was mewing and sighing and groaning. "Fuck me, fuck me. Don't stop."

It wasn't spoken internally now. I'd said it. I looked him in his piggish face and I was all desire, no disgust.

"Fuck me," I whined. "Finish it. And then fuck me again."

He was smiling. It was an evil, mischievous smile.

He held there, inside me. I half expected a sudden flow, a gut-wrenching drenching to rival that of the beer.

But he was withdrawing from me. And I wanted to cry. I clutched for his buttocks, trying to hold him inside me.

But he laughed and pushed my hands aside.

I was exhausted. I had just realized that. When he was inside me, everything had been focused on that monster shaft and begging it to reach further, to stretch wider. To throb and to flood me.

But now that was gone, I felt the loss of it. I whimpered.

He laughed. And then he reached down for me and lifted me off the bed and slung me over his shoulder.

He padded across the room and out into the hall. Down the hall to another closed door. He opened the door to darkness. He flipped on the light switch.

Again, spotlights on paintings on three walls, the fourth wall a solid sheet of glass overlooking the terrace and the sultry Bangkok night, the noise of a city that never slept spiraling up into the room.

I whimpered again as my eyes focused on the paintings. Three men now. One of them my Belgian satyr. The other another burly Westerner. Again a small Oriental youth between them. Three fuck positions. All doubles. Two cocks, fighting for dominance, within the small youth's channel.

On the bed, waiting for us. Naked and in full erection. Kamrod Tikka. Smiling. Hand encasing erect phallus.

"There," the Belgian boomed out, "I told you Mr. Tikka would meet us at the apartment."

"Oh god, oh god," I murmured. Not able to respond in any other way in my utter exhaustion.

As Kamrod held his rod stiff and licked his lips in anticipation, the Belgian turned me away from Kamrod and lowered my channel on his cock.

Kamrod encircled my waist with his arms and took my cock in one of his fists. He kissed me in the hollow of my neck.

I watched Jaguerman full in the face as he fisted my ankles, spread my legs up and wide and began working his cock inside my channel above Kamrod's already fully encased staff.

"Oh, god, oh, god, Oh shit." But it was barely a whimper.

After the Game

It's after the game and after he's showered. I've turned in the stats for the official record and the team has showered and bustled off in shouts of bravado and victory to the favorite "we've won" watering hole. It's just him, staying behind now. Waiting for me. Knowing that I'd be there. Having told me that I'd be there.

I've asked him to put on the tight pants again—but just them. No padding or cup. And I stop him from lacing up the crotch. The silky material is so tight over his ebony body that the material is spread there and his black, kinky pubic hair bushes out of the opening. He's so big and tall that my head comes up only as far as his chest, which suits us both as I move into him and press my lips over one of his nipples, the aureole of which is so big that I have to open my mouth wide to get my lips over it. He growls deep inside him as I suck his nipple, and he grabs my chest with his large, rough hands on each side, his thumbs latching onto my nipples and rubbing them hard.

My lips follow the trail of black hair down the deep crease bisecting his heavily muscled torso, and my tongue slicks down the pubic hair in the V-ing of his tight, silky leggings as my hands move around to cup his bulging, tight-muscled butt cheeks. The material is so thin and tight that it might as well not be there at all.

My tongue traces the line of his cock through the material, and I moan at the length and thickness of the tool—already half hard for me. My hands travel down the deep curve of his thighs. He's told me how he's going to fuck me, and I only now believe that he has the leg muscles to manage it. I shudder at the anticipation of what he's going to do to me. When he'd come over to me at the score table during the game and whispered in my ear what he was going to do, I was lost to him. I didn't believe him, but just the thought of it had me ejaculating in my pants as he laid a heavy paw on my shoulder and squeezed. I had teased him for weeks—put him off when he'd told me he'd wanted me and then let me know that he knew I'd want it too because he'd seen me on the massage table with the quarterback. He told me that, since I'd made him wait, I would get it rough and hard. When he left me my hands were trembling so badly that I could hardly put the stats in the right columns. I'd watched him walk away, my eyes going to the bulge of his buttocks and thigh muscles in the tight material of his leggings. And I melted.

I used my lips and tongue to work his cock by its root out of the V in his leggings. It seemed to take forever. I despaired of reaching the end, but when I did, I gasped at the size of the bulb. I opened my lips wide to pull it in, and it seemed to fill my mouth cavity. I managed to pull my tongue back to where I could press its tip into the slit in his cap.

I heard another growl from deep inside him, and he took my head in his hands and began to press in and then back. With each stroke he was reaching farther and farther back in my throat. I unhinged my jaw as best I could and grabbed hard on his curved thigh muscles for leverage and stability as, gagging and eyes watering, I gave up all control to him. My tease was over.

If he delivered on his promise, my maneuvering had paid out. The quarterback gave a nice, quick, athletic fuck. But I wanted it hard, rough, taxing, complete. This black monster god was the cruelest player on the team. I wanted to feel the fuck, to know that I had been totally taken.

From this point, I was his to do what he would with me. He had told me what he was going to do. He didn't make me wait.

His hands went under my arms, and he was lifting me with strong hands. I no longer had any doubt he could do what he said he'd do.

From that point, the contribution I made was to hook my knees on his hips, help guide the head of his cock to my hole, gasp as the gigantic bulb on his cock accomplished the miracle of opening the way past my sphincter to come to rest on my prostate and throb there, while he lowered his face to mine, the tips of his dreadlocks tickling my shoulders, and held my lips to his as he held there—teasing me with the false hope that he would give me a chance to adjust to him.

But there was no adjusting to a monster cock such as his, and as it started to move deeper inside me, I jerked my mouth from his and arched my back and screamed my scream of total invasion and possession. This was what I wanted. This was fucking. He laughed and pushed my torso down with his hands still on my sides, going with my first, involuntary arch away from him, rather than gathering me in again. I wrapped my legs around his waist, resting my calves on the shelf of his bulbous buttocks, rubbing against the silky pants he still wore.

I grabbed for his ankles with my fists as his hands went to my waist, pulling me up into his crotch, pulling my channel onto his long, thick cock. I was sobbing and blubbering, never having been so deeply possessed, penetrated, stretched before.

He was standing on those strong, muscled legs of his, bearing my full weight. And with the strength of his arm muscles and strong hands, he began to raise and lower me on his cock, pumping me slow and shallow and then—even as I was begging for the fuck—deeper and faster and then like a piston, deep, hard, fast, as I whimpered and moaned and groaned and cried out for him—and he strode slowly around the locker room now without missing a stroke . . . he did exactly what he said he was going to do with me.

And even as he was doing it, he was telling me how I was going to get it next time.

I was totally exhausted when he was done—when I felt him twitch and shudder and the warmth of his jism spreading deep inside me. But I was totally satiated too. This was what I wanted. This was good. I could savor this for some time to come. The quarterback would be weak vanilla after this.

He lowered my body to the cold, tiled locker room floor and stood over me, panting. I felt the tug of victory. He was panting for me. He had been exerted too. I had power over him too. We'd go back to the tease. He'd sniff after me and I'd shake my bottom and swirl away from him, making him beg for it. Showing that control wasn't all his. I wouldn't tell him how much I wanted it again.

Not now, of course. Now I was satisfied, exhausted.

I didn't hear him at first. The pounding in my ears hadn't subsided. I was still breathing heavily, my mouth hanging open, trying to gasp in great gulps of air.

"I said get up and run for it," he growled.

"What?" I squeaked breathlessly. Not comprehending. He'd said he was going to take me next like a hunted jungle animal. But we'd done it now for tonight. Surely he couldn't mean . . .

"Run, or I'll spike you right here on the hard floor."

He had a hand under my belly and the other fisted in my hair, and he was pulling me up off the floor.

I could barely stand, my knees were so wobbly. I turned and looked at him, still in his steel-blue football leggings. His cock and balls hanging out the front. His monster cock hard as a rock.

I moaned and swiveled away from him.

"Run, fuckin' run!" he commanded.

A stinging swat on the butt sent me reeling across the room and stumbling for the door to the corridor.

I made it only as far as the doorway to the massage room before I felt the strong, calloused hands on my waist, spinning me into the room.

I was facing the massage table. The same table where the quarterback had fucked me two nights previously, me stretched out on the table on my belly, him doing all of the work. Doing pushups on my back, leveraging off hands pushing into the table next to my biceps, his long, thin cock jacking up and down inside me in a cadence just like he would call out in formation. Impersonal, almost clinical. No talk at all, just grunts and groans. Getting his rocks off to help him play better, to release the tension. Me giving my ass up for the team. Not even a thank-you after he'd shot off. Just climbing down off the table and trotting off to the showers. Asking me questions about his stats as he was suiting up, with no mention whatsoever of what we'd been doing twenty minutes before.

Nothing impersonal about this black monster. He growled like an animal; he fucked like an animal. He sweated and dug and talked dirty to me. And told me what he was going to do to me—and did it.

He pushed me up against the edge of the massage table, the edge cutting into my lower belly. I cried out at the sharp pain, and he laughed. Standing close behind me, he bent my torso over the surface of the table by pressing down on my back with his heaving chest. He hooked his chin on one of my shoulders and his dreadlocks hung down over my shoulders and onto my chest.

With one hand cupping my belly, his other hand went to my buttocks, spreading the cheeks, the fingers going to my hole.

"Spread like you've never been spread before," he whispered in my ear in a deep, gravelly voice.

I whimpered, knowing he would do what he told me he would do and then I cried out in anguish as the fingers invaded me, spreading, probing, turning, then churning.

I spread my arms wide and planted my fists on the edge of the massage table, wide, to hold steady. I widened the stance of my legs to open as much as I could. I was up on my toes, but the strength of the plunging of his fingers—I don't know how many, but surely at least three inside me, all long and plump and hard-calloused, was raising me off my feet in rhythm.

His cock was entering me between the fingers, which slowly extracted the deeper he buried himself in me. Then the fingers of his hand were fisted in my hair and he was arching my back toward him. And thrusting up and up and up. Faster and harder. The silky material on his thighs were chaffing the backs of my thighs and making a rustling sound that was harmonizing with my whimpers and groans and his grunts and mutterings of "Fuck you, fuck you hard," "Fuckin' feel that, dontcha?" "Sweet white boy ass," and "Who's the boss; who's yer daddy?" He didn't wait for answers, but neither of us questioned who the boss was.

He stopped, breathing hard, and leaned into me. "You want it to stop?" he murmured in my ear.

"No, oh god, no," I moaned in reply.

I felt him come again deep inside me. I'd already done so three times over the eternity of the two fucks and my balls ached from the milkings.

His hand released my head and went to the root of his cock, which was still hard inside me. He rotated the tool inside me, and I moaned my pleasure, yipping breathy little "yes, yes, yes," encouragements. I felt his hot breath at my ear again. And then he told me what he was going to do to me next. And I groaned and my eyes filled with tears.

"You want it?" he growled.

I groaned and my eyes filled with tears. "Yes, oh god, yes."

"Yes, what? When? Where?"

"Yes, Daddy. Anytime, anywhere."

The Bonus

"Welcome to Key West, Mr. Jabril. You were quick getting out of the airport. Tuesdays are good days for traveling here."

Scotty was standing there on the curb outside the baggage claim area at the Key West air terminal much like last time and the time before that. He was leaning up against a red Jaguar XK-8 convertible and looking oh so preppy: spiky frosted hair, blue blazer over pink Polo shirt, white Ferrari Chino trousers, and brown loafers, polished up to a mirror shine. His smile was open and mischievous.

"Ah, you remembered me." It wasn't so much a pleased expression as it was a "You damn well better have remembered what I looked like" expression.

In contrast to Scotty's preppy blondness, Jabril was olive-skinned and dark haired. And muscular in contrast to Scotty's graceful litheness.

"Want to take a ride?"

Jabril didn't answer, and, indeed, Scotty didn't need an answer. He was here to pick Jabril up from the airport and deliver this luxury convertible. Of course he wanted a ride. It was just what Scotty said every time he picked someone up at the airport.

Jabril folded himself into the passenger seat, while Scotty folded his suit bag and computer case in the car's tiny trunk, came around to the driver's side, and slid in.

Most travelers flying into Key West rented a Mustang convertible. That was the standard rental of the Florida key. It had once been Chrysler Sebring convertibles, but tastes had changed in the past decade. And it was precisely because every other temporary driver on Key West seemed to be driving a Mustang convertible that Jabril had chosen a Jaguar. He had to pay a lot more at the Exotic Car Express than at Hertz, but it was worth the distinction from other travelers and it had its perks. He looked over at Scotty, his hair ruffling in the wind, his aviator sunglasses setting off his young, handsome face.

Scotty was just one of the perks. Scotty drove the Jag east around Roosevelt Boulevard, which semicircled the eastern edge of the key, turned west on Flagler and then north on Kennedy toward the eastern harbor and the baseball stadium. Just short of the baseball stadium he turned into the small, one-story building with the sign, "Exotic Car Express" over the plate-glass window and showing a Mercedes convertible on the showroom floor and drove back around behind the three-bay service wing off the showroom. He pulled in close to the building, turned the engine off, and lifted a set of keys to dangle between him and Jabril.

"The keys to the house are here too. Same place as last time."

As he held the keys out, Jabril held a fat envelope out and the two exchanged their treasures.

"Count it," Jabril said.

"I'm sure it's there. $1,500, right?"

"Right. I'll be back by 11:00 in the morning on Thursday. I have a flight at 12:30. You'll drive me to the airport." It wasn't a request.

"Yeah, sure," Scotty said as he opened the driver's door.

"Aren't you forgetting something?"

"Yeah, right." Scotty got out of the car, but only long enough to take off his blazer and lay it down on the fender of the Jag. While he did so, Jabril moved the passenger seat back as far as it would go and reclined it. Scotty got back in the driver's seat; titled the steering wheel up as high as it would go; and, swiveling toward Jabril, unzipped Jabril's trousers and fished out his plump cock.

Jabril kicked off his right shoe and propped his foot up to where the windshield met the edge of the car door. Using his hands, he guided Scotty's head down into his lap and groaned a deep groan as Scotty's lips opened over the bulb of his cock and slid down the sides of his engorging shaft.

After a few minutes, in a voice thick with satisfaction, Jabril whispered, "Suck my balls too."

* * * *

Jabril had donned stark-white Jocko David shorts with a Jocko mesh muscle shirt on top and white Crocs loafers to drive from the house on Virginia Street he'd been given the keys to just the few short blocks to the Bourbon Street Pub on Duval. He parked right out in front of the club by the fire hydrant and revved the engine before turning the car off, knowing that the men gathering around the entrance to the club would take notice of what he was driving and then, when he got out of the Jag, what he was wearing. And how good he looked in it.

He knew he looked good. He'd spent quite some time picking these clothes out and hiding them away for this occasion. His dusky skin, swarthy good looks, and well-cut body were set off perfectly in these clothes.

He was propositioned twice on his way into the club, but he brushed them both away with a smile. These guys looked like they wanted the same thing he did.

He bellied up to the bar, ordered a beer, and swiveled around to take in the scene while he waited for the drink to arrive. Even though it was a weekday night, the crowd was pretty good—and very good looking. Men were at the tables, making out and making deals. Men were on the dance floor, rocking against each other and fondling whatever they could grasp. And there was a cute young trick playing the pole at the other end of the bar.

Guys were brushing past Jabril and giving him the eye. He was giving a disinterested look back at most, but some of the smaller, cuter guys were getting smiles and meaningful looks back. The guys with piercings—not everywhere, but on the eyebrows and promising nipple rings as discerned under tight Ts—got special scrutiny. It didn't take long for the guys swirling around Jabril to catch the signals of what he was interested in.

When the drink arrived, Jabril pulled a twenty off a fat roll fished from the pocket of his shorts and put it down on the bar in full view of anyone looking and, when the barman picked up, Jabril signaled he was to keep the change.

In short order, a slim, blond guy with a small ring in an eyebrow and a ball piercing in his tongue slid onto the barstool beside Jabril. He appeared something on the younger side of twenty and had a pretty face and wavy blond hair. He had blue eyes and a sensual smile, with thick lips.

"Hi," he said to Jabril and flashed him a studied shy smile.

"Hi," Jabril answered back, giving the young man's eyes his undivided attention.

"The beer good?" the blond asked.

"Good enough," Jabril answered, although he hadn't had time to take a swig yet. And he knew full well that the young man knew that—he had appeared as the twenty was taken up by the barman. "You don't have a drink. You want one?"

"Yeah, sure, thanks. I'll take what you have."

Jabril didn't call the barman over, but he took the roll of bills from his table, flipped five twenties off the roll and laid them down, fanned out on the counter between him and the young man.

"Wow, I don't think the beer here is that expensive," the young man said. But the smile on his face showed that he wasn't being that naïve. "You got an oil well in your pocket or something? You one of those Arab sheiks?"

"It's not for the beer, of course," Jabril answered, just smiling and dipping his head at the young man's inferences.

The young man smiled. "My name is Trax," he said, as he laid a hand with long, slender fingers on Jabril's thigh.

"They'll have a pile going soon downstairs," he said. "You want to start down there? They have cubicles too."

"I like my privacy. And I have an idea where I'd like to go. You want a ride in a Jag?"

The young man looked dubious, but by the way he licked his lips when the Jag had been mentioned, Jabril figured he'd heard about the nice one sitting outside.

Jabril took the wad of cash out and reeled off another hundred and laid it on top of what was already there.

Trax lost any squeamishness he'd had about going away from the club with Jabril then. He flashed Jabril a big smile and said, "Sure, I'd love a ride in a red Jag convertible."

So, Jabril thought, he'd seen it. He knew it was red and a convertible.

"Steve," Trax called out to the barman, who walked over. "Here, can you hold this for me? I'll be back in a while." He handed over the cash and the barman took it as if this happened every day. And Jabril decided that it probably did. The kid had looked young—and vulnerable—which, along with the piercings and his size and erogenous look had been what had attracted Jabril. But it was OK if he was a professional. For this money, he'd give Jabril a good time.

The money passed, Trax looked at Jabril and gave him a mischievous smile. He reached over and took Jabril's beer glass and downed a good third of it. He wiped his mouth with the back of his hand—which, in itself, made Jabril's cock twitch, and said, "You didn't tell me your name."

"The Jag is outside," Jabril said as he stood up from the barstool, not answering the question.

They fucked on a beach by a breakwater in the shadows of the walls of an old Civil War fortress, Fort Zachary Taylor, on the southern tip of the key. Trax was impressed that Jabril knew the best beaches to go to for a gay coupling, and Jabril had his assessment of Trax confirmed when his name was whispered in greeting from a couple of nooks and crannies in the breakwater as they found their own spot and Jabril spread out the blanket he'd found in the trunk of the Jag.

They weren't alone on the beach, but they weren't doing anything that everyone else wasn't doing, and the backdrop of sighs and moans and grunts and groans only added to Jabril's arousal.

Once naked, Trax had let Jabril initially take the lead. The young man laid back on the blanket and Jabril straddled his chest with his knees and fed his cock into Trax's experienced, but still soft mouth and enjoyed the play of Trax's tongue ball in the underside of his cock.

Once Jabril was hard and panting, though, Trax turned him onto his back and was the one straddling Jabril's hips, lowering his channel on Jabril's shaft, and riding him to a first, swift ejaculation. Trax had a control of his channel muscles, which assured Jabril that he knew exactly how to please a man and made a good living from it. For two hundred dollars, Trax realized that the one coupling would not be enough, and after Jabril had come, he pulled the swarthy man's torso up to his, and they sat there, facing each other, rocking back and forth, and kissing and fondling each other until Jabril had regained his stamina.

Then it was Trax laying on his back, legs raised and spread, while, his thighs shoved under Trax's buttocks, Jabril took over the stroking. His lips were lowered to the rings in both of Trax's nipples, and the young blond, as he no doubt was trained to do, was moaning and sighing how good a fuck Jabril was giving him.

Afterward—and following a period of holding each other and cooing like they were a pair of schoolboys discovering sex for the first time—they gathered up the blanket and their clothes and stumbled, arm in arm, toward the parking lot.

Trax stopped, though, as they heard short, sharp cries of passion from a pocket of sand surrounded by rock farther up on the beach. When he stopped, Jabril did too. "That would be Jewel. A tranny. Ever done a tranny?"

"No, never," Jabril said with hesitancy.

"She's fun. And she can make you come just with her sex moans. Fifty for her and another fifty for me, and you can do her."

"Here, now?"

"Yeah, why not?"

"You saw me lock my roll up in the car."

"We'll trust you for it. Come on. It will be fun."

Not getting an objection, Trax pulled Jabril over toward where the sounds had been coming from. They had subsided now, though, into just murmurings. When they came into the secluded circle, what they saw was the figure of a slim, black transvestite, with her skirt hiked up and white vinyl booted legs spread wide. They got a shot of both her asshole and her dick, so there was no question what she was. But other than that, she was a beautiful woman, with big tits jutting out from where her top had been pushed up to her neck.

Crouching next to her was a big bruiser of a truck driver type, his flannel shirt open and flapping around a heavily muscled chest and his lower extremities bare. His cock was nothing special other than the heavy ring in the bulb. This alone, though, struggled for Jabril's attention with the luscious tranny flashing her goods at him. Jabril had so wanted a cock ring himself. But, of course, he couldn't have one.

"Interested in seconds, Jewel? He'll give you fifty. And," Trax continued, turning to the bruiser, "you can do me for fifty too."

"Thirty," the truck driver growled.

"Forty," Trax countered.

But by then Jewel had opened her arms to Jabril and whispered, "Come to Momma" in a sultry voice and Jabril was sinking between her spread legs. One of her hands guided his face to her coin-sized aureoles, which he immediately went to sucking. Her other hand was guiding his cock inside her ass. Her channel muscles were even better trained than Trax's had been, and when she moved the palms of her hands to Jabril's butt cheeks, she began controlling a fuck that was sending Jabril into paradise.

He turned his head to see that Trax was on his back and the truck driver was between his thighs and holding his legs up and spread with fists gripping the young man's ankles. Jabril's eyes went to the cock crowned with the heavy ring entering and pulling out of Trax's ass. All the way in and then all of the way out.

Jewel fucked him for forever, and sometime during the coupling, Jabril felt another set of hands on his buttocks and a tongue in his ass. This had never happened to him. This was an utterly fantastic feeling.

But then there was a new feeling at his entrance. Not a wet tongue. Something cold and metallic.

Jabril cried out and tried to pull away, but Jewel, with a surprising strong grip, laughed and pulled him closer into her smothering embrace.

"It's OK, honey. You'll like it. Just relax and go with it. Feel that cock ring?"

Jabril certainly did feel the truck driver's cock ring. And the cock that went with it. He thrashed and screamed, but it was no use. His cries turned into moans and grunts and then into sighs and whimpering; his thrashing moved to writhing—both of which only helped the truck driver to drive farther inside him—and eventually led to his body—the pain obliterated by the pleasure—joining with the rhythm of the fuck.

He knew he shouldn't be enjoying this. But Jewel's big tits and the way she could grip his cock and pull him inside her and her muscles undulating over his shaft—and that thick cock ring inside him and being filled and pumped, the ring punishing his prostate. Making him moan and leak and twitch—he was going . . . over the . . . moon.

Later, when he was laying in a hot-water bath in the two-bedroom bungalow on Virginia Street, soaking his sore, swollen ass, and sipping wine, Jabril reasoned with himself that he had come for the adventure—that he'd wanted to experience the heights of arousal and sexual pleasure—and that, even though unplanned and something he'd never want to do again, he'd certainly climbed the heights this evening.

He fondled his cock, pressing his thumb into the slit of the bulb, wishing that he could get a cock ring too.

It had been all new and it had taken him to one height. But it hadn't really been what he had been looking forward to the most. Trax had seemed young and innocence, but he had turned out to be a professional. The Bourbon Street Pub obviously hadn't been the right place. There was just tomorrow now. He'd have to try again.

* * * *

Jabril walked down to the grill at the edge of the South Street beach for breakfast. He was in shorts and a sports shirt open to his chest. But he wasn't cruising; he just was after some breakfast and thinking that a walk would help ease the pain in his ass.

Six hunks were out on the beach in skimpy bathing suits, playing volleyball. One of them must have recognized Jabril, because he went around to the others and whispered something, and they all kept glancing over at him while Jabril ate his eggs and bacon and they continued their game.

Now that he thought of it, the guy who had started the whispering looked vaguely familiar. He probably was from the bar the previous evening or maybe even some earlier trip here, but Jabril couldn't remember much more than a hazy sense of knowing what he had inside that Speedo that was painted on him. So, probably an earlier trip. Jabril felt flattered that maybe the guy remembered him.

Their game apparently concluded, three of the guys came over and asked if they could sit with him. He was just finishing up his coffee, but he was polite and assented.

They were just talking about life around Key West and asking general questions of him in the context of their banter. But when their discussion got into the huge gay community on the key and then, more pointedly, when they mentioned the Middle East situation and asked him whether he thought that hurt the flow of oil from there more than it had, Jabril politely started to extract himself from the conversation and left them there. They didn't seem to mind. They were hunks, but this was his last day here. This wasn't what he was after.

Jabril had had such an exhausting night that his breakfast had come at 1:00 p.m. And still he felt hung over. So, the day half spent, he decided he needed a nap. He went back to the Virginia Street bungalow, swam laps in the pool that took up much of the lot, and then napped until late afternoon. When he got up, he padded to the refrigerator and took two steaks out of the freezer to start thawing. Step one of his plan complete, he went into the bedroom and picked out the most nonthreatening clothes he had to wear. In the end, he picked what he'd planned to wear back on the airplane—khaki pants and a checked sports shirt. Nothing flashy; quite conservative.

Then he got in the Jag and drove down Duval toward Mallory Square. He parked there and started walking his way back, looking for a coffee shop. He followed along behind families with small kids, thinking they'd hone in on someplace that wasn't gay. He found what he was looking for on Fleming, just off Duval. An Island Joe's coffee shop and café. He went into the café, ordered a coffee and a sandwich, and sat near the back, where he could watch all of the tables.

His attention was drawn to a young, sandy-haired guy with glasses sitting at a table near the window, hunched over a computer. It seemed like his attention was focused on the computer, but as Jabril watched, he saw the young guy looking at other guys as they passed. He looked very nervous. But when other guys looked down at him—and especially if they smiled— the young guy would dip his head back into the computer.

He was good looking enough. A good build. But the glasses detracted. He was wearing baggy shorts and a T-shirt from some university. All Jabril could make out was "Florida."

The longer Jabril watched, the more he thought the guy wanted a hookup but had no idea how to go about it. This was the guy Jabril had been looking for.

He'd finished his sandwich but still had half of his third cup of coffee. It was good coffee, but Jabril decided to invest it in his cause. He stood and moved toward the front of the shop, brushing by the young man in passing, and "accidentally" splashing his coffee on the guy's university T-shirt.

"Oh, god, I'm sorry," he said, as he started dabbing at the young guys chest with a napkin. The guy was firm under there.

"Uh, it's OK."

"No, it's not. I'm really sorry. I'll have to get that cleaned for you."

Without asking for permission, Jabril plopped down in the seat next to the young man. By the time they'd sparred on what Jabril wanted to do to apologize and what the young man didn't want to bother with, they had established that the young man's name was Gill and that he was a student in chemistry at the University of North Florida in Jacksonville—and a member of the university's baseball team. He was on a semester-at-sea course and his ship was docked at Mallory Square for the week.

"I'm in here hoping they put the Dolphins-Redskins preseason game on that TV up there. We don't get reception on the ship."

"That itty-bitty screen up there? You'll hardly be able to see it even if they have the game on. And you are going to watch it alone?"

"I don't mix much. Sort of shy."

"Nobody should watch the games alone. Which team are you a fan of?"

"The Dolphins, of course. They're a Florida team."

"Me too. I'm just going home to watch it myself. Some guys were coming over, but they all bugged out. And no one should have to watch a pro football game alone. Where's the fun in that?"

"I don't know."

"Say. Maybe you'd like to come watch it with me."

"Uh, I don't know. It's about dinner time and . . ."

"I was going to serve steaks. They're already thawing. And we could get that T-shirt clean for you. I dirtied it; I should get it cleaned for you."

"I don't know . . ."

"I live nearby. Nobody should have to watch a pro football game alone."

"Well, I guess . . ."

* * * *

As Jabril hoped, the young Gill couldn't hold his beer all that well, and in the third quarter of the game, he already was woozy and nodding off. He was shirtless because his was in the dryer—and as a gesture of camaraderie Jabril had taken his shirt off too.

Gill had been impressed at the widescreen TV in the Virginia Street house pointed directly at a futon sofa. He'd also been impressed with Jabril's Jag convertible and with the jazzy bungalow on Virginia Street and even more at the pool that ran the length of the bungalow and took up much of the small lot the house was on.

He asked Jabril if he was some sort of Mideast sheik and if this was where he lived. And Jabril just smiled and said this was one of his homes away from home.

They popped Gill's T in the washer and Jabril laughed and said he'd go skins then too, and they sat on the patio with the lights on in the pool and ate their steaks and drank beer, waiting for the game to start.

Jabril became increasingly friendly and as Gill got increasingly blotto from the beer, he became increasingly yielding and his guard lowered and he began, slowly and in subtle ways, to reveal that he, indeed, had known before his ship docked that Key West was one of the gay capitals of the world, that he had heard that the gay activity was free and easy here, and that, yes, he'd always been curious, although he most certainly had never done anything about it. But his being in Key West had made him tingly and he had come off the ship and out into the town on his own just because it was arousing to think of possibilities and what fantasies he could pick up.

He was jolted into consciousness in the fourth quarter of the game to find that the back of the futon sofa had been lowered, that both of them were naked and stretched out beside each other, that Jabril's hand was encasing his cock, that his other arm was embracing Gill to him, and that he was kissing Gill's neck. What really brought Gill awake—well, half awake—though, was that Jabril was working his cock into Gill's passage.

Gill drunkenly struggled, writhing in Jabril's embrace, and objecting in thick-worded babbling that made little sense.

Jabril shushed the young man, saying that he had told Jabril that this was what he wanted, that Gill knew this was what he wanted, and that Jabril was in the saddle now already. That Gill should just lay back and enjoy what he knew he wanted.

Gill quieted down, but he sobbed and moaned and buried his face in Jabril's shoulder when he ejaculated under the attention of Jabril's pumping hand.

Jabril too had ejaculated into the bulb of his condom in the waning moments of the game, and they just lay there in each other's embrace, Gill softly crying and still trembling as the Redskins trounced the Dolphins.

Jabril reached over for the remote and clicked off the commentary, knowing Gill wouldn't want to be reminded of defeat. And they lay there, neither speaking, both trying to regularize their breath.

"I asked for it?" Gill weakly said in a whisper, at length.

"Yes. I guess the beer loosened your tongue. You told me that you'd come to the coffee house looking for a hookup and when I appeared, that you hoped it would be me."

"I did?" Gill seemed to be confused, not being able to remember saying what he, of course, never said. But also unable to call it a lie. It had been obvious to Jabril that this was what Gill really wanted.

And this is what Jabril had come to Key West to do—to pop some young guy's cherry.

"I've got to go," Gill whispered.

"You'll want to shower. The pool looks inviting, though. Let's take a swim first."

"I've got to go," Gill repeated.

"You told me you wanted to swim. You told me you wanted me to fuck you in the pool. This is what you came to Key West for."

"I don't . . . I just don't . . ."

"Did you come off the ship to be fucked or not? Did you take this cruise because you knew it would stop in Key West and this would be your chance, or not?"

They went into the pool naked. Gill moved lethargically through the water, still dizzy from the beer buzz and the shock of what he had done—what he'd allowed this rich Arab to do to him, what he'd had to admit that he wanted.

Jabril moved to him in the water and embraced him and turned Gill's body to his. He wrapped one hand around his neck and brought his mouth in for a long, deep kiss. The other hand encased their cocks together and began to stroke. Gill trembled and shuddered and moaned as Jabril's tongue invaded his mouth cavity and took his breath away.

The second time Jabril fucked Gill was on the patio at the edge of the shallow end of the pool. Gill was on his back on a towel, his legs raised and spread over the water of the pool, gripped in Jabril's hands, as Jabril stood in the water and slow-fucked Gill's channel at the lip of the pool.

Gill sobbed again through the fuck.

"Remember, I've never before . . . before today . . . please be gentle"

Jabil slammed his dick home and started fucking hard. "You want it hard, I know you do."

Gill just sobbed and took it.

"Are you OK?" Jabril asked at the front door where they were both standing, neither really knowing what to say. Gill seemed sad and confused still—and embarrassed. Jabril was doing what he could to mask his elation.

"I've got to go," Gill whispered. "There's a curfew on the ship. I've got to get back."

"Do you want me to drive you?" Before the sentence was completed, however, Gill had faded into the darkness of Virginia Street, headed for the night lights of Duval.

Jabril showered and slipped, naked, between silken sheets, pleased with himself that the trip had gone so well. He'd have to get up early in the morning to get everything in the house back in exactly the shape he'd found it. When he returned the keys to the bungalow to Scotty, Scotty would want assurances that the owners would have no idea anyone had been there when they returned from their trip to the Redskins-Dolphins game in Washington, D.C.

He masturbated himself to sleep, reliving the moment when his cock had breached the young man's sphincter and Jabril had claimed his innocence. The young guy's virginity. What was his name? Jabril really wanted to remember the names of his conquests. He'd probably remember in the morning.

At 10:00 in the morning, while Jabril was finishing up with his housecleaning, there was a knock at the door.

He almost didn't answer it; there wasn't supposed to be anyone here. But he could see through the side window by the door that it was the young guy from last night—Gill. He remembered now. That was his name.

"Ummm. Hi. I just came by . . . I wondered . . . oh, god, I want . . ."

Jabril moved out onto the front porch and brought the door close to shut behind. "Uh, this isn't a good time, Gill. I've . . . I've got my stockbroker with me. But come back at 2:00. I'll have something for you then. I'll do you fine then. That's what you've come back for, isn't it?"

Gill hung his head and studied the toes in his sandals, unable to speak. Too embarrassed to say it. "Uh, OK. 2:00, then. I'll be back."

Jabril leaned over, cupped Gill's chin with his hand, and brought their lips together in a kiss.

Gill looked guiltily up and down the street when they parted, but he was smiling and there were tears in his eyes.

"Good-bye, Gill . . . for now."

* * * *

The flight into Baltimore-Washington's Thurgood Marshall International airport was an hour late arriving, but Angelo lived just a few minutes away, in Colombia, Maryland, so he had plenty of time to retrieve his Ford pickup in the distant shuttle lot and get home before Cindy was home from work and the kids were back from school.

He arrived in time to unpack and to hide his Jocko wear and the Speedo bathing suits in the bottom of the duffel bag with his tennis gear before he heard the lilting voice of his wife from the entrance hall.

"Hello! Is Mr. Gianinni on the premises? Mrs. Gianinni is home. Your truck is here; you can't be far behind."

"Hi, babe. Missed you. Have you missed me?" Angelo said as he walked slowly down the stairs and took his wife in his arms. He gave her a deep kiss and fumbled with the material covering her breasts.

"Down, boy, I hear the school bus. The urchins will be invading any moment now. Of course I missed you."

Later, when the kids had gotten the presents Angelo had brought them and had been bundled off to begin their homework, Cindy put a cup of steaming coffee down on the kitchen island counter, and Angelo perched on a bar stool.

"Everything go OK in Atlanta? The weather good? You got what you needed done?"

"Yep, everything good," Angelo said. "It rained Tuesday night, but I'd made it to the hotel by then." Angelo had quite carefully checked the weather in Atlanta every day he was gone. This was a standard Cindy question. She always asked it—just to have something to ask him about his business trips. It wasn't like she'd ever check. Angelo was so dull and predictable.

"Business was good too. I got everything done I went there to do." Angelo lifted his coffee cup to hide the sly little smile that that statement had brought to his lips. "But I'll have to go back in a couple of months. There always is more to do."

"They work you too hard at the office," Cindy said.

"It's a job. There are so many without jobs now. I have to keep plugging away at this one."

"Yes, I know. But you never get out to blow off steam anymore. When was the last time you played tennis?"

Angelo's heart skipped a beat at the mention of tennis and his thoughts went to whether that duffel bag was a good place for his stash. But, yes, of course it was. That didn't have anything to do with Cindy's mention of tennis.

"I have a good life. We have a good life, Cindy," he said as he reached over and took her hand in his.

"Yes the salary's good. But they really should give you bonuses—you deserve a good bonus for all these trips you take."

"I don't really see the possibility of that," Angelo said. But this wasn't the thought that came to mind. What he was thinking was how grateful he was that his boss gave bonuses—good ones. His most recent one, the one that took him to Key West, was for $5,000. But the best part was that his boss hated the IRS so much that he gave the bonuses under the table and admonished his employees not to let their spouses talk about them, which meant, of course, that none of them even told their spouses about the bonuses—so no one but he and his employees knew about them.

Coaching Change

"The forehand. Move in and take those serves with the forehand."

The voice had cut through all of the noise in the stands at the Fitzgerald tennis center. Zach had been getting plenty of support from the stands surrounding the tennis court—which stood to reason, as he lived and trained here in Washington, D.C., a hometown boy, living in the Mclean suburbs across the Potomac in Virginia. But this was the first real piece of possibly useful advice he'd gotten on how to beat Petr Zhong.

On the next serve Zach moved in closer to the backline and to the left. He'd been covering for an angled serve that his coach, Stanislav Federov, had told him was Zhong's style. But Zhong hadn't used that serve for a set and a half. What he'd done was jam the serve into Zach's body. Zach was beginning to wonder if Stan had scouted out Zhong at all.

The ball was whipping its way to him, and he was in place now and instinctively struck at it with a forehand. He connected with it in the racket's sweet spot, and he watched the ball zing across the net and at an angle that Zhong couldn't reach. A cheer went up from the crowd.

Zach wanted to smile and strut, but the cheer that was going up was more of a relief that he wasn't going to be humiliated. It was really too late to bring this match around, but maybe he could keep himself from being embarrassed. The first chance he got, he looked up into the stands in the direction from which the helpful prompting had come and was surprised to see a familiar face. Bojan Nikolic, the number three seed, was sitting there in the first row. And he was smiling at Zach. This obviously was where the instruction had come from.

Zach was impressed. Bojan Nikolic had come to see him play. Zach had come through the qualifying rounds of the Legg-Mason tennis tournament, a feeder tournament for the U.S. Open, at the end of July. His coach had said he should wait until next season to try, but his dad had wanted him to see what he could do, and Zach's dad had pretty much called the shots in Zach's tennis development. All three of them, including Zach, had been surprised that Zach had qualified, but he'd done so in what the *Washington Post* sports section had said was brilliant form. Then he'd won through the first round as well. Of course, since he virtually was a hometown boy, the *Post* would give him all the coverage and support it could. But it looked like his dad was more right than Stan was—that Zach was ready to make a run at the pro circuit.

Losing to Petr Zhong would be no disgrace. Zhong was the seventh seed. But still, Zach couldn't say his coach had been much of a help in recent months. Zach wanted to change coaches, but he knew that wasn't going to fly with his dad. It was really unfair. Stan was still around because of what Zach's father wanted, not because of what Zach needed now in his present stage of development.

Stanislav Federov's reputation was what had brought him into the Thomas' camp. He'd coached three top ten players in his career. And that's all Zach's father, Kenneth Thomas, could think about. His dream was for his son to be a top-ten player. All of his life had been focused on Zach's tennis future—so much so that Zach's mother didn't stick it out and now was out on the West Coast raising some other man's family.

Well, today it was advice from one of the other players, from the stands, that helped Zach keep his head up. He lost the second set too, but not without rallying and putting up a fight that had the crowd cheering for the effort of their hometown boy. Already holding his own—well, almost—in the pros and barely eighteen.

The surprising thing was that Bojan Nikolic was still at the tournament at all. He'd lost both his singles and doubles matches in the first round. The singles match had been a real battle in which Bojan had just run out of gas. He was twenty-eight now and on his way back down the rankings. His best performances now came in doubles. But he'd been scheduled to play the doubles virtually back to back with the singles, and the singles had wiped him out so that he hadn't won the doubles match either.

Normally a player losing like Bojan did in early rounds of one tournament would be off preparing for the next one on his schedule—or rearranging his schedule to try to find another tournament to play in.

So, Zach was surprised to see Bojan in the stands—and much more surprised to have received coaching from him. It was flattering that Bojan would be there—and would bother with Zach at all.

At the end of the match, while Petr Zhong was sending his victory tennis balls into the stands and a courtside commentator was trying to get his attention for an on-court interview—and after Zach had received his round of applause "for trying," everyone lost interest in Zach and he gathered up his rackets and other gear, stowed them in his duffel, and headed for the exit tunnel, forgotten now, at least for the moment.

Or so he thought. Bojan Nikolic was leaning over the railing from the stands at the corner of the tunnel as Zach was passing by.

"Nice match," he called out to Zach.

Zach looked up to see the Serbian player smiling down at him. "Yeah, after some nice guy from the stands pointed out what I should have known I was doing wrong," Zach called back.

"Meet me at the player's door after you've showered. I'll treat you to a beer at the Corona tent."

Zach showered quickly, ecstatic that a top-fifty player wanted to have a beer with him. All of this good press he'd been getting was something very new to him. And a top-fifty player was showing interest in him. Was this great feeling what came with being in the hunt with the pros? Zach didn't know, but it certainly was nice balm for having been knocked out of the tournament.

"Thanks for the pointer in there," Zach said when they were sitting at a table as much in a corner of the food court area as they could to try to avoid Bojan being recognized. That wasn't working, though. They were continually being interrupted by fans who wanted to connect with Bojan. And Bojan was smiling for them all and bantering with them. Zach was immediately impressed with the Serbian player. He was attractive and built like a million dollars and had a radiant smile and a friendly personality. Zach would have expected more of a sullen attitude from someone who now was losing more than he was winning and was likely dropping twenty spots just over this season. But if Bojan was concerned about this, he wasn't letting it show.

"You were doing most things right. You've got great form. A few adjustments and you're going to be in the majors."

"You think so? Zhong certainly did a job on me."

"You were just too far gone before you adjusted. You did great after that. You're going to need to be in top condition to move to five-setters, however." Nikolic reached over and felt Zach's bicep and then dropped his hand and felt his thigh. "Pretty good conditioning, though. Just some more work in the gym. You got a steady practice partner?"

"Stan hits with me—and my dad. My dad's good. He could have been a pro if he gotten the chances he's giving me."

"Ah, Stanislav Federov. He was very good . . . once."

Zach was tempted to pursue that, but this was another player on the circuit. He remembered what his dad had told him. "It's war out there, son," he'd said. "Don't give up your strategies or air your camp's dirty linen in public."

Nikolic didn't seem to be fishing for signs of trouble in the Thomas camp, though. After he'd responded to a greeting from a fan, he turned and said. "Would you like someone to hit with you for a couple of days? I've got time to kick around until Saturday. If I could find a place to stay . . ."

"That would be great. And you could stay with us . . . with me and my dad. And with Stan. He lives with us. Our house is just over in the Virginia suburbs. You'd really hit with me—and give me some pointers."

"I'd love to."

* * * *

They'd managed to snag a practice court at the Fitzgerald center after their chat over the Corona, which Zach had already told his father he'd try to do win or lose his match against Zhong. So, Zach's father and Stanislav Federov had already left the venue. Zach had driven there in his own car.

They stopped in Roslyn, in Virginia, just cross Key Bridge from Washington, and ate dinner at the Vantage Point rooftop restaurant at the Holiday Inn, so it was straight to bed for both of them when they got to the Mclean house.

They were both out early the next morning on the private court below the rear terrace of the Thomas house, though, hitting balls and talking technique.

It was the usual hot, muggy August in Washington, so they were practicing just in shorts, and Zach was impressed at the shape Bojan was in despite his rather advanced age for a tennis player. He remarked on how well cut Bojan was, and Bojan came to him and ran his hand along Zach's own muscles, telling him what he needed better definition in the muscles for to serve the various ball stroking techniques and telling him what exercises and how many daily reps of these Zach needed to do to get his body in the proper shape to be competing at the pro level.

The younger man was impressed with what Bojan knew and awed at all he hadn't learned about preparing for the business yet—and he felt a warmness at the nearness and touch of the handsome Bojan that had nothing to do with the temperature.

As they were playing, Zach noticed that Bojan's attention had gone up to the terrace above them, where both his dad,

Kenneth, and coach, Stan, had now appeared and were watching the two younger men practicing. Zach had telephoned his father last night and told him that Bojan was going to be there for a few days, hitting with him, so there was no surprise for the two older men that the tennis player was there. And Bojan had been installed in the studio apartment over the garage at the Thomas' Mclean house the previous evening.

Zach's face flushed in embarrassment, though, when he saw that both of the older men were just in robes and were sitting quite close together as they drank their morning coffee. He had hoped that Bojan wouldn't see anything like this. He looked across the net at Bojan, and although the tennis player had briefly shown a look of surprise, he quickly turned his attention back on Zach and immediately went into an exercise of hitting lobs.

When the two came up for a late breakfast and to hit the showers for a rest before an afternoon practice session, Kenneth and Stan were no longer on the terrace.

As soon as Zach and Bojan entered the house, however, it became obvious where the two had gone. The door to Kenneth's bedroom was slightly ajar, and both Zach and Bojan could clearly hear the sounds of sex. They even were able to see that the two men where on the bed, naked, and that Stan was fucking Zach's father.

"I'm sorry," Zach mumbled, only now realizing that bringing Bojan here hadn't been a good idea. "Please go back to the terrace. I'll bring you some coffee and toast. If you want to leave after that, you can just go straight to the apartment over the—"

"No, it's OK, Zach," Bojan said. "It's OK. I knew about them. I knew about Stanislav. All the guys know. But I thought it was you. . . . Well, that's his usual arrangement. We can just sit in the kitchen. It's OK."

"Me? Oh, god, no, not me," Zach answered in a tone of horror as they went to the kitchen. The house had an open plan. They still could hear the sounds of sex, but they also could get a glimpse of it across the great room through the half-opened door. "But now you know why I can't change coaches. You said 'Stan was a good coach once . . .' and I didn't say that I had my reservations about Stan continuing to coach me, because my father and Stan . . . well, you can see. My father pays for all of this, and he's not going to be favor of a coaching change." Zach said this as he was pouring coffee for both of them and perching on a stool at the kitchen island across from Bojan. The Serbian had opted for a bagel over the toast and was making short work of it.

Zach was still red-faced at the sounds coming from the bedroom. They were reaching some sort of climax, although Zach knew from experience that it would just start all over again. Stanislav was a real bull. In fact, when Zach had first reproached his father for the relationship with Stan, his father's only response, given as if Zach should be able to understand and appreciate it, was that Stan was a real bull.

"Doesn't that bother you?" he asked Bojan.

"Not in the least," the Serbian answered. "It doesn't seem to bother you all that much either other than wondering what I think. It sounds like they're having a good time. Haven't you ever thought of . . . ?"

Zach felt the fingers on his arm. Bojan had reached across the table and was lightly stroking the hairs on Zach's arm—and smiling at him that glorious smile. Zach shuddered. God, he was beautiful. And his body was beautiful. The Serbian's nipples were hard, protruding nubs. Zach had seen that happen with both his father and Stan when they were working their way into doing it. And they fucked openly, not caring if Zach saw them. And Zach had seen them in high fuck.

Sure he'd thought about it before and was attracted to it. He couldn't have moved in his father's circle of friends and not known they were interested in him or not to have had time to think over whether he might be interested as well. He looked into Bojan's hazel eyes. He knew that look.

"We could both shower in the apartment over the garage," Bojan said in a low, hoarse voice.

Bojan fucked Zach under the running water in the shower. Zach's chest and belly were pressed against the wet tiles of the shower stall, and the underside of his hard, upward-curved cock stroked up and down on the slick tiles as Bojan stood close behind him, holding his raised arms against the wall with fists on his wrists and fucking up into him from behind. After Zach came, Bojan half carried him into the bedroom and pushed him down, still wet, on his back on the edge of the bed; gripped Zach's ankles; spread his legs wide; hunched in close over him, capturing Zach's eyes with his own as his cock entered Zach's channel again; and fucked him to Bojan's own ejaculation.

It was clear that Bojan had done this before and was very good at it—and that it would become a part of the regular practice routine.

Although the love play between Zach's father and coach had piqued his curiosity, Zach had no idea until now how good being fucked by another man—and one with experience at it— could be. Bojan was ten years his senior and it seemed like he had spent that ten years learning the techniques that would make Zach moan deeply and beg for more.

As they lay entwined with each other afterward— building up, Bojan whispered, to another session that he described to Zach in detail and that had Zach hard again already—Bojan murmured, "If I was your coach, I could live here and we'd do this twice a day."

"My coach?" Zach said, surprised. "You're a player. You'd leave that for coaching?"

"If I had someone as promising as you to develop, I'd turn to coaching."

"You'd do that for me? You think I can be that good?"

"You're almost that good now. Federov isn't going to develop you further. And, as you know, my own standings are faltering. This is the usual signal to change to coaching. I can't ignore that."

"But you've seen. My father isn't going to let Federov go. And it has nothing to do with my tennis. And without my father—and his backing—I can't go on the circuit. I certainly couldn't pay you a salary."

"I might have a plan?"

"A plan? Tell me."

"I will. But first we fuck again."

"You could tell me first and then we could . . . oh, shit. Oh, fuck. Yes! Oh, god, Yessss!"

76

Kenneth Thomas came home late—near twilight—on Friday evening after the regular partner's meeting he was obligated to attend every Friday he was in town because he was the senior partner in the law firm. He was tired and irritable. He didn't really like it that his son had brought Bojan Nikolic into the house. It had disrupted the balance somehow. Bojan was giving entirely too much tennis technique instruction to Zach, and Stan was beginning to complain about that. He was even talking of maybe leaving. But Kenneth couldn't have that. He wasn't a young man anymore. He couldn't just go out and find someone who could fuck like Stan could and was as well endowed.

Kenneth suspected that Bojan was spiking Zach. The signals of that were too clear. But beyond being slightly jealous because Bojan was such a hunk—and so young still—it was neither here nor there if he was fucking Zach. Zach had to grow up someday. And better someone like Bojan than Stan help him do that. There had been signs that Stan wanted Zach, and this would kill Kenneth. He couldn't compete with his son if Stan turned in that direction. But, regardless, the balance had been upset in the household. Something would need to be done.

He drove up by the front door and got out of his car. He looked over at the garage and saw that a light was on in the studio apartment above it.

Were they up there fucking, he wondered. He had half a notion of stealing up the stairs to see what he could see. Both Bojan and Zach had bodies to die for and were young. Bojan was ten years older than Zach, but Kenneth was twenty years older than he was, so all of that was relative. He'd enjoy watching two superb young bodies vigorously fucking. Even if one of them was his son. Maybe especially if one of them was his son.

He was about to enter the house, when muffled sounds caught his attention and he looked over to Stan's old Mercedes sedan, parked in the shadows near the garage.

The car seemed to be rocking back and forth. Kenneth hesitated, instinctively afraid of what he'd see if he went over there, but curiosity and the need to know that it wasn't what he thought it was enticed him to slowly and silently close the distance between the front door and Stan's Mercedes.

It was exactly what his subconscious was afraid he'd find.

Two naked bodies in the backseat. The familiar back of Stan, knees planted on the floor of the commodious backseat of the old sedan and torso hunched over the other body, facing Stan, his legs spread wide and raised, the balls of his feet leveraging off the ceiling of the car, his fingernails digging into Stan's shoulders.

"Oh, god, oh holy shit! It's so big. It's too big. I don't know if I can . . . oh, shit. Oh Shit! Yesss! All the way. Yessss!"

Revelation one: Zach's voice. First silly thought: Of course it's big. He's horse hung; that's why he's still here.

Later, when Kenneth was sitting at the kitchen island, slugging scotch down, beginning to calm down and he and Zach were listening to Stan driving his Mercedes away—for the last time—Kenneth began to understand the result of the tantrum he had thrown.

"He's gone. He's really gone."

"I'm sorry, Dad."

"It's not your fault. It was just a matter of time. But I don't believe it. He really left."

"I can find another coach, Dad."

Kenneth turned a glassy-eyed stare on his son. "You don't understand. He's gone."

Zach latched onto the realization that his dad wasn't talking about him losing a tennis coach. He was mourning another loss altogether. Up to that point, Zach had regretted, just a little, the plan he and Bojan had concocted. And then, after being fucked by Stan, he had the added regret that it had been just that once with Stan and that it had been abruptly interrupted. Bojan could cock—but Stan could *really* fuck. And the size of that cock—Zach was in awe that he had been able to take it all. But he didn't have much in the way of regret anymore. He'd lost his tennis coach, and despite all of his dad's talk of giving it all up for Zach's tennis development, all his dad could think of was losing his personal fucking machine.

"Bojan can coach me, Dad. He says he's ready to retire into coaching. And he's already helped me so much—"

"We'll talk about it in the morning, Zach."

"But it's the perfect solution. All around."

"Yes, I hear you. We'll talk about it in the morning. I can't think now. I've got to have time to regroup."

In the morning, Zach waited out on the court for a half hour past the usual time for Bojan to appear. But he didn't. And when Zach went to Bojan's apartment above the garage, he wasn't there either. If Zach had taken a good look, he would have seen that Bogan's stuff was all gone too. But Zach didn't do that. He assumed that Bojan had gone to the tennis center to catch the quarterfinal matches—although he gave no thought to how Bojan would make it there.

Zach was almost as confused still this morning as his father had been last night. He couldn't get out of his mind the working of Stan's monster cock in his channel. He had a new appreciation for why his father had been so captivated by the coach.

He half thought that maybe he just hadn't remembered correctly that Bojan wasn't going to hit with him at home today. The more he thought, the more he seemed to remember that Bojan had said he wanted to go to the Fitzgerald center and that they could use the practice courts there as well as the one here.

So, Zach dressed in tennis togs and gathered his rackets and other gear in his duffel and drove off for the Carter Baron center in northwest Washington, where the Legg-Mason tournament was ending its first week.

The practice courts at the Fitzgerald center were rimmed with trees, so Zach was all the way up to the fence of the one that he heard Bojan's voice emanating from before he saw who was on the court. Bojan at one end, of course, but at the other end . . . Stanislav Federov. They were hitting balls, and Stanislav was giving instruction in the booming, demanding voice of his.

Zach just stood there at the fence, his legs going numb and his heart rising in this throat.

Seeing him standing there, both Bojan and Stanislav walked over to him.

"I don't understand," Zach managed to mutter. "Bojan . . . you are going to coach me."

"Coach you?" Bojan said, leveling that "no cares in the world" smile at him. "Why would I do that? Stanislav is free now and has agreed to coach me. I know I've got a couple of more good years of tennis in me. All I need is a winning coach to help give me a boost back up."

"So . . . so, all of that . . . was just . . ."

Stanislav was standing close to Zach now and had placed one hand on his arm and another on his waist. He leaned down and murmured softly in Zach's ear, "You were great last night. We didn't get to finish. I have keys to a trainer's room. We could . . . I know you want it."

"Sure, why not?" Zach answered, turning a steely glance at Bojan. A plan was quickly forming in his mind—he was learning the ins and outs of the business by leaps and bounds. But even if he hadn't any notion of a plan, he wanted Federov's cock inside him again. And he had gathered some sexual tricks from Bojan that just might impress Federov. "And then perhaps we could talk about coaching changes."

Bojan suddenly didn't look quite so sure of himself.

Made to Fit

"He's coming around. Do we have that feeding injection ready?"

"Yes, we have it right here. And the expunge tube too. It's too bad that we couldn't get the feeding and defecation refinement perfected for this one, though. Sheath4 is a magnificent specimen. Wherever did you find him, Dr. Wilson?"

"You can thank Jack for that. He's a sports buff. Saw this one playing arena football and then again later in the season for the city's basketball team."

"He's just perfect. So tall and muscular. He must be six-seven."

"No, six-eight and a half. And everything inside him was in such perfect shape. It was almost a pity, really."

"But you got everything functioning again?"

"Yes, of course. Not as he formerly was, of course, but there were further refinements we put in this one. Sensors along the channel. He'll enjoy it."

"While it lasts."

"Yes, well, one of these times we'll have the balance right."

"Pity about the feeding and defecation system, though."

81

"Yes, but maybe with Sheath5 or 6."

"Where did you capture him?"

"He was coming out of a gym. This was his whole life. At least with the sensor technology all of his work will have been worth it. This will be the height of his life."

* * * *

Perry woke in confusion. Where was he? He could remember waving good-bye to his mates in the gym and going out on the street. Nothing since then.

He was on a gurney, strapped down, but the straps on one of his arms were loose. If he worked at it for a while, he should be able to free an arm—then, with his strength, he should be able to get off of this. Then what?

He didn't know.

He felt funny. All hollow inside—well maybe not completely hollow, but like stuff inside there had been moved around. But he didn't hurt or anything. Maybe a dull ache. But he'd always been able to play through the pain.

Ah, yes, he was loose. He started feeling around his body. He was naked, but everything felt like it was there—it was just this hollow feeling . . . holy hell! What was this? His ass was a fuckin' tunnel. He could get his fist in there . . . hell, he could get both fists in there. Fuckin' A, what's—?

"Naughty, naughty, Sheath4. You aren't ready to get up yet."

Perry's arm was seized and strapped down again.

What's this Sheath4 crap? Perry wondered.

The gurney was been wheeled down a long, wide hallway. Some sort of hospital? The walls were stark white. The faces looking down at him were smiling and telling him that it was all going lovely.

The room was dark. Or at least very dim. After the bright light of the hallway, Perry's eyes weren't adjusting quickly to the difference in light.

He heard a loud, deep wheezing sound—perfectly frightful really. And a clucking and snorting noise.

He was being unstrapped and lifted off the gurney. Really too many strong hands to struggle with. And he felt weak and hollow.

He was being lifted against a wall, and his wrists and upper arms were being bound to some sort of chains on the wall—not plastering him to the wall; holding him suspended in space, his body arching out from and hanging down from the wall.

Then the controlling hands were gone and the lights went up.

Perry lifted his eyes . . . and screamed.

What he was looking at was a monster. A man, surely, but still a monster. A good twelve feet tall, the musculature of a human, but everything exaggerated—gigantic. Its face wasn't ugly—but it wasn't beautiful either. Perry appreciated perfectly cut man flesh, and so he should have been in awe of this creature. Everything was proportional, but it was all so huge—and threatening.

No, it wasn't all in proportion. What hung from the monster's crotch was way out of proportion even as gigantic as the rest of it was. The monster's thick cock dragged on the floor, and the balls of the creature almost reached the floor themselves.

Perry's eyes met those of the creature, who had been hunched over and snuffling loudly. What Perry saw in those eyes—lust—make him shudder, scream again, and tug uselessly against his bonds.

The monster smiled at Perry. It reached down with a gargantuan hand and encased the base of its cock. Perry looked on with horror, as the cock quickly began to rise off the floor and harden.

"No, no, no, please no!" Perry cried out, as the monster moved toward him, reaching out for him, grabbing his ankles and lifting and spreading his legs, moving the gigantic head of that cock to Perry's hole that Perry himself had discovered earlier was now as open as a train tunnel.

Perry continued to scream as the cock slid—not too easily—into that tunnel. He writhed and fought against it. Panted and moaned, grunted and groaned.

The cock was only half inside him when Perry went limp and his eyes rolled back in his sockets.

Unmindful, the creature kept feeding its cock inside Perry.

Back in the booth on the other side of the one-way mirror, the doctors were conferring.

"It's no go. Cock3 is just built too big. No matter how large-bodied the sheaths are, they won't take Cock3. Their torsos just don't have the room to enlarge the tunnel to the necessary dimensions."

"Just wait. I haven't turned the sensors on yet. We'll see. The cameras are rolling, aren't they? That's so important."

Dr. Wilson flipped a couple of switches. Both Perry and the monster came alive. The monster let out a groan and arched its back. It grabbed hold of Perry hips and began to stroke Perry's channel on its embedded cock. Perry's eyes popped open and he moaned in long waves, hooked his legs on the Cock3's hips, and reached out for the monster's bulging nipples.

The creature was fucking hard and fast. Perry shot a load up his belly and then the creature came too, its cum burbling out of Perry's mouth and down his chin. Not just once, but four times, coating his chest with white cum.

Cock3 reached up and jerked the chains binding Perry's wrists out of the wall. It tenderly carried Perry, who just flopped askew in unconsciousness, over to a creature-sized mattress on the side wall. It laid Perry's body gently on his back on the mattress, and positioned Perry's legs in an open position with pillows under the small of his back. Cock3 stood away from the bed to where it could position the head of its still-hard cock at Perry's tunnel and then pushed in to where it could go between Perry's thighs with its knees.

The creature began slow fucking Perry again and was humming its pleasure. Perry lay there, unconscious, his tongue lolling out of his mouth. Cock3 leaned over and lowered its lips to Perry's and gave him a long deep kiss. Then it moved its tongue down Perry's chest, cleaning up the cum it had spouted from Perry's mouth.

"Sheath4 is gone," Dr. Wilson's assistant declared. "That's all—"

"No, it's not all. Watch Cock3's behavior. It wants more sex; it senses there is more to be had. Always before when the sheath was expended, Cock3 lost interest. Cock3 has never kissed a sheath like that before. It's never taken a spent one to its bed before. Let's see more of this. I think it's the sensors. Turn the power up. And keep those cameras rolling."

Perry's body began to twitch and jerk, Cock3 let out a big groan—and began to pump in earnest. The creature also went into a frenzy of kissing Perry and sucking on his nipples and holding him close to its chest while it pumped.

The scene was going on at great length, and the two men in the booth agreed that the sheath must be expended by now; that no man's insides could take what Cock3 was doing to Perry's body.

But still, the young man's body writhed just as if he were alive. The assistant remarked on this, but Dr. Wilson answered that it was probably the strength of the charge coming through the sensors.

That charge certainly was fine with the creature, because once more cum poured out of Perry's mouth and onto his chest and multiple spoutings. And at the point of ejaculation, Perry's eyes flew open, he let out a cry, and his hard cock ejaculated as well.

"Merely mechanics," Dr. Wilson muttered. "But such a good show."

The creature was prodding and patting Perry's body, without reaction. It got off the mattress and went over to the center of the room, turned from Perry, crouched down in position sitting on its legs, its cock now streaming out on the floor before it, and began to rock. There was no telling if this was a sign or satisfaction or of loss.

"Show's over, I guess," Dr. Wilson said. "Very interesting. A bit of progress here."

"No wait," the assistant exclaimed, putting a hand on Dr. Wilson's. "Don't turn off the sensors. Sheath4 is stirring."

"Excellent," Dr. Wilson said. "Improbable but excellent." He checked the cameras to make sure they were operating properly.

Perry gingerly picked himself up from that mattress. He stretched and groaned. Then, he more stumbled than walked over to Cock3 and sat down—on Cock3's cock—in front of the creature. Cock3 looked up, surprise written on its face, and gave a shy little smile. Perry went up on his knees and leaned into the face of Cock3 and kissed the monster's mouth. With a sigh, Cock3 embraced Perry close to its chest with its arms. Perry reached between them and twisted Cock3's nipples until the creature's hips started moving in a roll. It was already hardening, but Perry reached down on each side and stroked the side of the engorging cock.

Cock3 lifted Perry high into the air in front of it with hands encasing Perry's waist. The cock came up at a 45 degree angle. Perry grabbed for his ankles, and spread his legs. Cock3 rubbed the upper side of its cock along Perry's hole as it moved Perry's body back and forth.

"Turning the sensors up on the rim now," Dr. Wilson muttered in the control booth.

Perry threw his head back and howled his pleasure. After a few moments of this, Perry cried out, "Fuck me. Oh, god, fuck me again!"

Perry was skewered again on the cock, facing the seated Cock3. The creature was pulling Perry's channel back and forth on the cock, close enough into his body that Perry could hang his heels on the monster's shoulders. Perry's body was arched back and way from Cock3's heaving chest. His arms were dangling at his side and he was crying out, "Yes, Yes. Deeper. Fuck me. Fuck ME!"

Cock3 was making deep, guttural sounds of supreme pleasure—and pumping hard and deep.

The two doctors in the booth had high fived, and Dr. Wilson was now going wild with the sensor controls.

The bulb of Cock3's cock emerged from Perry's mouth, and Perry had his tongue out of his mouth, flicking it over the glans. Perry spouted up at Cock3's face once, twice, three times. And then Cock3 repeated that doubly in a display of short-timed spray over both of their chests.

When Dr. Wilson turned the cameras off and turned to his assistant, Cock3 and Perry were stretched on the mattress,

Perry's back cuddled into Cock3's chest and encircling embrace. Sheath4 was serving its purpose with Cock3 and Perry was sighing and moving his hips forward and back, giving gentle friction to the cock buried inside him.

"So, that was a success," Dr. Wilson's assistant answered.

"Yes, now with Sheath5 we need to get that feeding and defecation refinement in place. We can use Cock3 again. He's got a taste for it now."

"And the films from today?"

"To the Internet—to our special subscribers there, of course. We'll make a mint on this one alone. It's what keeps our important research going."

"And Sheath4? Leave him in there?"

"For now. After a few days, if he's still functioning, set him up with The Ram."

"The Ram? But we suspended that study."

"I know. But it was always a favorite film of the subscribers. And I like to watch too."

Appalachian Trail

I'm not all that sure how I got roped into going to Ken's daughter's place up on Blue Mountain near Front Royal. It was something about the Appalachian Trail, though, I'm sure. We were sitting at the bar at Scotties, a truck stop bar in Opal where Route 17 breaks off east from Route 29, south of Washington, D.C., to go over to Fredericksburg and the Eastern Shore, and Ken mentioned the Appalachian Trail.

"I've always thought it would be fun to hike a section of that," I'd said. "But I haven't gotten around to it yet. There are the mountains right over there, with the trail running along the top of them, and I haven't found time to hike them yet."

"You're probably still hitting the books pretty hard at that college you're going to," Ike the bartender had said. "You got no time for hiking."

"Yeah, I guess," I'd answered. "But a guy can waste his time away hitting the books 24/7—and that sometimes just leads to spending all your time working after you're done with college. I've met a lot of guys who have never been up on the Blue Ridge mountains—never having found the time—even though they are right out there where we all can see them."

"Hiking the mountains can be pretty rough," Stan, the guy who owned the gun shop and firing range in Opal said from down the bar. "You look like you could handle it, though. You on the football team over at that college?"

"No," I answered. "We're too small to be in a football league. I wrestle, though—and work out a couple of times a week. And I ride hills with my bike. When I'm exhilarated, I just have to get out on my bike."

"Yeah, you look like you work out a lot," Ken, who had saddled up to the bar next to me, said. "Lookin' real good."

I didn't know if I was supposed to melt to that or not. Ken had been nosing around me for several weeks now. I'd found this guy's bar only recently. I'd been going into Washington, D.C., to meet guys—there was a full-service club on O Street near the southeast Washington waterfront, where the Anacostia flowed into the Potomac. But that was a long way to go. I'd hooked up with a couple of young, good-looking guys here at Scotties, so I'd come here when I didn't have time to go into D.C.

It wasn't really my kind of bar for what I wanted, though. There weren't too many young, in-shape guys coming in here. It was mostly lonely truckers who worked the eastern seaboard and local service worker types who could get pretty rough. And older guys, of course. Those guys were always around gawking and doing their wishful thinking thing. That was Ken—two out of three. He was a trucker, kind of a redneck. Hard muscled, but wiry and older, probably in his mid forties. He was uglier than a fence post, and he didn't seem too bright. About all he could talk about was his truck route and sports— and my body. Not at all the kind of guy for a young college student to hook up with.

Whenever Ken came into the bar when I was here, he tried to saddle up to me and bring the conversation around to complimenting me on my body and getting suggestive about going with him.

"You really want to do some hiking on the Appalachian Trail, you should go up to my daughter's place on Blue Mountain one of these days," Ken was saying. "She's got a house right across the road from where it runs by on its way to the Skyline Drive along the top of the Blue Ridge. You could start with just walking a section of the trail there. There are a couple of entrances to it along the road running up the mountain to her place."

"Yeah, that would be an idea," I'd said. I just said it to be polite, though, and those of us gathered around the bar went on to talk about the rain we'd been having leading into October.

"It'll be a great year for leaf watching," Stan said. "We'll have a lot of tourists coming through as early as the weekend to go up on the drive. The show should be spectacular this year because of the rain we've been getting."

"I'd sure like to see that," I said. On hindsight, I guess that's where I made my mistake—giving Ken his opening.

"I'll be up there, at my daughter's, week after next," Ken said. "I'll be dog sitting. Her and her husband are taking a Caribbean cruise, and I've agreed to house and dog sit for them. I'll be having a gathering up there—doing some hunting and some cookouts for neighbors up there I know. You've got some sort of fall break comin' up from college, don't cha, Dan? You could come up for a couple of days and walk a chunk of the trail. There's plenty of room at the house. I could take you up there when I went."

"Yeah, that would be nice," I said. I wasn't really thinking on what he was saying, though. I was giving the eye to a young hunk who had just come into the bar. I was pretty sure I'd seen him at the Sheetz gas station. He was some sort of shift manager there, I thought. He was a real good looker and strutted around like he had something special. And maybe he did. I was surprised to see him in here. Sheetz was nearby, up at the intersection where 17 broke off from 29, so he must know what sort of bar this was.

He was looking right back at me. Showing interest. So, I wasn't paying all that much attention to what Ken was saying.

"I could pick you up at the college next Friday afternoon and take you up there for a couple of days. Four o'clock in the afternoon suit you?"

"Yeah, sure, that would be nice. Thanks," I said, not fully listening to him. My eyes were on the Sheetz guy, who had sat—or, rather, slouched—at a table, with his chair turned sideways, pointed at the bar, his tight-jeans-clad legs spread and his hand on his crotch. He was still staring directly at me and giving a little smile.

When I went over to his table, he said he had a new Camaro I might like to see. And then he asked me if I'd ever been fucked in a Camaro.

After all of Ken's beating around the bush, I found this guy's direct proposition refreshing. "Not until abut fifteen minutes from now, if you've got the time and the dick for it."

He drove me into the car wash building over behind the Sheetz that was supposed to be closed this time of night and shut the line down so we were alone. After he'd sucked me off, he moved over into the passenger seat and I sat on his cock and concentrated on not letting my head bounce off the ceiling of the low-slung sports car.

This had been worth all that time of putting up with Ken trying to zero in on me.

* * * *

"Uh, I'm tired, Ken—and I've had too much beer. If we're going to walk the Appalachian Trail tomorrow afternoon, I need some shut eye. OK?"

"Yeah, sure, we can go on upstairs."

"You probably need to clean up down here first, though. Didn't you say there'd be some families arrive tomorrow morning for a cookout before we hiked?"

"Yeah, maybe, although they may not come before Sunday. They didn't commit to a specific day. We could leave this and clean it up in the—"

"Sure, if it's there in the morning, I'll help you with it. Goodnight." I didn't let him finish his sentence and my feet were already on the stairs to the second floor. I went straight to the bedroom at the end of the hall he'd said I could use and shut and locked the door, thanking the heavens that the bedroom had its own bathroom. I wouldn't unlock the door until morning.

I could see what he was doing—what he wanted. He kept saying without really saying it that there would be families up here with us. But we'd gotten to his daughter's house after he'd taken me to dinner at the Apple House at the foot of the mountain, and his daughter and her family were already gone. There were just two hound dogs here, which seemed happy to see Ken.

I guess he thought that if he bought me dinner, I'd let him fuck me all night up here.

The time that any other people—any families—were coming up here was conveniently receding into later days than he'd suggested. If I'd known he was going to get me up here without others around, I wouldn't have come.

He was old, and rednecky, and ugly—and not the sharpest knife in the drawer. There was nothing he had that I wanted. I was into younger, good-looking guys.

He'd tried his best to carry on a conversation with me in the evening, but he finally gave up and found a college football game on ESPN. Neither one of us gave a crap for either of the teams playing, but we were both more comfortable with that to focus on than fumbling at cross-purposes with each other. The beer had been flowing, but I didn't want to get drunk with him. He was one of those bottomless pits who never seemed to get drunk no matter how much he'd had. I'd noticed that down at Scotties.

He must have thought I was getting drunk, though, because he came over and sat close to me on the couch while we watched the game. He had an arm in back of me on top of the couch back. When I felt the touch of his fingertips on my shoulder, I made like I had to go to the can. And when I came back, I made a point of sitting in one of the armchairs rather than back on the couch—and as soon as I could feign some yawns and remark on what an exhausting week I'd had at school, I escaped to my bedroom and locked the door.

Ken wasn't there the next morning when I got up. He left me a note about having to go down into Front Royal for some groceries and had left some breakfast for me.

When he came back he was all smiles and good humor, saying that we could pick up the Appalachian Trail up here near the house and walk a couple of miles back toward the foot of the mountain and then turn and come back and that this would be a good introduction to the trail to me.

He seemed to have decided I wasn't going to let him fuck me and was making the best of the situation.

We went out on the trail after lunch, and now I was glad I'd come up here. The forest was a riot of autumn colors. And it was so quiet and everything was so lush and dreamy and mysterious that I was almost having a religious experience out here.

As we approached the intersection of the trail with a pathway that Ken said went back to the road and to a parking lot next to the communications towers that were at the very top of Blue Mountain, we heard muffled voices of men. Right where the other trail came in, there were two young men hikers, sort of sitting on large rocks beside the trail.

"We're foreign students taking a year off and hiking the whole way up from Georgia to Maine," one of the guys said when we approached them and struck up a conversation. They both looked like they were fully capable of doing so. Both were muscular and good looking. They were wearing tight T-shirts, with back packs; cargo shorts; and hiking boots, and they seemed oblivious to the chill in the air.

The blond, clean-cut one said his name was Hans, that he was from Amsterdam, and that he was studying to be a doctor. He was the heavier and taller of the two, but was solid rather than fat. The darker-haired one, with a profusion of curly body hair and a heavy five-o'clock shadow was named Alain; he said he was just studying to study. I thought their English was exceptionally good for foreigners. I also thought they were both so sexy looking that I had trouble keeping my eyes off them.

They and Ken took to each other immediately. They told me they were resting from coming off the Skyline Drive portion of the parkway and were looking for someplace to change into warmer clothes as it was getting chilly.

"Hikers usually follow the warmer weather by hiking down from Maine in the fall," Ken said.

"We know that now," Hans said, with a laugh. He was the more jovial and outgoing of the two. He also seemed to be the "take charge" one and the one ready to make an instant decision and get on with it.

94

"We're from a house just up the trail there," Ken said. "And we're turning back from here anyway. If you want, you could stop at our house and change your clothes there. Maybe take a break from the hike."

"You live together in that house?" Hans asked. He turned to me and gave me a penetrating look.

"We're there, yes," Ken said.

I wanted to correct the impression Ken was giving, but I didn't have a chance.

"Ja, sounds good to me," Hans said.

The three of them turned immediately and headed back down the trail, toward Ken's daughter's house. I followed along behind.

Not far from the cutoff back to the house, though, I tripped on a tree root in the trail and went down hard, twisting my ankle.

The three men in front of me heard my pained grunt when I went down and stopped and turned.

"You OK, Dan?" Ken called back.

"It's my ankle. I may have sprained it."

"Here, let me see," Hans said, and he crouched down beside me and started unlacing my hiking boot.

"We're not far from the house," Ken said. "You think you can make it?"

"I don't know," I answered.

"You could go on ahead," Hans said. "I'll look at this. I have bandages in my pack I can wrap it in and we'll be along shortly."

With no more than that, I was alone in the forest with Hans on the Appalachian Trail. He had gotten my boot off and was gently massaging my foot, feeling for strained tendons. He attentions were both painful and sensual. I grimaced. But I also was trembling under his touch. He was a hunk and was overpowering as he leaned over me. He was exactly what I melted to—when I could get it.

"You live with the older man? You go with men?"

"No. I mean, yes," I answered, flustered. His hands on my foot and ankle and massaging up onto my calf was disconcerting. "No, I don't live with Ken," I said.

"But yes you go with men? I saw the looks you gave me and Alain. In Amsterdam we know what those looks mean."

I paused without answering a bit too long. He gave me a knowing smile and moved in closer between my spread legs and let his hand move up onto my thigh.

"Perhaps you go with younger men then Ken?"

"Yes, I go with younger men—when I like them," I answered in a small voice.

"Perhaps you like me, Ja? I am, what you say, hard for you," he said in a low voice. "You go with me? You let me fuck?"

"Here? Now?" I asked, shocked, but also melting to him. His knowing forwardness was disarming.

"Yes, of course. Off the path, of course, but where is more beautiful for making love than here in the forest? I give you good fuck."

He raised my bare foot to his lips, licked up the sole, and took my big toe inside his mouth. After he had sucked for a moment, he let it free and moved his hands to my crotch. "Let us see what we have here," he murmured.

"You said off the path," I responded in a strangled voice. "Here, anyone could . . . Oh, god!"

He picked me up and carried me downhill from the trail. Within a few yards we were invisible from the trail in the lush foliage. He found a mossy area and lowered me on the ground on my back, stripped off my jeans and briefs, and moved his knees between my legs. He bent over and took my cock in his mouth, and I moaned for him, and, in short order, was begging for the cock—which he was all too willing to provide.

His fucking was straightforward, no-holding-back plowing, as if we were doing the most natural thing that two healthy young people did in the forest. I was completely taken with the matter-of-fact sensuality of it. Just two young, attractive men getting their rocks off on a pleasant afternoon. I rolled my hips up and lifted my legs over his shoulders, both of us taking care with my ankle, even though I now could feel that it had been just a twinge and didn't hurt anymore, and we locked eyes on each others, enjoying the reflection back and forth of the pleasure we both were having.

After Hans fucked me, we stayed in that position, panting, slowly regaining our breath. I wanted him again, almost immediately. His virility was obvious in how rapidly he was hard again.

He rose to his feet, and extended his hands down to me. "Here, I carry."

"It's OK," I said. "The ankle doesn't even hurt now. I just rolled it, and it's already OK. I can walk on it."

"No, I show you what I like to do with small men like you. You be my baby." He then reached down and pulled me up. He crouched a bit, bending his legs, while he pulled my ass into his crotch and my channel onto his cock again. I wrapped my legs around his waist and nuzzled my face into the hollow of his neck. His hand cupped and spread my buttocks and, while he stood there in the forest with me draped on his hips, he used the strength of his cupped hands on my buttocks to rise and lower me on his cock until both of us had come again.

Then, with me still whimpering my surrender, and following my directions to the side trail that went to Ken's daughter's place, he carried me to the house.

When we entered the house, we found Ken and Alain sitting in the living room, drinking a beer. They both looked at us bug eyed when they realized I was impaled on Hans's cock.

"We were wondering where you were," Ken said. "Is Dan's ankle—?"

"Where is his bed?" Hans asked.

"Upstairs, last room on the left down the hall. Do you?—"

"Come with me, Alain," Hans interjected. "We have need of you too."

In my bedroom, Hans laid me on my back on the bed and then he and Alain whispered to each other as both started to undress. I assumed they were changing their clothes.

I assumed wrong.

When I'd been stripped as well, I was turned and raised to my knees on the bed by Alain, who stood on the floor behind me, his arm wrapped around my belly, holding me up, as he entered my well-lubricated channel strongly with his engorged cock and began to stroke me deep. Hans came around the other side of the twin bed and fed his cock between my lips.

I had two sexy, young hunks going down on me at once. I'd never done this before, but it was highly arousing and I had absolutely nothing to complain about.

Alain was pulling out of me, but then I was being skewered again. He was thicker and was reaching deeper with his cock this time. And now he was playing me, not just fucking me. He'd pull his cock back and punish my prostate with his bulb, and when I was moaning deeply, he'd thrust deep. He'd stroke until I thought we were in a rhythm. And then he'd change the rhythm, keeping me off guard, making me gasp, not knowing what was coming next—except that it would take me to newer heights of satisfaction.

I don't know when I realized it wasn't Alain fucking me anymore. It might have been the stronger grip on my hips—or the bigger hands. But I looked back and saw that it was Ken fucking me, not Alain.

I no longer cared. Ken was a master of the fuck, and he was playing me like I was an instrument made exclusively for his attention. I suddenly realized the advantage older men had. Ken had the experience of knowing exactly what pleased a bottom and brought the most intense pleasure out of them.

He was still fucking me when the two young hikers were gone. He no longer was ugly to me. I wanted to be fucked on my back now, so that I could watch the tight muscles of his chest contract and expand with his stroking and I could reach out and feel the sinews of his lean, but well-defined muscles and the veins sticking out on his arms because they had no fat to travel through.

"You what?" he exclaimed when he'd brought both of us to climax. "You want to do what? You didn't like it? And your ankle—"

"I loved it," I said. "I just have to get on my bike and pump up hills when I'm this excited and exhilarated. And my ankle will be fine; I need to keep it loose. I'll come right back. I want it again—when you get it up again."

"I can get it up for you right now," Ken said, reaching for me again.

"I saw a bike out by the garage. I can use it, can't I? I'll be right back."

"Sure, knock yourself out," Ken said and he rolled over on his back on my bed—and I could see that he, indeed, could get it right back up for me.

I rode across the top of the mountain, back toward Front Royal, climbing a bit to the peak at the communications towers, where I would turn and come back—being sincere that I wanted him again, could hardly wait to get his dick back inside me, playing me like a violin.

When I hit the rise at the communications towers, I saw them—Hans and Alain getting into a sedan that had been parked in the parking lot there. They hadn't been walking the trail up from Georgia. They'd entered the trail at the communications towers—exactly where we had come across them in the first place.

And then what I had fleetingly seen back at the house when they were dressing hit me. Ken had let off fucking me briefly and he turned to them and I'd seen a flash of green.

He'd paid them.

I'd been stupid. It had all been a setup to help Ken get his cock inside me.

I turned and started peddling furiously back to the house. But my pleasure was more important to me than my pride. I didn't fool myself. I was peddling back to get more of Ken's cocking, not to dredge up any scheming that was in the past.

Trawler Initiation

On a shrimp boat trawler well out to sea, you and a big muscle-bound bruiser of questionable intellect are telling me while we are taking a coffee break in the trawler I'd signed on for my sophomore summer in college that the senior crew all have privileges with the new guy. Just an initiation—like crossing the equator for the first time. But more fun.

What privileges and fun for who? I think, fear rising from my gut.

I'd been avoiding the bruiser because I didn't like the way he looked at me. But you've been nothing but friendly to me and have shown interest in who I was, why I was spending the summer working on a trawler, how old I was, did I screw all of the coeds—stuff like that. This, though. This, here and now, doesn't seem friendly—or maybe it seems too friendly. It has got me off balance.

You say you know I take cock because I'd been with the captain in his cabin the previous night and the bruiser heard how well I liked the captain's cocking. He says the captain was crowing this morning, saying he'd won the crew poll on who would be first.

Would it make any difference if I told you that the captain had gotten me drunk, and that I'd never done it before, and that, other than the soreness, I wouldn't be half aware that I had done it last night? Somehow I don't think you'd care—or that the bruiser would care either. And the captain said he wouldn't tell anyone if I came to his cabin again tonight. And he said it in such a way for me to understand that it wasn't really a request—out here on the open water, where it's just those of us on this trawler.

Flustered, I say I don't know what to say. What I'm thinking is how the bruiser heard. The captain's cabin isn't anywhere near the quarters for the rest of the crew. But what I say is that I'm not easy like that, and will think about it.

I'm trying to remain calm—cool. Trying to cool man my way out of the cabin. But if they'd seen me riding the captain's cock that second time last night they'd have a right to think I sniffed after it anywhere I could get it. I'd just been letting loose. And he'd gotten me drunk. Three months on the sea completely free from the constraints of land and college. And the captain was a stud and a half and he wore practically nothing, just a Speedo—just like all of us when we are out to sea. It was just a fling. Just a summer madness to mark the end of the school term. And he got me drunk. I'd thought about it, yes, and I'd fantasized about it when I was thinking of signing onto the trawler, because I'd heard what could happen on these isolated vessels out on the open water. But I'd never done it before last night.

"Think fast," you say and turn to the bruiser and say, "What do you think, Big Jim? Right here on the table?"

The bruiser giggles, stands, and pops the biggest cock I've ever seen out of his Speedo. I'd been eyeing his basket for days, wondering who would be up to taking it that big. That was part of why I'd been staying away from him. In shock, I stand. You reach out and grip my forearm, but I brush your hand away and lurch for the hatch out to the deck.

I hear you both laugh as you start in pursuit. I make it only about thirty feet, in the bow and below the bridge. The bruiser pounces on me and brings me down on a coil of roping. I land on top of him, and he snakes heavily muscled arms around mine, pinning me to his chest. You lean down and pull my Speedo off my legs. The bruiser's legs then lace in between mine, and he lifts and spreads his legs, so that mine spread and lift as well. I feel his thick, hard cock in the small of my back, snaking almost all the way up to my shoulder blades, it seems. I start to hyperventilate, but I know that won't help, so I start taking breaths in large gulps.

You are standing, looking down at me, and smiling. You push your Speedo to below your balls, showing that you're hard for me too. You go down on your knees between my legs, and I cry out as you slowly work your way into my ass.

I struggle, but it's useless, the bruiser is too strong for me. And the struggling only helps you move deeper inside me. I whimper as you stroke and stroke and stroke. I'm determined not to cry, though, to take it and then get as far away from here as possible. But what is far away on a trawler on the open seas?

Seeing that the captain has come out onto the deck of the bridge above us, I call out to him. He smiles and waves, takes a swig from his coffee cup, and turns and calls to the mate to join him. I see that he's pushed his Speedo down and is stroking his cock. No relief there. The black guy, Horace, who provides a lot of the muscle on moving cargo, has come up from the stern, hearing that something's going on. He's wearing a big grin and comes and stands beside us. He's got his cock in his hand.

"Relax kid," you say. "It's just the new guy initiation. When everyone's had a piece, we'll let you choose your two favorite for the rest of the voyage. Maybe they'll both enjoy you at once." You, the black guy, and the bruiser laugh.

I feel you jerk and come and then you are out of me and helping the bruiser free his cock from between his groin and my back. You are helping the bruiser find my hole with his staff. And when he has and I feel like I'm being split asunder, I start screaming anew. The mate is next to the captain on the bridge deck now. They are embracing and kissing and have taken possession of each other's cocks.

I can't stop complaining loudly from having the largest cock in the world pumping inside me. This isn't anything like the captain's. It isn't anything like I had from either the captain or you.

"Scream all you want, kid," the bruiser says in my ear in a hoarse voice. "There's empty ocean in every direction you can see from here, and we'll be out here for three months. And," he giggles, "a screamer makes me horny. And when I'm horny, I can go all day."

I believe him. I moan, starting to calm down, because the pain is turning into pleasure and I'm taking the biggest cock in the world. I'm taking the biggest dick in the world. I can't believe I'm managing the biggest dick in the universe. I'm wondering if it can get deeper from a different position. I shudder. I don't want to know that. But . . . but, of course I do want to know that. I'm taking the biggest dick in the world.

"Sweet ass," bruiser whispers. "And you like it. I can tell you like it. You wanna bunk with me tonight? I'll show you tricks you never knew. Maybe Horace can join us. You'll like that, kid. I can tell."

I'm thinking of the captain. I've got to go there tonight. But will he keep me all night? And, if not, will the bruiser be waiting for me? Can I take it? Maybe I'll need to be drunk tonight. Three months. Oh, fuck.

God he can fuck. God he can fuck.

I look up to see the captain and mate coming down the stairway, cocks in hand, smiling. I can barely hear what the captain is saying. "Great lay. Tight ass. Had him three times last night. I can tell you what he likes."

Guitar Me

The name on the awning of the taverna struck me and brought up memories so rapidly and fully that I wasn't completely aware of the guitar music wafting up in my brain. If I had been I wouldn't have climbed the two terrazzo steps to the terrace level of the Tree of Idleness restaurant and sat at a table under a spreading olive tree. Even then, though, I knew I was tempted to enter the restaurant because of its similarity to the one Adrianna and I had often frequented in the village of Bellapais in the northern, Turkish, enclave of Cyprus. As it was, the memories brought back so much pain that I collapsed more than sat, breathless, in one of the straw-bottomed chairs, and was pinned to the spot because the young Greek Cypriot waiter was so quick to take my order of a bottle of chilled Palamino wine and a plate of sheftalia.

I was on somewhat of a pilgrimage of nostalgia to try to hang onto memories of the good times with Adrianna—the years before she had contracted breast cancer and our world was sent spinning. But this was, perhaps, too much nostalgia too quickly. And running into a restaurant named the Tree of Idleness was more than I had bargained for. Adrianna and I had met at a restaurant called the Tree of Idleness in northern

Cyprus. She ran her own seaside pool bar west of Kyrenia on the northern Cypriot coast, but her then husband, Jalil, was a musician at both her bar and the Tree of Idleness, and I went to the latter restaurant in Bellapais one evening. I was in my first year following journalism school and was traveling around Europe. I told everyone that I was looking for out-of-the-way vacation places and was compiling a tour book, but I acknowledged to myself that I was hiding.

Jalil wasn't playing his set when I went into the restaurant. If he had been, I wouldn't have gone in. The open terrace under a spreading olive tree was nearly empty except for the usual elderly Turkish men, lining the wall in their straw-bottomed chairs, drinking the sludge they called coffee, and ogling all of the pretty girls walking through the Bellapais central square.

There was a girl for me to ogle too. She was sitting alone at a table and looking pensive. I was bold and asked her if I could sit with her while I drank an Efes beer. She was amenable to that. She was a mere wisp of a girl—a young woman, surely, but waiflike, with dark hair in a pixie cut, which made me think of her as a girl. I discovered in chatting her up that she was English. She said that she was there to hear the guitarist who would be playing in a few minutes. I almost left then, the mere mention of a guitar being what I was trying to escape, but the young woman—Adrianna—seemed almost to beg me to stay with the look in her eyes.

Then Jalil, a dark, handsome Turkish Cypriot man, who wasn't much older than I was and was strongly built, perched on a stool next to the door into the interior of the taverna and began to tune his guitar. Adrianna stopped speaking in midsentence and almost looked frightened when Jalil first appeared. But when Jalil started to play his soft, but insistent, Spanish guitar music, she became mesmerized. So did I for that matter, much to my chagrin. Jalil was as compelling as his music was. His features were rugged in a way that promised to make him ugly in old age, and he was powerfully built, evoking surprise that he was strumming a guitar rather than working on a fishing boat. But he was beautiful now, and there was a sensuality in what he played and how he played it that seemed to hold Adrianna in thrall. It did me, certainly.

When he'd finished his first set, he came over to the table and demanded—I can't say asked, as it certainly seemed like a demand—that Adrianna tell him who I was. She introduced us and then, almost immediately, said she'd have to leave. I started to rise when she did, but Jalil asked, almost with a pout, if I wasn't going to stay to listen to his next set, which would be his last for the evening. As compelled as I was to do so, I would have said no, but Adrianna insisted that I do so as well.

The music of his concluding set was so compelling and sensual that I almost couldn't speak when he finished and came back to my table.

"You seemed to enjoy that," he said, with a smile.

"Yes, it was incredible," I answered.

"I watched you as I was playing. It enhanced my playing, I think," he said in a low, hoarse voice. "It was almost like having sex, wasn't it?"

"Yes," I murmured in answer. It was exactly like that. That's what I was hiding from, and that's why I probably should have left as soon as he started playing.

"That was my last set, but there is more that I'd like to play for you. I live on the coast, down west of Kyrenia, but I have a room here too, above the taverna. Will you come with me?" he asked.

"Yes," I said, instinctively knowing what he was asking of me.

And then in a lower-register voice, his eyes drilling into mine, and his fingers lightly brushing the hair on my forearm, causing chills to go up my spine. "And will you come for me?"

"Yes," I whispered.

Later Jalil told me about the pool bar on the Mediterranean coast that he and his English wife, Adrianna—he only told me they were married after he'd fucked me—ran, and he invited me to move in with them and use the bar as a base to do my tour book research.

I accepted. I knew it was a mistake to do so, and perhaps if he didn't play the guitar so divinely . . .

Once I'd moved into the pool bar house, I found that Jalil was often drunk and, when so, was a brutal, rough lover. I could take it—in fact I rather enjoyed being taken totally and roughly and slapped around a bit. But he fucked his wife this way too.

In time, after she'd been brutally assaulted in the night after the pool had closed down and I had to sit in my room and listen to his taking of her—knowing exactly how it felt to be grabbed and slapped and forced down under him on the bed and have my legs forced open and the hardness of him thrust up inside me and the plowing start as he choked the breath out of me—I could not ignore it anymore. I never reached the stage of trying to intervene. We were in his country, with its traditional laws. She was English and I was American, and she was his wife—almost his possession, in Turkish terms. And as long as he played his guitar for me, I was virtually his possession as well.

But later, after he'd left her sobbing to go drink himself further into a stupor, I'd come to her room and comfort her and tend to her bruises. In time, comforting her included giving her the gentle fuck that her husband wouldn't give her.

All the time he was fucking me too. When he found out that I was fucking Adrianna, we had to flee him and northern Cyprus. We went to London, where I wrote and she worked in a pub. We married when her divorce from Jalil went into effect, and we returned to Cyprus—this time to the Greek side—where we opened a small boutique hotel and taverna on the southern coast, near Limmasol. It did well—and my travel writings were doing well also. When Adrianna contracted breast cancer, we owned and operated a larger boutique hotel in the Lake District of England.

It took Adrianna two horrible years to die. I sold the hotel and went wandering, enabled to do so because writing about this was my bread and butter. But in my wanderings I found I was both seeking and hiding from something— something that I now was free to do, but that I still thought was wrong for me to do.

My wanderings and search for places Adrianna and I had been happy brought me back to Greek Cyprus. I was lodged at the Nicosia Hilton now, in the interior capitol of Cyprus.

Restlessness had sent me walking in an ever-enlarged circle around the hotel. And that was what brought me to the taverna, on the small side street, named the Tree of Idleness, just as the taverna on the square in Bellapais on the Turkish side had been named.

I was still deep in reverie when the music began. The guitarist hadn't come out to the patio under the olive tree. He sat on a stool inside the taverna, which was really used only in the colder winter months, so he was the only one inside. It was dusk and he was under a spotlight, though, so he was hard to miss. He was playing Antonio Carlos Jobim's "Corcovado," which had been one of my favorites in college when I heard Cat Ralston play it.

I couldn't leave now. I was a prisoner to the music—and to the guitarist. He was considerably older than I was, maybe forty-five or so, of medium height, but he was hard-bodied in a sinewy way and with rugged features that showed wear and tear but, when put together, exuded power and sensuality. I couldn't help myself, I was already thinking of him as a lover and wondering if he'd be gentle or rough—was he long, thick? Jalil was both.

I shook my head. What was I thinking. Just because he played the guitar divinely and was sensual looking didn't put us in bed together. I'd finished the sheftalia and nearly finished the Palamino. But suddenly I knew I couldn't leave—at least not until he finished for the evening and left. When the waiter came by, I ordered a brandy. He didn't care how long I stayed. When Greeks came to a taverna at night, they were in for the night.

There was something about the guitarist that wasn't completely Greek. If he were in the movies, he'd play a gangster part or the grizzled cowboy, long experienced to the hard life of a ranch.

When he finished the set and left the little platform he'd been sitting on and disappeared into the back of the taverna, I felt like I'd been in a trance. For the first time I noticed that there were CDs on the tables. On the front was a photo of the guitarist, set half in shadows. A black-and-white shot. It only added to the rugged sensuality of his aura. I looked at the name. Paul D'Alessandro. That wasn't a Greek name. There was a short bio on the case. He was Cypriot back to the period in which the Genoese owned the island. So he was of mixed Italian and Greek origin. It was a good mix, I thought.

I found myself reading the bio, looking for any evidence that he was married. And then laughing at myself. Jalil had been married and it hadn't mattered. I had been fucking Adrianna during the same period that Jalil had been fucking me and it didn't matter. Still I chastised myself for having any fantasy of a hookup with this guitarist. I had foresworn all of that. This was why I was backtracking and trying to capture all of the good times I'd had with Adrianna. I was determined to keep her and what we'd had for seven years firmly in my mind.

"You like the music?"

I looked up sharply. He was standing there at my table, his guitar in his hand.

"Yes, yes, I liked it very much," I said.

"My name is Paul. Paul D'Alessandro," he said.

"Yes, I know," I answered. And then, embarrassed, I pointed at the CD. "Oh, sorry. My name is also Paul. Paul Matisen. A coincidence."

"Yes, a nice coincidence you come to the Tree of Idleness. You come here before?"

"Yes. No, not this Tree of Idleness."

"Ah, you have been to the one in Bellapais then."

"Yes. Years ago. But . . ."

"Yes, I know about the one on the Turkish side. That's the original one, but it belonged to Greeks. They opened this one on the Greek side when the Turks invaded and pushed the Greeks off their land there."

"Oh." I didn't quite know what to say after that. It naturally was a sore subject with the Greeks who had been dispossessed of their homes and businesses on the Turkish side, much the same as the Turks who had lived on the Greek side of the line experienced.

"No matter what brought you. It's good you found us. I watched you while I played. It was as if you were spinning on every note."

"Spanish guitar music does that to me," I said with a nervous laugh. "It's so . . . so . . ."

110

"Sensual?"

"Yes," I answered in a small voice.

"I could see that in your face as well. That was what I meant by spinning—the thought of you spinning on what I might have for you. I believe it made me play with more feeling."

I felt I would hyperventilate. I'd heard that line before—the declaration that I made him play with more feeling. That's what Jalil and said right before he told me he was going to fuck me—and I had almost begged him to.

"Well . . ."

"'Corcovado' is a nice song. But someone like you, I think a bachata in flamenco style is for you."

"Bachata?" I asked. "Flamenco I've heard of."

"Yes. Something very Latin. Something for lovers. Like Ravel's 'Bolero.' You know 'Bolero'?"

"Yes, doesn't everyone?" I said with a catch in my voice.

"I play a bachata in flamenco style for you. For you, I play 'Mon Amor' now. Not the famous song by that name. A bachata by that name. One I have often played . . . for a lover."

"Really, anything you play will be fine," I answered hurriedly. "I have to leave soon anyway. Your playing has been—"

"And then you come with me, yes? My sets will be over. I have a room nearby. I play just for you. Then I play you, yes? I make sex with you like I make love to my guitar."

I froze. Before I could say anything, though, he had turned and gone to his high stool and was preparing to play.

The music was mesmerizing. It began slow and the tempo and volume built. I had an insistent, pounding rhythm to it when it got into full swing and it, indeed, was just like the rhythm of the fuck. I found that I was holding my breath and that my hand had gone under the table top to my engorged cock through the thin material of my trousers. His eyes were locked on mine and mine on his and I felt we were having sex as he played. He said he wanted to make sex with me like he was playing the guitar. I watched his fingers caressing and brutalizing the strings of the guitar in term—and that's what I envisioned him doing with my body. The image was overwhelming.

111

He reached a crescendo and I couldn't take any more. I threw bills down on the table, far more than I owed for the food and drink, and stumbled off the patio and onto the street. At the corner of the building, I turned into the darkness, moved behind a thick stand of bougainvillea winding up a trellis, unzipped, and barely got my cock out when, the clearly heard music reached an even higher, more insistent pitch, and I ejaculated against the stuccoed wall.

I stumbled back to my hotel room, took a shower, and got into the bed naked. Weaving a scene in my mind then with Paul D'Alessandro, I masturbated to another ejaculation and fell into a deep sleep.

* * * *

Jalil wasn't the one who taught me the sensual effect that classical guitar music—and guitarists—had on me. That had already happened and, in many ways, was what had brought me to Turkish Cyprus to begin with—to hide from myself and my weakness.

I studied journalism at Georgetown University, in Washington, D.C. While there I met a young woman my age who was going to American University and studying Latin American studies. Inez was her name. She had dreams of being in the Foreign Service and serving in South America. Although my dreams weren't limited to South America, I too wanted to travel the world. She was shy, as was I, but that drew us together, not apart. She was serious in everything she did and wanted to study all aspects of every problem closely. I was just a dumb kid who narcissistically groomed myself to look hot without having any inkling of what the goal of that was. We were contemplating a lasting relationship, and she initiated sex—to ensure, I guess, that I was what she really wanted.

She didn't say I wasn't good at it after we'd rather clumsily, I thought, fucked a couple of times. She seemed to remain on track to her goals, one of which was me. I was just going with the flow, assuming that marriage was something you did upon graduating from college—although both of us intended to go on to graduate school and we both had the means and grades to do it.

Another of Inez's goals was to become a proficient classical guitarist. To that end she was taking lessons from Cat Ralston, who was a quite well-known and well regarded classical guitarist, credited with bringing Brazilian guitar music to the American ear and who owned and played at the Cat's Meow, a nightclub in the Maryland suburbs of the capital.

The first time I saw and heard Cat Ralston was at a New Year's Eve party Inez dragged me to at the Cat's Meow. His music moved me that evening, although he himself didn't. In keeping with the atmosphere of ringing in the new year, it was crowded in the club and they were a rowdy bunch. They mostly quieted down during the sets that Ralston played, backed up by his brother on the bass. But, although I was fascinated—and felt a little warm—from the music, Inez kept saying that Ralston wasn't playing his best—that he was irritated by the noise. And, indeed, he scowled through his playing and, Inez said, cut his sets short.

He wasn't a young man. He was probably pushing fifty and was mostly bald on top, although his arms were muscular. He had a sensitive face, though, which I kept wishing wasn't set in a scowl. And when he closed his eyes while he was playing, he seemed to soar onto an upper, sensual plain. His fingers were, of course, limber and expressive, and I tried looking at them rather than the irritated frown on his face. I found myself soaring with him, although at the time I connected the buzz I was getting and the urge—which I followed—to feel Inez up while he played to the cheap champagne we were drinking.

Inez, who was clearly disturbed that Ralston was on edge, suggested that we leave early. I was ready to go, because Ralston's irritation somewhat irritated me too. It was his club. If he didn't want a boisterous crowd in on New Year's Eve, he should tailor the deal, I thought. I stopped in an art museum parking lot on the way home—it was already after midnight— and we fucked in the backseat of my Sebring convertible. It was my second most successful performance with Inez ever. I didn't then connect it with the guitar music, although it was what kept

113

going through my mind while we fucked—mostly Ralston's rendition of "Corcovado."

Inez was clearly disturbed that I hadn't heard or seen Ralston at his best, and as he was like a god to her, she insisted we go back the next weekend, when the crowd would be smaller and would be there solely for him.

She was right. His performance was magnificent that second night, and he clearly was in a much better mood—although he still soared to the heavens by himself while he was playing. I found myself soaring there too, trying to be with him, but content to be somewhere near the same cloud with him. Once when I opened my eyes well after he'd struck the last cord, I saw his eyes on me.

He stopped at our table after that set, which I could understand. Inez had a lesson with him once a week. He sat at our table briefly, asking Inez to introduce me to him.

"You seemed to really feel the music, Paul," he said.

"Yes. I don't know what it is about the music, but it makes me feel so . . . so . . . ."

"Sensual?" he asked in a low voice.

"Hmm, maybe, I'll have to think about that." I was embarrassed. He'd defined the feeling exactly, but I had no idea people were actually permitted to talk like that in polite company.

He and Inez chatted for a few minutes and then, as it was apparent Ralston was about to go on for another set, he turned to me and said, "Do you play an instrument?"

"Piano," I said.

"Any good at it?"

"I studied it a long time. I guess you'd say I could hold my own doing background at a party."

"Any interest in taking up guitar?"

"I've never thought about it," I said.

"You could try taking lessons from me. I have a spot open on Thursdays. At 6:00 p.m. Last lesson of the day."

Inez piped up, "I think there's now an opening on Tuesday's right after my lesson. We could come together."

"I think that slot has filled," Ralston said. He was looking at me. His eyes were intense, and I thought he was trying to convey something. But I had no idea what it could be.

Of course I accepted. If I was at all good at the guitar—and being able to say I took lessons from Cat Ralston—well, it would be quite a coup.

It was rather curious at the time, but when he played the next set, he didn't close his eyes and appear to be riding the clouds. He kept his eyes locked on mine. And he played as if he was playing just for me—almost like he was playing me. When my heart began to race on a passage, he pushed it. When I began to tremble and move with the beat, he sped up the rhythm. I was sweating and hard when he finished.

I fucked Inez in the backseat of my Sebring in the nightclub parking lot, not being able to wait. And it was the best of my performances, bringing moans out of Inez I'd never heard before and letting me know exactly when she'd had an orgasm. I couldn't have positively said she'd even had one before then.

I felt a little tense going into my first guitar lesson with Cat Ralston. We were in an all-black room—black carpeting, black padded walls, black ceiling in a small room off the main nightclub floor. When I later remarked on the blackness to Ralston, he said he played best with no distractions. Remembering his irritation on New Year's Eve, I could well understand what he was saying. There was a bench and a couple of straight chairs, an ottoman, and a fancy bank of electronic equipment. There were three guitar stands, all with a guitar on them that looked like it probably was priceless.

Ralston came into the room wearing bagging shorts, an Hawaiian shirt unbuttoned to reveal a hairy, beefy chest—not quite fat, more barrel-chested muscle than meat—and open-toed sandals without socks. He was drinking a beer. I would have been surprised except that Inez had warned me that he was eccentric and was prone to dress really casually. On stage it was always a formal white shirt, with the top three buttons unbuttoned to reveal a gold medallion nestled in curly chest hair, black trousers, and black dress shoes.

"Today, you get a feel for the guitar," he said. "Here, you sit straddling the bench, forward please. I'll be sitting behind you. You will be playing with your fingers, but I'll be doing all of the playing. My method is to show how to place your fingers for the wanted sound by the feel of it."

"OK," I thought, although I was on edge, nervous. I assumed that was natural the first time, though. Still, I gave a little shudder when, with guitar in hand, he straddled the bench too and sat close behind me. His arms came around my shoulders and the guitar was in front of me.

"Here, put this hand here—with this finger there and those on these strings. And the fingers of the other hands here. Yes, that's right. You're trembling. Don't feel embarrassed. I do this with all of the new students."

He was holding me close; how couldn't I feel embarrassed. I could feel the hardness of his cock at the small of my back, for god sake. Or was it hard? I couldn't tell, and why would it be hard?

He placed his fingers on mine and he guided them through a few scales and then a few simple nursery rhyme tunes. I felt like I was fumbling under his guidance, but he told me I was doing fine.

"Now something at the other end of the scale," he whispered. "Just so you can feel what a moving tune feels like."

The tune was sensual, starting off slow and picking up speed. "And this interval part. Notice it uses only one hand."

While using only one hand for this demonstration, though, he was unbuttoning my shirt with the other and running his hand from my chest down to my belly. I was breathing hard and had my eyes tightly shut, dancing slowly on that cloud. I guess I knew what he was doing, but I was too much into the music—and the effect the music was having one me—to object. And when I didn't object, Ralston moved his hand on down to my basket.

"You're hard. You truly know what this music is for, don't you? This is the music of the fuck. So, we will fuck now."

I whimpered, unable to form words. He was right. I was under the spell of the music. The thought raced across my mind that the two times I thought I'd fucked Inez well, it really was because of the music.

He put the guitar aside, but there was still music. It was still Ralston playing the guitar—this sensual song. But it was coming out of loudspeakers now. It had started back at the slower part at the beginning.

With his arms still around me, he unbuckled my belt and unzipped my trousers. His chin was on my shoulder. His hand was on my cock. He stroked me to the increasing beat of the music. I watched the movement of his toes in his sandals. The man had perfect rhythm. Even his toes scrunched and expanded right on the beat of the music and his stroking of my cock. When I ejaculated, he kissed me on the neck and murmured. "Very good. Very musical. Right to the beat."

I was confused. It was him keeping the beat. I did nothing but not fight him. In contemplating my confusion, I had to ask him to repeat his next direction.

"Slip off your trousers and briefs, please. I will fuck you now."

I moaned but did as he commanded. He grabbed hold of my hips and pulled me back on the bench. Then with the palm of his hand in the center of my back, he pushed my chest down onto the bench, and I felt the bulb of his cock at my hole.

"Concentrate on the music," he murmured. And I did so, but I sobbed and whimpered and grabbed the legs of the bench in a white-knuckled grasp as he worked his cock inside me. When he was all inside, he paused and his heavy breathing was matching the rhythm of my panting.

"Superb," he muttered. And then I heard the music start all of the way over again.

"Belly on top of the ottoman over there," he whispered.

He pulled out of me and, like an automaton, I struggled over to the ottoman and laid down on it on my belly, with my arms and legs spread wide and my head hanging over the top.

I gasped as he entered me again, able to get in deeper in this position.

"Concentrate on the music," he murmured. And, again, I did. He fucked me in rhythm to the music. As it accelerated in speed and intensity, so did he. He kept commanding, "Yes, yes, good. The music. Perfection. Concentrate on the music."

I grabbed at the carpeting with my fists, dug my toes in, took a fold of material from the side of the ottoman in my mouth, and chomped down to avoid screaming. But most of my attention went to where it was directed—reveling in how Ralston's cock was able to keep perfect time with the increasing beat of the recording.

He ejaculated at the height of the music.

"Supremo," he exclaimed. "You can feel the rhythm and you can now play with passion. The lesson is over; I'll see you again next Thursday afternoon."

I had only three lessons before I pulled myself away from Ralston's clutches, during which I learned little of how to play the guitar but much of what a man could do with another man. I also cut it off with Inez soon thereafter. I had enjoyed being fucked by Ralston far more than I had enjoyed fucking Inez.

As soon as I graduated, I was on a plane to Europe to start my grand journalist experience. Luckily I had the means to do so.

What I was to find out, however, was that I didn't have the means to resist classical guitar music and guitarists.

* * * *

I arrived at the Tree of Idleness and took a quick look around, but I didn't see Paul D'Alessandro anywhere. I turned to leave, but there he was, carrying a net bag with a few provisions in it.

"I knew you'd come back," he said with a smile. "I do not play tonight. It is one of my off days. I live up there, though," he continued, pointing to the two stories of flats above the restaurant. "You come with me?"

"Yes," I answered, the guitar music already starting in my head and my mind going back to that other Tree of Idleness and that other guitar player. I was prepared for him to then say, "And you come for me?" as Jalil had done. But he didn't. He was more direct than that.

"And I fuck you, yes?"

"Yes."

118

"You stay the night, and I fuck you all night?"

"If you wish," I answered.

"Do you wish?"

"Yes . . . I think so."

We sucked each other off as we slowly undressed, discovering each other's bodies. Me in awe and a little frightened of the size and thickness of him—but quickly in heat over the hardness of his body, sinewy and lithe, not an ounce of fat, the muscles well defined and the veins popping out on his arms with no layers of fat to go through. His legs were strong. I suddenly felt I knew what "all night" was—that he could go all night.

"Where? The bed?" I asked, motioning to a twin bed in the corner of his studio room.

"Not the first time," he said. He moved a straight chair with arms in front of a full length mirror on the wall next to the entrance into his kitchenette. He opened a closet door half way across the room. Another full length mirror was on the inside of the door. I could see that being positioned at the chair would mean that much of what happened between the mirrors could be seen in the mirrors. This alone made me tremble.

"Lean into the chair," he said. "Your hands on the arms of the chair, legs spread, please."

When I did so, I could see that I was able to use the mirrors to watch what was happening both at my front and at my back. D'Alessandro knelt behind me. I felt my butt cheeks being parted and then his tongue at my hole. I watched a hand come between my legs and take my cock and he was milking me while he tongued my hole. Occasionally he'd let loose of my cock and give my balls attention. And periodically he also pulled my cock back through my legs and gave it suck.

I sighed, enjoying the view and the sensations and the buildup of it. This was what Jalil never did. There was no buildup. This had me in heaven—well, almost heaven. Why had I been resisting this, I wondered. I can't believe that Adrianna would object. She had known that Jalil was fucking us both. Was it just that the experience with Ralston and then Jalil had been so traumatic.

I came in a flow that was more calming than explosive. Paul laughed and took my cock in his mouth and cleaned it off.

He bounced up and went over to the counter dividing the kitchen from the main room.

"Five," he said, counting out the condom packets on the counter. "I like your body. It gives me so many ideas. I wonder if this is enough."

"I have more in my trousers," I said.

"So, you knew."

"I had hoped," I said. He laughed and rolled a condom on his cock, which was looking both formidable and mighty proud. As he moved to me and put his hands on my hips, I murmured, "Music. Could we have music? Your music, please."

"So you want to fuck to music, do you?"

"Always."

"And mine? Nice that you want it to be mine. I'll give you extra good fuck for that. And good music too. The flamenco style of bachata I told you of. Good fuck music. The song 'Mon Amor.' I'll put that on."

The music started and he was close behind me again. During the initial, soft part, he entered me, slowly and deeply, while I took heavy breaths and groaned and set myself rigid.

"Relax," he whispered in my ear. "Just relax. I have far to go yet and I want to take you fully. Just relax. I'll make sure you don't fall." He moved a strong, broad hand to my belly and palmed me there, giving me support. He was holding the root of his cock with his other hand, rotating it in my channel, helping me to open to him, pulling deep groans out me, flying me to heaven.

When he had bottomed, he just held me there, both of us panting, waiting for I knew not what.

And then I understood. The music moved into the passage where the beat picked up and the music became more insistent, louder.

My belly still palmed with one hand, he cupped my chin with the other and arched my back to him. And then, right on the beat, he began to pump me, faster and faster, right with the music, bottoming deep on the down beat, pistoning me while I moaned and grunted and cried out to him on how high I was flying, one with both him and the music.

Before the music ended, with both of us ejaculating simultaneously, I realized that this was exactly the same song that Cal Ralston had first fucked me to.

Bound to Bait

"The offer is tempting, yes," The elegantly clad Guiovani Lucano, president of Unipro, said, "but the French cosmetic firms are eager to have whatever dragobotania we can produce. There's really no sufficient incentive I can see to change that and sell to the United States instead."

He was talking to the American chemical dealer, Nicholas Reynolds, as they both sat, drinking coffee, at a café table on the terrace of the Grand Hotel Tremezo on Lake Como above the hotel swimming pool, which itself looked like it was suspended over the surface of the lake. But he wasn't looking at the beefy early-middle aged American. His interests and attention were riveted elsewhere.

He had been watching a lithe, blond youth swimming laps in the pool below. His gray eyes had flared and his patrician nostrils had twitched when the youth caught his attention when he had gracefully risen from a chaise lounge by the pool, glided to the low diving board, and made a perfectly arced dive into the blue surface of the pool at the beginning of his swim. The thought of a dancer had entered the tall, thin, graying-templed Italian manufacturer's mind. Guiovani had specific, refined tastes. They included young, blond male dancers.

123

He gave a little shiver of pleasure as he watched the young man rise from the pool, effortlessly climb the ladder, and stand there in his skimpy Speedo, briefly, tossing his blond curls from side to side to flick off droplets of water and then move, mincingly, to the chaise lounge, retrieve his towel, and wick his perfect, hairless torso off with the fluffy hotel towel. Guiovani slitted his eyes and licked his lips, imagining the young man bound and suspended over his bed in his villa outside Milan.

"The French companies offer incentives above the deals they put on the table?" Reynolds asked. He kept an innocent, unsophisticated-American look on his face. A look of "please educate me in the real world of European business."

"Yes, well, there are age-old business customs in Europe," Guiovani said, tearing his eyes away from the titillating sight of the young man toweling himself off by the pool below to look directly into the clumsy American's face. The young man had one knee kneeling on the surface of the chaise lounge. The angle of the leg was making Guiovani hard. His refined tastes were quite specific.

"I'm sure we can do business on that basis," Reynolds said, knitting his brow like he was searching his mind for what he might offer. "We could provide these directly to you, I assume. No need for them to appear in any records."

"Yes, of course," Guiovani said, but even as he said it, he sensed the presence of someone at the table, standing between him and the rays of the afternoon sun. He looked up, expecting to see the waiter—and to bristle, as the waiters at as fine a hotel as the Grand Tremezo should know to watch for the signal that they were wanted when it became bill time.

But what he saw instead of a waiter made him take his breath in and set his coffee cup down in fear that it would tumble out of his suddenly trembling hand.

"I'm bored, Dad. Can't I go into the casino?"

"No, Ryan. I'm doing business here and I could not clear my mind if you were out of my sight. And it's impolite just to intrude like this. Do sit down over here rather than standing over us and getting us wet."

Guiovani almost cried out that he wanted the young man standing by him, as close as possible right now and here. What

124

he would really like would be for the youth to be trussed up and at his mercy.

"Excuse us, Signore Lucano. And please excuse my son. I have just retrieved him from his boarding school in Switzerland. I'm afraid I've kept him sequestered far too long. It's time for him to start learning his proper way in society. This is my son, Ryan. Ryan, this is Signore Lucano. He owns the chemical company we're here to do business with—if we can reach a mutually acceptable arrangement, that is." He gave a searching look at Guiovani.

Reynolds had a hand on Ryan's shoulder as the young man sat down in a chair across from Guiovani at the café table. Guiovani wanted to scream that there, of course, was a possible deal in the offing as he looked at Reynold's hand on the bare skin of his son with envy he was having a hard time concealing. But he kept control of himself and merely smiled benignly at the youth and said, "I am happy to meet you, Ryan. And, alas, I'm afraid they don't permit minors in the casino."

Ryan had been looking down at his lap shyly, but when Guiovani spoke, he lifted his head and fluttered his long eyelashes over his baby-blue eyes and gave the Italian patrician a winsome little smile. He exuded appreciation that the man noticed him and was talking directly to him. But of course Guiovani noticed Ryan. He was close to hyperventilating on the spot. Only many centuries of the best of breeding kept the Italian noble from leaping across the table and onto the beautiful blond youth.

"Oh, Ryan could go into the casino," Reynolds said, breaking the spell—thankfully for Guiovani, who wasn't all that sure that his breeding was enough to hold his libido in check. "He's eighteen. He just looks young for his age. He doesn't really need my permission now to do whatever he wants to do. I've been a protective father; perhaps overly protective. Of course you can go to the casino, if you wish, Ryan."

Ryan looked at his father and smiled. He reached up and took Reynold's hand in his two hands and interlocked their forearms on the café table.

Guiovani was beside himself with need.

"Thanks, Dad. Maybe later. I'm so bored here."

125

"That's terrible that you should be bored in such gorgeous surroundings," Guiovani said. He spread his arms, sweeping them across the view of the lake of the Bellagio across Lake Como. "I don't think there's a more beautiful sight in the world."

"I feel so tight and bloated," Ryan said. "I need more exercise."

"There's the pool," Guiovani said. "You swim very well—and dive too. I saw you down there."

"Did you?" Ryan asked, turning a radiant smile on the Italian gentleman. "I like competition, though. At school we were always into sports. I love tennis. But Dad doesn't play tennis, and there's no one else here . . ."

Everything suddenly seemed so clear to Guiovani—the way to his heart's desire. "Tennis? My son, Guido, plays tennis quite well. And he's your age. He's coming home, to Milan, this weekend. Would you like to play with him?"

"Wow, that would be great," Ryan said, his voice full of enthusiasm. "Could I, Dad?"

"I just said you were now old enough to do as you like, son," Reynolds said, with a laugh. "But I have other business to do in Rome this weekend. We have hotel reservations—"

"If you like, I could take Ryan back to my villa in Carro Maggione, outside Milan for the weekend. We have a tennis court. He and Guido could play, and then I could drive him to your hotel in Rome. And we could, of course, discuss business possibilities further then—when I've had time to speak with my staff on possibilities." Guiovani was having difficulty toning down the excitement in his voice for the idea.

"Could I, Dad?" Ryan asked, his voice full of enthusiasm. Guiovani nearly laughed with pleasure—a sensual pleasure—at the little puppy dog aspect to Ryan's enthusiasm. Just like a little puppy dog wagging his tail. A vision of Ryan's well-rounded buttocks in his Speedo as he moved on the deck of the pool below earlier sent one of his hands to his basket under the table.

"I don't know . . . it would be such an imposition on Signore Lucano," Reynolds said, his brow knitted and showing concern of having pushed the man he wanted to make a million-dollar deal with beyond the edge of hospitality.

"No imposition at all," Guiovani interjected quickly. "Guido would also be bored this weekend without someone his own age to be with. And he loves tennis. It wouldn't be an imposition at all; I would see it as a valuable incentive. And there are the business discussions to be had at the end of the weekend." He turned his eyes on Nicholas Reynolds, wondering if he'd put enough emphasis on the word "incentive" for the dullard American to catch on to what he was offering. But apparently he had. Reynolds was giving him a whole different look now.

* * * *

Guiovani walked around the perimeter of his king-sized bed, looking at camera angles. He had four video cameras on tripods pointed at the bed. Satisfied, he reached up and gave Ryan a little push, sending his suspended body swaying in the air above the bed. Ryan emitted a little whimpering sound through the black, plastic ball gag in his mouth, and Guiovani laughed a little appreciative laugh.

Both were naked. Guiovani's nakedness revealed a body that was very well kept for a man of fifty—trim and well muscled. In contrast to the slimness of his body, he was equipped like a horse, and his balls, popped out by the leather strip wrapped tightly at the base of his engorged cock, were big as tennis balls.

Ryan's nakedness was a trussed one. He was facing down toward the bed, suspended on a rope hanging directly down from a hook in the ceiling above the center of the bed. The rope was connected by roping around the young man's chest at one point and ropes leading to his ankles at other points. Ryan's legs were bent back so that his heels nearly touched his buttocks. His legs were spread by other ropes attached at one end to hooks in the ceiling above and below the bed frame and then to his ankles.

Ryan was built like a young boy, but his ping-pong-ball-sized balls were popped out, like Guiovani's were, not only by a

127

strap around the base of his cock but also by leads from this with lead weights on the end that dropped toward but did not quite reach the surface of the bed.

Earlier, he had not been able to see where tennis courts fit into the back garden of the Lucano villa when they drove up to it in Guiovani's Maserati. A pool surrounded by privacy-providing funeral cypress trees seemed to take up all of the space within the stucco-walled fence around the house. The villa was located at the top of a hill, and the countryside, with no near buildings in sight, undulated around it in folded ridges of pastureland

"We have a community tennis court," Guiovani had said. "But, until Guido arrives, you can swim in the pool."

Ryan had thought that Guiovani implied when they were driving there that his son would already have arrived at the villa.

Ryan was swimming laps in the pool when he looked up and almost swallowed water in a gasp at seeing Guiovani standing, naked, several lengths of nylon rope dangling from his hand, his majestic cock hard and curving up toward his flat belly, by the pool. He was smiling blandly and watching Ryan swim.

Guiovani dove neatly into the pool and stroked hard, reaching a retreating Ryan as he touched the lip of the pool at the shallow end, where he trapped Ryan's diminutive body up against the wall of the pool. As he held a writhing Ryan against the poolside with the weight of his torso, he got ropes tied around the young man's ankles and to rings on either side of where they were standing, which stretched Ryan's legs out wide to either side. Then he reached over and tied Ryan's wrists together above his head.

Ryan was crying out and otherwise objecting, but he quieted down when Guiovani laughed and pointed out that there was no one within a mile to hear them. Ryan had wondered why he'd encountered no servants in the house, but now he knew why.

"I'm sorry I can't provide any proper seduction," Guiovani whispered in Ryan's ear when he had him trussed up, his heaving belly on the warmth of the terrazzo surface of the decking surrounding the pool, "but you are just too luscious. I can't wait longer."

After that he had only waited long enough to roll Ryan's slim hips up and tongued his hole to open him up, and then he was hunched over Ryan's back and fucking him deep as Ryan whimpered and sobbed.

"It's done now," he murmured in Ryan's ear afterward, as his chest pressed into Ryan's back. "It can't be undone. Think of the important deal your father needs to negotiate with me and think about where the money comes from to keep you and send you to that private school. I want you again already. But not here. Inside. You aren't going to fight me, are you? There's no going back."

"Guido isn't coming this weekend, is he?" Ryan asked through his sobs.

"There is no Guido," Guiovani said, and then he laughed. Ryan wasn't turning his invitation to go inside down.

Guiovani used a remote to set the four video cameras to whirring and then he climbed up on the bed under Ryan's trussed body. He took hold of the leads to the weights from Ryan's balls and swung Ryan's body back and forth gently. He was rewarded with moans from Ryan's gagged mouth. Guiovani's mouth went to the young man's perfect little cock. He was pleased that he was making it engorge and that he could still hear the moans.

When he could hold off no longer, he rose up from under the swinging body and positioned himself between Ryan's spread thighs. He thrilled at the sight of Ryan's bent legs—both of them bent. All of Ryan completely at his mercy.

Ryan was swaying back and forth. When the arc of his sway moved back to where Guiovani's cock head was cradled between Ryan's butt cheeks, Guiovani grabbed the youth's hips and held him in place until the cock bulb was positioned at the hole. Then he pulled back hard on Ryan's body, pulling his channel unto the cock with deep penetration. Ryan sobbed and writhed as he was able, while Guiovani pulled him back and forth, with increasing speed, on his cock, ejaculating with a cry of victory after nearly a half hour of pumping his bound captive.

Leaving Ryan trussed about the bed, Guiovani went to his marble bathroom after he was done and stood under the shower for a long time, devising his next bondage position for the sweet young blond.

When he padded out of the bathroom, toweling off his naked body and having decided to have Ryan next in the basement room, strapped to the wall, Guiovani stopped dead in his tracks and gasped.

Ryan was gone. There was a folded piece of paper on the surface of the bed, and the Italian manufacturer ran over to the bed and read what it said.

> *I am sure you have had incentive enough, but to be doubly sure, I have taken the film from the video cameras. I also filmed your playtime at the pool earlier today. By the way, Ryan isn't really eighteen.*
>
> *Nicholas Reynolds*

$* * * *$

Nicholas Reynolds had been cajoling the meaty chocolate brown giant most of the late afternoon. Their table on the terrace of the Pearmont Walmont Hotel in Gaborone, Botswanna's, Grand Palm club and casino enclave was already in the shadows of the wall of bougainvillea that marked the back boundaries of the patio. The table was inside a framework of steel tubing, with drapes that could be pulled around it, making it usable as a private cabana.

Kugiso Malema was being a very hard sell. But he had the corner on the market of all dragobotania growing in the South Africa region. Reynolds was the buyer for the U.S.-based cosmetic firms actively trying to muscle the French out of the skin care products market.

Ryan sat between the two men, being just as demure and as enticing as he possibly could be—which was quite enticing indeed. For the first hour he had been afraid that Nicholas's research had been off—that maybe this black giant wasn't into the kinks that Ryan and Nicholas served. But as the table went into the shadows, and Ryan laid a hand on Malema's thigh, the owner of ClaroBolel enterprises turned a corner in cooperation.

He also turned a corner in looking at Ryan while he was talking to Nicholas, something that the two Americans had expected him to do much before this.

"We must think of something that would sweeten the deal and make it worth my while," Malema said to Nicholas.

Both men heard Ryan gasp, but neither, with effort, turned to look at him. Malema had reached under the table and taken Ryan's hand from his thigh and placed it on his basket. Ryan had gasped at the size of what he'd found there.

Malema had been paying attention to Ryan all along. He was hard as a rock.

Still talking about the possibility of negotiations, Malema put his beefy hands on Ryan's shoulder and pushed down. Ryan got the message and slipped under the table.

When he unzipped the African's trousers and a monster cock with a thick silver ring in the bulb rolled out, Ryan gasped again. The Botswannan's skin color was a rich creamy chocolate, but his huge cock and his meaty balls were jet black.

Reynolds and Malema continued their bandying deal making as Ryan made muffled slurping and gagging sounds from under the table as he worked the giant's cock even larger.

"Do we have a deal, then?" Reynolds asked at length.

"Maybe. I fuck him now?"

"Here? Now? On the terrace of a hotel?"

"Pull the drapes around the table," Malema simply said, used to taking the direct route and finding simple answers to complex problems.

Reynolds stood, pulled the drapes, and started to leave the enclosure.

"No, I want you to stay and watch. I am fucking your son with the biggest dick you'll find in Botswanna. I want to know how badly you want this deal."

When Reynolds had sat down again, Malema pulled Ryan up from under the table and set him in his lap, facing Reynolds across the surface of the table. He pulled the Speedo Ryan had been wearing off his legs, and Ryan's eyes started to water and he was huffing and puffing as Malema set his entrance down on his bulb.

"Take his ankles and spread him farther," Malema directed.

Reynolds stood and leaned over the table and did what his was told. Malema grabbed Ryan's waist with his hands and pushed the young man down hard onto his cock.

Ryan groaned and grunted and sobbed all the way to the bottom of his sheathing. Malema's mouth went to the hollow of Ryan's neck and his hands went to Ryan's nipples, and with a low moan and a sigh of satisfaction from Malema, Ryan grabbed the rim of the table with his hands for leverage and began fucking himself on the jet-black monster cock.

"Do we have a deal?" Reynolds asked when Malema had ejaculated.

"Maybe, yes. It requires some thought still."

"Would it be a definite yes if we went to our room in the hotel? I have a strong four-poster bed in my room. And plenty of rope. I've been led to understand—"

"Where is this room?"

After Ryan had been trussed up, Reynolds interjected his body between the lumbering naked form of Malema. He, no less than Ryan, had trouble keeping his eyes off the man's jet-black cock and low-hanging balls—and, especially, that punishing silver cock ring—but he stood his ground against the man intent on getting to Ryan.

Ryan was suspended in air above the surface of the four-poster bed. He ankles and wrists were bound in fur-lined cuffs that had strong rope leads going up to the top four corners of the bed. Luckily the posts were strong and thick, something Reynolds had methodically checked out before booking this hotel. To relieve the strain on his spread-eagled arms and legs, the small of Ryan's back was slung in the pad of a black leather plow belt, and the hand holds of that were tied by ropes to the middle of the sides of the top bed frames. A silk scarf gagged Ryan's mouth. Especially after seeing Malema's equipment, Reynolds didn't want to chance that Ryan's screaming would summon curious hotel staff and guests.

"You have seen what you can have," Reynolds said to the impatient African giant. "I have the contract papers on this clipboard. Sign and you can have him."

"I can have him if I want him," Malema growled.

There was a tense moment, when the two men stood there, glaring at each other. Reynolds was sweating heavily and hoped it didn't show, because he knew, as well-muscled as he was, he wasn't a match for this black giant.

Malema broke first, though, and his mouth went to a smile. "One last twist to the deal, perhaps. I can supply you twice the amount of dragobotania as the contract specifies—and at the same price. But I want this now, and tomorrow I want him delivered to my house—not the house you know of. Another house. My special playhouse."

There was a pregnant pause as Reynolds considered. "For how long."

"This is Africa. I like gifts. He would be your gift to me."

"You wouldn't hurt him, would you?"

Malema smiled a cruel smile and let that sink in. "I'm going to hurt him now. Tomorrow . . ." He just let that trail off.

Ryan was struggling within his bounds. It was clear that he heard what they were negotiating.

"Twice the dragobotania? Same price per kilo?" Reynolds asked.

"Yes."

Another brief moment, punctuated by the muffled objections of Ryan. Reynolds applied the point of the pen to all copies of the contract. "Initial where I've changed the amounts and sign at the bottom, all copies. Write out the address you want him delivered to on this notepad. I'll have him there no earlier than 2:00 p.m."

Reynolds watched as Malema signed all of the copies as demanded; then he stood aside and reviewed the documents for proper signature, while Malema climbed up on the bed. Kneeling on his knees between Ryan's thighs put him at the right height, but he had to cup the young man's buttocks and roll them up to get the desired angle.

Reynolds was at the door to the corridor before he turned and took a look at the tableau on the bed. Malema had already been inside Ryan's channel, so the second time wasn't the chore that the first one was. Still, Ryan was twisting and turning his body as he was able, giving Reynolds a wild-eyed stare, and emitting muffled screams. Malema had bottomed inside Ryan's sheath before Reynolds got into the corridor. He hurried to the next door down the corridor and slipped into their second room. He arrived and clicked the remotes to the cameras trained on the bed in the other room just in time to catch Malema beginning to pump Ryan hard and deep.

When Reynolds was sure Malema was gone, he clicked the cameras off and slipped back into the hotel room with the four-poster bed. Ryan just sort of sagged down on the bed in an exhausted heap, as Reynolds released his bonds. Ryan himself untied the scarf gag with weary hands.

"That's that," Reynolds whispered. "I think you took that well. It certainly filmed well."

"Did you see that big, black cock, Daddy? Have you ever seen anything like that?"

"Liked that, did you?"

"Yeah, I liked it. I fuckin' loved it. But it made me want you." Ryan slithered to the floor at the foot of the bed and clung to Reynold's leg. "Do me, Daddy. Please."

"Let me get the film out of the camera first. And we'd better clear out to the other room. He might come back. For a minute I thought we might have a problem. He still might have another thought and come back with goons."

"Fuck me, Daddy, please," Ryan wheedled. His fingers were on Nicholas's zipper. The older man laughed and brushed Ryan's hand away.

"God, you're a slut. I'd worry about you being taken by these guys if it hadn't been all your idea. I swear you can't get enough cock. I'll do you, you can bet on that. It was hot watching the black monster at work. But it's unsafe here. We'll pull everything into the other room. That's registered to another name. If that hard-dealing bastard comes back here, he won't have the slightest idea where we've gone."

"Tomorrow . . . you wouldn't . . ." Ryan sounded a bit scared now.

"Nah. We have plane tickets for the morning. He won't start looking for us until mid-afternoon. By then he'll have my e-mail with a sample video attachment and me letting him know I know his wife's family owns most of the business. He'll keep to the deal."

"On the floor like a dog," Reynolds commanded when they got everything moved to the adjoining room.

Ryan complied, murmuring his pleasure while Nicholas used joined cuffs on his wrists and ankles. Then he secured Ryan's thighs close together also with restraints high up under his buttocks.

Ryan panted and moaned as Nicholas, naked now, knelt behind him, He separated Ryan's buttocks with his hands and started to work his entrance with his tongue. Ryan's channel was still slack from the reaming Malema had given him.

Nicholas crouched over Ryan's back close and fucked him like a dog for a few moments, both of them enjoying the tightness of Ryan's channel thanks to the strappings holding his legs close together. Ryan turned his mouth to Nicholas's and they kissed deeply.

After a few minutes, when his cock was fully sheathed, Nicholas reached for the plow belt that he'd used to give Ryan's belly support when he was trussed in the bed next door and he whipped that around Ryan's belly and grabbed the handles of the plow belt, stood, and flipped Ryan's body off the ground so that his full weight was on the plow belt holding his belly up, and the sway of the fuck was being controlled fully by the movement of Nicholas's cock in Ryan's tightly constricted channel.

Ryan murmured "Oh, Daddy, oh, Daddy," to their shared ejaculation.

Later, when they were on the bed, legs and arms entwined and mewing to each other in postcoital reverie from multiple fuckings in various inventive bondage positions, Nicholas gave a little laugh.

"What?" Ryan asked, turning his smiling face to Nicholas's for yet another sweet kiss.

"The gullibility of those guys," Nicholas said. "You and I don't look a bit alike. Yet, they have all believed that I really was your father."

"And that I was underage," Ryan whispered. "You tell them that I'm not eighteen, and right off they assume I'm underage and that they're in extra trouble. When I'm almost twenty."

"But I'll always be your daddy," Nicholas said.

"And I'll always be your little boy," Ryan answered. Then he reached over and picked up a pile of restraints. "Again, Daddy. Do me again."

"You are such a fuckin' slut," Nicholas said, as he reached for the restraints.

Doing College

"That's the last of the equipment inventoried, Bobby. You know why I stayed back with you this evening to help you do this, don't you?"

"Yes, coach," Bobby, the manager of the university football team, said. He was trembling a bit and licking his lips.

"OK, then. Hit the showers."

"Yes, Coach."

"Come here first."

"Yes, Coach."

Ed Tolivar, the football team's offensive coach sat back on his desk top, pushed Bobby down on his knees between his spread thighs, grabbed the hair on the back of the small guy's head with one hand, pulled his own dick out of his gym shorts, and beat the young man with it lightly around his face, while Bobby chased the shaft with his open mouth. With a laugh, Tolivar gave Bobby his cock for several minutes of suck.

Then he lifted Bobby back up onto his feet, turned him, slapped him on the buttocks, and said, "I've got the drill schedules to map out. Then I'll meet you in the training room. Lock the doors on your way back."

"Yes, Coach."

Bobby padded into the locker room, close to hyperventilating on what Coach Tolivar was about to give him. Bobby knew he was going to get fucked when the coach told him they were doing an equipment inventory this evening and that the coach was going to stay to see that he did it right. The inventory wasn't due and it certainly didn't need Coach Tolivar. The coach was fucking him more often now. That was OK with Bobby. He wanted to keep his manager position and all of the perks that came with it. Beyond that, he considered the coach's cocking as one of the perks.

So, he came knowing he'd be fucked. He just didn't know how totally he was going to be fucked.

As, stripped, he reached the shower room, a hand came out from the side of the entrance, grabbed his wrist and pulled him into the showers and under a shower head, which the freshman third-string tailback, who Bobby only knew as Stud, turned on full blast.

"Suck me," Stud demanded, pushing Bobby down on his knees and grabbing his head and holding it in place under the heavy stream of water. Bobby resumed on Stud what he'd just been doing with Coach Tolivar. He didn't mind this too much either. Stud was the hunkiest player on the squad, built like a bodybuilder and good-looking as a movie star and with the cock and balls of a horse. Bobby had been wanting to be taken by him since practice for the season had started.

"Gonna fuck you good."

"Shit, yes, but coach is waiting. He'll know."

"I want him to know. All the time I'm fuckin' you, I want you to remember to tell Coach that I'm a team player, a versatile player. I'll do for him what you're gonna do for me. Grab your ankles. And grab 'em good, 'cause I'm gonna lift you off the tiles."

Bobby did as directed and whimpered and panted, as Stud leaned him forward, held him by the hips, and started the long journey of his cock up Bobby's channel. Fully saddled, Stud moved one hand to Bobby's belly, grabbed Bobby's chin with the other, and pulled Bobby's body up to where it was plastered on Stud's torso.

"Now, lock your fists behind my neck and your ankles behind my thighs, 'cause we're goin' downtown."

Bobby complied and was fucked fast and furiously until he shot his load onto the wet shower room floor and was sagging like a rag doll on Stud's pistoning cock.

Stud let him fall in a heap on the floor and left the shower room. Bobby was still whimpering and burbling his complete capitulation when Coach Tolivar, naked, and looking like the trim, powerful Marine he once had been, came looking for Bobby. The coach came down on his knees beside Bobby, asked him what had happened, and listened to Bobby tell him exactly what Stud had told him to tell coach.

Coach Tolivar gently picked the small figure of his team manager up from the floor, carried him carefully down the corridor and into the training room, tenderly laid him on his back on a massage table, jerked his legs wide, and fucked the stuffing out of him.

* * * *

Stud looked up at the bookcase facing the foot of his bed and frowned. Dragging off his bed for the third time in the last fifteen minutes, he rearranged the books on one shelf again and then went back to his bed. Giving a sexy smile toward the bookcase, he laid back and threw one arm over the back of his headboard, puffing his chest muscles out. He slowly moved his other hand down his naked body to his horse-hung dick, which he took in his hand and slowly worked himself up to Clydesdale proportions.

His roommate, the team's freshman first-string quarterback who everyone knew as Slick, entered the room, straight from the showers, just a towel around his waist. As his eyes went to Stud, Slick dropped his towel. He stood there for half a minute, his mouth agape; his tall, lithe; well-cut Nordic blond body trembling. Then he sank down on his rump beside Stud's thigh, whispered. "Oh, God, Stud," and reached for Stud's cock.

Stud brushed his hand away and grabbed for, and managed to grasp, both of Slick's wrists with his fists. Slick was

139

strong, but he was no match for Stud. He had every reason to know that he wasn't.

"Don't tease me, Stud," he whined.

"You can't have it until you promise you'll talk to Coach—that you'll tell him that you want me on first string with you. We came here as a pair; he'll believe that you need me as your primary receiver."

"You know how hard that will be, Stud. You got here because I said I wouldn't come without you—but you've seen the guys ahead of you at the position. And you're not going to be able to make the grades anyway. But don't hold off on me, man. Cock me. You know I gotta have it."

"You let me worry about the grades, Slick. You have to do your part. You want any more cockin', you're gonna talk to Coach. All you gotta do is tell him that you need me."

"I need ya, Stud. You know how bad I need ya."

"On the playing field. You gotta tell him you need me on the field."

"I don't know, Stud."

"Come on, ya big lug. Assume the position."

Stud sat up on the bed and turned, allowing a trembling Slick to come up on the bed on his knees and to move up toward the brass headboard. He grasped the rails, as Stud went down on his back and slid between Slick's spread thighs. He lifted his mouth to Slick's cock and his hands grasped Slick's butt cheeks and pulled them apart. While he sucked and Slick set his pelvis into a roll and gasped his pleasure, Stud's fingers went to opening up Slick's channel. After few minutes, Stud slid out from underneath Slick's butt and knelt behind him. He pulled Slick's dick back between his buns and alternated between sucking that and his balls and tonguing his hole, while Slick groaned and began a litany of "Fuck me, Stud, fuck me, fuck me now, please."

Stud rose up on his knees and covered Slick's torso closely with his. The underside of his horse-hung dick was rubbing across Slick's crack, worrying his hole.

"Now, now. Shit. Now!"

"You gonna talk to Coach about me?"

"Yes. Yes. Yes!"

"And who's the quarterback in this room? Between you and me, who does the stuffing?"

"You do, Stud," Slick whimpered.

"And who does the receiving?"

"Me. I'm your receiver. All of it, Stud. Give me all of it. Please. Stuff me."

"OK," Stud said, with a laugh. "But ya gotta fuck yourself if you want it."

Stud pushed Slick aside and flopped down on his back on the bed, his feet facing the bookcase at the foot of the bed.

"Ride it. No, facing away from me."

He held Slick's waist with his hands as Slick slowly skewered himself on Stud's cock, facing the bookcase, and began riding Stud's cock under his own power. After a few minutes, Stud rose up behind him, embraced his chest with one arm and worked Slick's cock with the other to a lurching, spouting ejaculation.

"Chest on the footboard, up on your knees," Stud commanded. Slick did as commanded, grabbing the legs at the foot of the bed with his fists, as Stud thrust inside him from behind and began fucking him hard and deep. He grabbed a head of hair and arched Slick back so that the bookcase got the full effect of the expression on Slick's face as he got gloriously fucked by the lover he had brought to the university with him.

* * * *

In the manly world of the little death
There is one Lord; one slave
On victor; one vanquished
One over; one under
One sword; one sheath
The raging battle ends
In an embrace of the little death
A demand for surrender; a cry for mercy
A flash of victor's sword; a surrender of vanquished's sheath
Thrust and moan; thrust and groan
One Lord; one slave
Thrust and moan; thrust and groan

One victor; one vanquished
Thrust and moan; thrust and groan
One over; one under
Thrust and moan; thrust and groan
The embrace of the little death
Thrust of sword; and moan
Thrust, thrust, thrust; and groan
The flood of victory
The sigh of the little death

Stud had thought long and hard about the grades problem, probably the hardest of the two problems facing him. Being third string, he was here on a half scholarship. That wasn't enough for him to be able to stay—not nearly enough. He needed a full scholarship and some spending money. A first-string football player got a full scholarship. He'd never had trouble finding spending money.

The grades were harder. Slick was a whiz in math and the sciences, so he'd keep Stud above a C with that. The tests would be a bear, but Slick would do the homework. That would keep Stud above the level. Slick couldn't help with English. And then there were two electives.

"You're taking poetry for your English credit?" Slick had asked, incredulously. "From Professor Moyer? That fairy? And archeology and filmmaking for your electives? You should be taking balling and beer drinking for your electives."

"I got a plan," Stud had said.

A week later, after his first one-on-one session with the dried up old maid Megan Rogers, the archeology instructor, an interesting still shot could be taken of Stud moving out into the hall outside of her office, zipping his pants up and buckling his belt, while Ms. Rogers was splayed in the chair behind her desk, hem of her skirt up around her waist, her tits flopping out of her blouse, and a silly, sloppy grin on her face. If what he was muttering could be discerned, he'd have been heard saying something about digging to China and handling artifacts well enough to last a semester.

Todd Baxter, the film professor, a rather flashy platinum-blond former bit player in the movies, with an attitude and a technique of scaring his students sick from the get go, had issued video cameras in the first class and told the students to come back with an initial film for him to critique at the next class. He took the class down to the faculty garage and showed them the fancy van the university had provided him for taking, processing, and editing film in the field.

The evening before the second class, as Baxter was leaving the university and had walked down to his baby-blue Mustang in the faculty garage, he found Stud, wearing only his gym shorts, his massively muscled arms crossed on his massively muscled chest, and showing his washboard abs to the best effect. He was holding a the video camera in his hand.

"Can't make your class tomorrow, Prof. Sorry, mandatory team meeting. But I rushed doing my film assignment, so that wouldn't be late."

"OK, give it to me. I'll—"

"I thought I did real good, Professor Baxter. I'd really like you to see it now and give me some pointers."

Baxter was in no hurry to deprive his eyes of the beefcake Stud was showing him.

"Uh, sure. We could go up to the studio."

"We could see it in the van, couldn't we? I'm sorta in a hurry. You showed us that everything needed is in the back of the van. And it's got a generator. You said the second class would be introducing the class to how the stuff works in the van. I could get a briefing in that and cover not being able to get to the class. I'd hate to start off the course behind the other students. I know the coaches would be grateful to you."

This helped. Baxter had been sniffing around Coach Tolivar for months. He was aching to be cocked by that hunky Marine.

"Oh, god. Is that? Is that?"

"Yes, Slick, our quarterback. He's a honey, isn't he? Am I doing him well?"

"Oh, god, yes," Baxter murmured, panting so hard he could hardly get the words out. They were only a few moments into the film taken from the bookcase of Stud and Slick having sex in Stud's bed and Baxter was already kneeling in the back of the van, facing the monitor running the video, and Stud was behind him, embracing him, unbuttoning his shirt, and unbuckling his belt. Baxter wasn't stopping him.

Half way through the first running of the film, Stud was crouched over the film professor, who was on all fours and still mesmerized by the film while Stud was fucking him like a dog.

Baxter made Stud run the film three times and demonstrate every position used on Slick in the film on him in the back of the van.

In the third class, Baxter announced that Stud would be his teaching assistant that semester, and the two made the van rock in every out-of-the way parking area within twenty miles of the university. Stud received an A in Introduction to Filming.

He also, surprisingly, got an A in English (and, of course, in Introduction to Archeology).

Elijah Moyer, a distinguished-looking Van Dyke graybeard in his early fifties, was not a man to be impressed or influenced easily. Tall and thin and elegantly dressed and speaking in what he at least presumed was the highest class English accent, he strutted across the stage, asking probing questions of students pulled out of the nervous classroom, in a rapid-fire manner and usually answering the questions while the student was mumbling and sweating and then making pointed, witty, and cut-off-at-the-knees remarks on the insufficiency and idiocy of the student's response.

Stud sat in the first row of desks—or rather slouched—dressed in gym shorts, an athletic T, and flip-flops. He exhibited a disinterested, glassy stare, as he watched a spider walk across the ceiling.

"Mr. Austin. Mr. Austin. Are you with us?"

"Me? You're talkin' to me? I go by the name Stud."

Professor Moyer's lip curled. There was always an athlete like this in his class. He always had to cow them from the very beginning to get them under control.

"We are adults in this class, Mr. Austin. We give each other the respect of addressing each other formally. Perhaps while I have your attention—if only for a moment of limited attention span—you could tell the class who your favorite poets are."

144

Stud turned his face to the professor and smiled a knowing, sensual smile. He had taken a front-row seat, so only the professor could see him.

"Well, Elijah—I can call you Elijah, can't I? I like William Shakespeare, of course. But I also like Richard Barnfield, Digby Mackworth Dolbein, Lord Alfred Douglas—and Noel Coward, of course."

Professor Moyer blanched and his jaw went rigid. All of these poets were known to write homoerotic works.

"I especially like Richard Barnfield," Stud said with a playful smile. He saw that he had Moyer's full attention now. He let a hand go to cupping his basket. "I like his 'The Affectionate Shepherd.' Doesn't it start?":

> *Scarce had the morning starre hid from the light*
> *Heavens crimson canopie with stars bespangled,*
> *But I began to rue th' unhappy sight*
> *Of that faire boy that had my hart intangled;*
> *Cursing the time, the place, the sense, the sin;*
> *I came, I saw, I viewd, I slipped in.*

"That will be enough, Mr. Austin. Now, Ms.—"

"What I can't quite understand, Elijah," Stud interjected, "is just what he means by 'slipped in.' But reading on in the poem—"

"We can pursue this later in private—in my office," Moyer overrode him. "We have much to cover in today's class. Shall we move on now?"

Stud was leaning against Moyer's car in the faculty garage, arms crossed over his chest.

At Moyer's home, in his four-poster bed, Stud made Moyer beg for the cock before he pushed the professor on his back at the foot of the bed, grasped his ankles and cruelly split his legs, and then gave him eight thick inches of what he begged for.

Moyer was spent and exhausted already, when Stud pulled him up off the bed and rotated him, and dumped him on his belly on a nearby red velvet chaise lounge. The professor's head and arms hung over the head of the chaise as Stud

145

mounted his trim buttocks and placed the bulb of his cock at the professor's throbbing hole. He grabbed a handful of head hair and pulled the professor's head up to where their faces were close together.

"I wrote a poem just for you professor. I hope you will give me extra credit."

"Please," Moyer murmured. He was shuddering.

"Please what, Elijah?"

"I want you . . . it . . . again."

"Let's do it to my poem, Elijah. The poem you're going to give me extra credit for. Let's begin. I call it 'Sword and Sheath.'"

"In the manly world of the little death"

"That's how it begins, Elijah. You know what 'little death' means, don't you?"

"It's a literary allusion to an ejaculation. Please, Mr. . . . please, Stud, I need it."

"Didn't know I would know that literary device, did you? That should be worth more extra credit." He was rubbing the underside of his cock across Moyer's hole. The professor was moaning and quietly begging for the fuck.

"There is one Lord; one slave
One victor; one vanquished
One over; one under
One sword; one sheath"

"You know what that means, don'tcha, Elijah?"

"You. You are the lord. You are in command," Moyer sobbed.

"Bingo. Which bring us to my next lines."

"The raging battle ends
In an embrace of the little death"

Stud wrapped his arms around the professor and held him close. Moyer was panting and whining.

146

"A demand for surrender; a cry for mercy"

"Oh, god. Please. Please."

"Please what, Elijah? The words are good. No word is too crude for what you want from me. Say them."

"Fuck me, screw me, cock me! Ahhhhhh. Oh, Christ almighty!"

Stud thrust his cock hard up inside Moyer as he cried out:

> *"A flash of victor's sword; a surrender of vanquished's sheath*
> *Thrust and moan; thrust and groan"*

Moyer gasped as Stud pulled his cock back and then moaned and groaned as Stud thrust up inside him again.

> *"One Lord; one slave*
> *Thrust and moan; thrust and groan"*

Stud matched the words, and, in turn, so did Moyer.

> *"One victor; one vanquished*
> *Thrust and moan; thrust and groan"*

Again

> *"One over; one under*
> *Thrust and moan; thrust and groan*
> *The embrace of the little death*
> *Thrust of sword; and moan*
> *Thrust, thrust, thrust; and groan"*

Stud screamed as he shot off deep up the professor's channel:

> *"The flood of victory"*

They both lay there, spent and reveling in the fuck. When Stud could speak, he closed his poem in a whisper.

"The sigh of the little death"

Stud pulled himself up off the professor's shuddering body, picked the professor up like he was a sack of potatoes, and dumped him on the carpet beside the chaise lounge. Then Stud sat down on the side of the chaise and spread his legs. He rocked back on the weight of his arms, his fists dug into the surface of the chaise next to his sides.

"That should be worth an A this week. If you want it again next week, another A. If that's a deal, clean my cock. Now."

With a moan, Professor Moyer rose up onto all fours and scuttled over to between Stud's thighs, and took the football player's cock in his mouth.

* * * *

Stud received the news that he had been moved to the first-string tight end position on the university football team straight from Coach Tolivar.

There were in the athletic facility's football program training room after hours.

Bobby, the team manager, lay, moaning, in a heap on a wrestling mat, having earlier been enjoyed, together, by both the coach and Stud.

But now, Stud was leaning over a massage table, belly on table, with the coach standing behind him, feeding his cock deep inside Stud's channel, and pistoning him hard. He moved his mouth to Stud's ear and told him of the elevation to the first string. Stud smiled. It had all fallen into place. He even had managed spending money by threatening not to visit his professors for special education again unless they wrote monthly checks to him.

Free Pottery

I needed to get away from Avis. I normally hadn't gone with her on her buying sprees for the boutique gift shop we owned and she ran in the well-heeled Buckhead suburb of Atlanta. I tried to keep busy managing the tennis program at Georgia Tech. I'd been a top twenty professional once and still played doubles in tournaments when I could get a partner willing to chase the balls down. At nearly thirty-five I wasn't up to that anymore. I had to rely on a power backhand and placement.

That's what I taught at Georgia Tech. Power backhand and placement, and I always had a student or two willing to show me power and placement of another kind when Avis was off on her buying sprees.

For some reason I'd lost my reason and agreed to go to Greece with her in search of exotic pottery for the store. A week of her yapping and arguing with Greek merchants had given me a headache. I volunteered to canvas the northern, Turkish coast of Cyprus, alone. Getting into that enclave was such a hassle and required such a convoluted travel schedule that Avis let me go by myself.

What Avis didn't know, though, was that I had been given some very good recommendations on where to stay and what to do in Turkish Cyprus—and that ever since that Turkish exchange student, Erdiz, had shown me that masterful backstroke of his the previous summer, I had been dying to have another young Turkish man between my thighs.

I arrived in Turkish Cyprus on a plane from Istanbul, having already made reservations at a gay boutique hotel east of Kyrenia on the northern coast. I hadn't given Avis anything but a name and a number and she was so wrapped up in herself that I knew she wouldn't check the hotel out—in fact that she wouldn't try calling me at all. The hotel consisted of six separate villa-style suites cascading down the Kyrenia mountainside below the artists' enclave of Bellapais and toward the Mediterranean coast. The rooms of the hotel clustered around a series of terraces and a swimming pool.

The man at the desk when I checked in, a heavily tanned, solidly built, muscular man in his fifties with a white-toothed smile, wavy gray hair on his head, and salt and pepper hair curling at the neckline and armpits of his athletic T-shirt, asked me if I was in Cyprus on business or for pleasure. I answered, "Both, I hope."

"I assume you know what sort of hotel this is," he asked, with a guarded smile this time.

I answered that I did, that it had been recommended to me by a previous pleased guest, and that I hoped that would be the pleasure part of my trip. I added, though, that I was here to buy pottery in bulk for a boutique in the states.

He gave me a big smile, a wink, and a second, lingering look.

He had a slight, young Turkish man lead me to one of the small villas, which was one large room, with full plate glass at the end pointed to the sea and a bath on one side and small kitchenette on the other side at the opposite end, with the entrance foyer between them.

The young man walked with mincing steps in front of me. He was close to being beautiful rather than handsome. Somewhat androgynous, but arousingly so, I'm sure, for anyone aroused by such a type. This didn't really include me, though; I preferred muscle men who would use me. He was wearing a white cotton shirt and trousers that were almost transparent. He had thong briefs on underneath. And he was barefoot.

When we arrived at the villa and he'd done the obligatory instructions on what was what and how it worked, he asked me if there would be anything else he could do for me—anything at all. It was quite obvious that he was offering himself to me.

I told him that he was quite handsome, but that he wasn't really what I was looking for.

He took it well. He asked me what I *was* interested in, and I saw no reason not to tell him directly and in detail. I was to find that all Turkish men took it well. I was also to find that if they saw something they liked, they took it—and they usually took it well.

My first experience of that came not more than two hours later. The invitation of the swimming pool and the dark-blue sea beyond were too enticing, and I changed into a Speedo and took my sunglasses, a book, and towels out to the pool and claimed a lounger.

I was the only one there, except for an older man across the pool and one terrace down who was availing himself of the hospitality of the young bellhop who had offered himself to me, without luck. They were entwined on a lounger, with the guest—who was probably northern European and whose body was going to fat—huffing and puffing as he fucked the young Turk.

I tried to ignore them and to get interested in my book and taking the sun's rays. I hadn't been there very long, though, before the man who had checked me in—who I was to learn was the owner of the hotel—put me in the shadows by standing between me and the sun.

He was a fine figure of a man. In fact, other than age, he was very much like what I had told the bellhop what I was interested in. He now was without his T-shirt. He was muscular, with a barrel chest, and his torso and arms were quite hairy. My tennis player, Erdiz, had been hairy too. It was part of what I enjoyed about him. Erdiz was much younger and trimmer than the man standing before me. He was also much more handsome of face. But this man had a rugged charm about him. And that ready smile. And his hands were big and his fingers long and thick. And I looked down at his toes in his open-toed sandals. They were thick and long too, and hair covered.

"I am Karamat," he said. "We met at the reception desk."

"Yes we did," I answered

"I own the hotel. I sent Musa with you to your room, but he said you were not interested—at least not in him."

"Musa is very nice," I answered. "But, no, he is not what interests me. He seems to be busy now."

We both looked over at the other lounger. Musa was on his chest, with his midsection and legs in the air. The northern European was holding Musa's legs at his side and fucking the young man like he was fucking a wheelbarrow.

"I'm not sure I've ever seen that position," I remarked, keeping my tone amused. "I certainly haven't tried it."

"You must like men inside you then," he said rather matter-of-factly. "And it's a fine position. You *should* try it."

"Yes, I do like men inside me. And maybe someday I will try that," I answered in the same vein.

He sat down on the lounger beside my thigh then, leaning over me, with his hand down beside my opposite side. "Would you like me to suck and fuck you, then? I assure you that I do it very well. Do you like Turkish men. Not boys, men."

"Yes," I said. "I like Turkish men very much. And before you ask, I like hairy men. But I've only had younger men."

"Bah. What do younger men know about fucking other men? You need to be at least fifty to do it well, to make men beg for it again."

"I've always thought that the second fuck was nicer than the first," I said. "You have your hand on my cock." And he did; he was lightly massaging my basket.

"Do you mind?"

"No. It feels good."

"Do you want to see what I fuck with?"

"Sure. Why not."

Karamat stood and dropped his shorts to the ground. I gasped at the size of him. He was in half erection. And the hair on his dark brown body was salt and pepper everywhere but on his head, which was gray, and his pubes, which were still black.

"See, my head is old, but my cock is young," he said. "The hair tells you." And then he laughed. "The best for you. My head knows what to do; my cock can still do it."

"That's nice to know."

"I suck and fuck you now, yes? I make your trip worthwhile."

I smiled and lifted my hips off the surface of the lounger. He leaned down and pulled my Speedo down my legs.

"Very nice," he said, giving what Turks must use for a wolf whistle, making a popping sound from his mouth with his plump thumb. "Many men fuck you? Your hole tight or slack?"

"Not many—and usually with weeks or months between one and the next. Tight, I would guess. Does it make a difference?"

"If slack, I have ways to tighten it up. Tight is good. You feel it good. You not afraid?" he asked. He was holding his cock and waving it at me.

"Yes, of course I'm afraid of what you're waving at me. But that's part of the enjoyment, isn't it."

"I like you. You're not shy. I give you good fuck, I think. It's always better to take it with joy," he said, with a broad smile on his face.

He fished around in the pocket of his shorts and brought out a tube of lubricant and three condom packets.

"Three?" I asked in mock shock.

"You said the second is better than the first, so we see what three is like." He was smiling again.

"We'll see about that," I said, with a laugh.

He sat back down on the lounger, opened the lubricant, and took some in his hand. Then he leaned his face over my groin, took the bulb of my cock in his mouth, and started to suck. I moaned and ran the fingers of both of my hands into his hair. I had every intention to get as much enjoyment out of this as he would give me. One of his hands went under my thighs, and I felt his lubricated fingers at my hole. He licked up and down my shaft and then took it all in—once, twice, three times.

153

I shuddered and lifted my hips off the lounger. He had moved a finger deep inside me.

I moaned deeply. It was obvious that he could give me much enjoyment.

He came up for air and said, "Yes, very tight. I like tight. Like taking a virgin. But we loosen it up a little, I think. You enjoy it more." He took one of my legs and lifted my ankle to his shoulder and then went back to sucking the bulb of my cock and worrying my hole with his lubed finger. Then two fingers, and he was moving them in and out, finger fucking me. His tongue was flicking my piss hole, and I was groaning and writhing under him.

"Young men do this to you?" he asked when he came up for air.

"No," I answered. "They are more direct and more insistent. They focus on themselves, their own needs."

"Ah, older men like me—and soon you—know how to savor it. How to have more pleasure; but more, how to give pleasure. And you are a guest here. We work to your pleasure."

Three fingers and I was grunting and groaning. His mouth was pumping down on my shaft. Quicker and quicker. I came in a flood into his mouth.

"Sorry," I whispered. "It was too good."

"Just one," he said with a laugh. "I make you come four times. Each one better than the one before."

He lifted the hand that he'd been fingering my hole with and flashed four fingers. He slowly and with a wink inserted each finger in is mouth, in turn, and sucked them.

"Oh, god," I croaked.

"Now me. First one very businesslike. You like second, so first one just to put us both in the mood." He stood up from me, straddling the lounger and my thighs and made a show of rolling a condom on his cock and lathering it up with lube.

"First time is for conquering," he said. "Once you are mine, we make love. Or maybe you don't—"

"Stop talking and fuck me," I said. "Yes, hard and deep. Take no prisoners. Make me feel it. Use me." I spoke in a low growl that I didn't recognize as my voice.

He gave me an intense look, grabbed my ankles and spread and raised my legs, pulling my pelvis up off the lounger as well. I rolled it up. He positioned the bulb of his cock at my entrance. I grunted and groaned as he worked the bulb inside.

And then he stopped, leaving his bulb inside the entrance, while I adjusted to it and tried my best to pull it further in with the muscles of my sphincter. This was working, he slowly was moving inside.

"Ah, good. You are good at this. I think we both will take our pleasure from this," he murmured. "But you are too anxious. More pleasure if you know your need for it enough to beg for it."

I began to pant, to beg for it. I scrabbled for his nipples through the matting of hair on his chest, trying to provoke him to plunge into me. He was smiling more cruelly now.

"Shit. Fuck! Give it to me!"

"We will see if a young man can do this for you."

I cried out as he plunged down, down, down. Out and then plunge, again. I cried out again and raised my pelvis to him. When he'd bottomed this time, he held deep inside. I plaintively begged him to fuck, pulling at his body hair, raising my mouth to his nipples and sucking hard, getting my hands around on his buttocks and squeezing the meaty globes and trying to pull him deeper inside me. I beat on his chest with my fists.

God, I wanted him to fuck me hard—more than I'd ever wanted in a fuck before.

He pulled away from me, and slipped out. Then he rose up on his feet, his legs straddling the lounger, and flipped me over. He grabbed my legs, pulling me up to where only my chest and cheek were on the surface of the lounger. With a laugh, he plunged back into me with his cock, and began wheelbarrow fucking me like I had remarked on about the fat guy and androgynous bell boy across the pool. I grabbed the upper legs of the lounger, hanging on for dear life, and cried out my passion while he pumped me hard and deep, not stopping until I had come again.

Karamat let me collapse on my belly on the lounger, and he came down, full length, on top of me. He had come too. I was so absorbed in my own ejaculation that I don't know if we came together or he came first or after.

I felt him go soft inside me while he ran his hands over my body and nibbled at the hollow of my neck. He moved down my body, kissing as he went, until he was crouched behind me. He tongued and nibbled at my buttocks, and then I felt him pulling my dick and balls through my legs. I moaned, widened the stance of my legs, and came up slightly on my knees, presenting my ass to his attentions.

When he swallowed my ball sack and began to roll my balls inside his mouth, I rewarded him with another deep moan. He was holding and slow-stroking my cock with a hand.

"Do your young men give you this attention? Has anyone else done this to you after a first fuck?" he asked.

"No," I answered with a groan. He moved his mouth to my cock and then my hole. Back to my cock and then my hole. And I ejaculated for the third time.

I heard him fiddling with a condom packet, and then he was straddling my hips and riding me in long, deep, slow strokes. He had his fists pushed into my shoulder blades, bearing the weight of his body, but then he slipped them around under my chest and arched my back up to him. I turned my face toward his and we kissed for the first time. He tasted of tobacco and brandy. He was palming my chest, rubbing both nipples between thumb and forefinger, and rocking my body back and forth on his cock.

This time I felt him ejaculate into the balloon of the condom inside me, and I sighed and murmured, "Thank you. The second time was even better."

"You are a sweet fuck," he muttered back in a matter-of-fact voice. "I leave you now for a while. I have to build up again after two and there is work to be done. If you want me to finish you, stay here and I'll be back."

"Finish me?" I murmured. "How could there be more?"

"Stay around and you'll find out," he answered. "I am Turk; there's always more."

I laughed at that—at the inference that I was some sort of project that needed to be finished well. But I stayed, on my belly, luxuriating in the pleasure I had gotten out of his mature, experienced body. And from his bull's cock.

I looked out over the pool. Musa, the small bell boy was riding the prone figure of the Northern European now. And nearby, two men were entwined on a lounger. I couldn't tell who was fucking whom. They were both Europeans and were young and thin. I decided they must be a couple, retreating here to do what they couldn't so openly do at home.

A young man was cleaning the pool. He had a gorgeously well-developed body and was wearing a skimpy black bathing suit. His body was a nutty brown, and he had a full head of black, curly hair and a Fu Man Chu mustache. He wasn't nearly as hairy as Karamat was, but there was a trace of matting under his pecs and a thin line running down to the waistband of his swim suit, which dipped down in front, permitting pubic hair to rim the waistband. When he raised his arms, though, there was a good bit of hair in his pits. His torso was tightly sculpted, and the veins popped out on his powerful arms.

I dozed, thinking of him. When I woke, not knowing why I had done so, Karamat was sitting beside me again, massaging my body with his strong hands. The Northern European and Musa were gone, as was the pool man. The young European couple were in the pool, one belly up to the side of the pool with his arms splayed out over the pool deck tiles. His partner was embracing him from behind and they were kissing—and, I presume, fucking.

"You are awake."

"Yes."

"You have not run from me."

"No."

"We know each other well now. Two fucks and we are friends. Now we will be lovers, yes?"

"Yes, please."

"I fuck you know like a Turk fucks his lover."

He stood and I watched him roll on a condom—the third one. He turned me on my side on the lounger, away from him, and then stretched out behind me. He pulled my body into his, and I turned my face to his, and we kissed, as we both explored each other's bodies to the extent that we could reach.

He pulled my pelvis into his groin and reached down and pulled my calf up so that my leg was bent. I felt the knee of his leg cover my other leg and pull it back a bit.

And then he was slowly entering me—and entering, entering, entering. One of his hands went to my cock and encased it and he slow fucked and slow stroked me to my promised fourth coming, his third, and to, indeed, what was the most sensual fuck of the three.

"You must lock your door tonight," he whispered in my ear.

"Why? I've heard that Cyprus is perfectly safe."

"If you do not lock your door, you may be attacked and raped."

I didn't lock my door that night.

In the darkest of night, I felt the weight of a body on my chest. And hands encasing my head. And a hard cock presented at my mouth. As I sucked, I ran my hands up onto his chest. Nearly hairless, trim but heavily muscled. Young, virile. The cock sweet in my mouth. Rock hard, but not especially long or thick. It wasn't Karamat.

He kneed my legs spread and pushed his knees underneath my buttocks. As he entered me, he leaned down over me, and we kissed. The silky smoothness of a mustache. I tongued his chest as he pumped me and ran my tongue up into his hairy pits, sniffing and appreciating the maleness of him, his musky scent.

He came inside me and I realized he wasn't crowned. I didn't care. I wanted all of him. I regretted he had come so fast. But surprisingly he didn't soften. Young and virile. He turned me on my belly and rode my ass until we came together—me for the first time, he for the second.

Laying full length on me, he spoke for the first time, in a whisper. "Sorry. I saw you at the pool—with Karamat. I wanted you too. You did not lock your door. I begged Karamat, and he said I could have you. He told me that I was his gift to you, that he fuck you tomorrow again."

"He didn't ask me. You must be punished, I think," I whispered back. "Lay on your back, or I will complain to Karamat."

158

We changed positions and I rode his cock into the dawn, as he gripped and spread my buttocks with strong, pool man hands—to open me for the repeated invasion of my spread hole with his ramrod cock.

* * * *

"Pottery? You want pottery? And you want to know if I know where this piece was made?" Karamat turned the coffee mug I'd given him over and over in his hands. He was smiling a funny sort of smile. "Sure, I know this pottery. It's from Kemal's. On the coast west of Kyrenia. I'll call and have them send a man to drive you there, if pottery is what you want."

"You know what I want, Karamat, but pottery is what is paying for this stay at your hotel. It isn't really necessary for you to get me a driver. I can get a taxi."

"No problem; they want to send a car for you," Karamat said. He couldn't seem to lose that lopsided grin. "I'm sure they will enjoy serving you."

He went into the office of the hotel to make a telephone call, and I went back to my villa to rest until the driver came for me.

It had been a tiring day. I hadn't gotten much sleep and was gloriously sore, but walking down in the castle harbor town of Kyrenia had helped me exercise muscles back into shape and deaden any pain I had experienced. I just wasn't used to so much sex of that intensity—and from two different men—in that short a period.

In Kyrenia I had moved from one souvenir or gift shop to another, seeking local-made pottery Avis would like. There were some vividly painted scenes of ancient Turkish warriors done on large display plates that I found were made in mainland Turkey, and I managed, with the help of the shop here, to order a shipment of those by telephone to be shipped directly to Atlanta.

But other than that, there was disappointingly little. That was with the exception of the unusual coffee mug I had found. It was of a tan earth color, rough pottery on the outside, with geometric designs etched into it while the pottery was still wet—

159

obviously by hand or a stencil roller but by a deft hand. Only the inside and lip of the cup were glazed before firing. I had found a few bowls of this and a set of wine glasses and a water pitcher, as well. I'd only bought the cup, though, so that I could show it to Karamat. The shopkeepers I'd asked concerning the origin of the pottery were only willing to obtain it for me. But I didn't want a middleman on the payroll or I wouldn't have come here directly.

I was dozing in my room when the telephone buzzed and Karamat was summoning me to take my ride to the Kemal pottery.

As I walked up to the hotel office, I saw that Karamat was talking with a young Turk, who, it seemed like all of the Turkish men here, was handsome, dark and sultry, and built like an athlete. He had a slightly thuggish look to him, like anyone who went with him would be used roughly, which gave me chills. He also cast on me the same speculative smile I'd seen others do since I came to Cyprus.

"This is Rafat," Karamat said. "He will take you to the pottery." They had been speaking with their heads close together as I approached. They both looked up and gave me brilliant smiles when they sensed I was there. They both were in shorts and droopy athletic Ts, with deep cuts in the armholes, showing thick matting of black hair in their pits, and curly hair cascading out of the dip in the neckhole. Such revealing wear seemed to be the casual apparel of choice in Turkish Cyprus. They both filled their clothes out very well—the mature, Zeus-like Karamat and the young, Apollo-like man talking with him.

Rafat and I were soon scuttling along the coastline on a bad road in an old Holden with so many knocks and squeals that I had to concentrate hard on what the young man was saying. I was watching his hands on the wheel, although his hands didn't spend much time on the wheel. He was being very expressive with them. They were good, sensual hands. The fingers were long, with curls of dark hair above the knuckles. He touched me a few times while we were driving and he was gesturing and even ran his hand down my chest once when he had flung his hand out, protectively, when we had taken a curve in the road hard.

"You stay at Karamat's hotel, yes?"

He damn well knew I was staying there. "Yes."

"Karamat, he treats you well, yes?"

"Yes, he's very hospitable." I knew what he meant by that. He'd put his hand on my thigh and squeezed as he shot me a brilliant, knowing smile. "And he's a master at what he does." I wanted Rafat inside me, and I wasn't going to be in Cyprus long enough to beat around the bush about it. He'd left no question what he wanted from me.

"You like hairy men?"

"Yes, very much so. And men who take what they want."

"Good," he said, flashing a big smile at me. "Karamat said you were very enjoyable."

Rafat let me off at the front door of a squat stuccoed building with picture windows on either side of the entry. Bars covered these windows. It had the look of an old, disused army barracks about it. Rafat urged me to go on in and look around in their showroom while he parked the Holden behind the building.

I entered the showroom to find, standing behind a counter—Rafat. Although he was quick to point out that he wasn't Rafat, but Selat, the twin of Rafat.

"Please, please. Look around. Uncle Karamat told us what you were interested in—and what you were looking for in pottery wholesale. He say you like the half glaze ware."

"Yes, that intrigues me. I don't think I've ever seen any pottery like that. It's just glazed on the inside." "Uncle" Karamat, I was thinking. He hadn't told me they were related. Perhaps that was why he'd given me such a sloppy grin when I'd shown him the coffee mug.

"Yes. That makes it cheaper. But we find many tourists like it—even better than our more artistic, full-glazed pottery. But, please, look around. We make you a very nice deal. Yes, very nice indeed. Uncle Karamat tell us what you like."

I knew he wasn't talking about pottery any more, not really. I felt myself going hard—especially as Rafat had just entered the showroom. Seeing the two of them together was very arousing.

161

As the two talked to each other in whispers and undulged at furtive looks at me, I wandered around the store. The half-glazed pottery, indeed, was very enticing—as were many of their fully glazed and decorated pottery pieces. They had pottery with vine leaves either etched into the raw clay or painted on the surface that would, I believed, sell very, very well in Buckhead. Yes, very enticing. I looked at the twins, standing there and smiling at me, proud of their work and hopeful of its sale. They were very enticing too.

"Are these all the samples?" I asked. "Any more somewhere?" I couldn't hide that I was looking for some place more private than the showroom.

"Yes," Selat said, with a broad grin. "We have more. And a very special collection in the back. You come back and see?"

"Yes, please," I said. Selat ushered me toward a doorway covered with a beaded curtain. I saw that Rafat was at the shop door, locking it and turning the sign to "Closed."

The room Selat led me into was not large. Three sides were lined with shelves, containing pottery. A double bed was set against the fourth wall, between two shuttered windows.

My eyes went to the double bed and lingered there.

"Selat and I take turns sleeping here at night," Rafat said. "For protection of the shop. We also fuck here."

I turned my gaze toward Selat, being slightly embarrassed that the young men were so openly hitting me and were so assured. Of course, I had given them every reason to be assured.

"Perhaps this pottery will interest you," Selat said, as he led me over to one wall.

Arranged on the shelves, using the half-glazed technique were a dozen or more cups, bowls, and pitchers.

"Pick one up," Selat said. "Examine it closely. I think that you'll like it." Rafat was standing close behind me. As I picked a cup up—and then almost dropped it as I saw the images etched into it—I felt his hands go to my hips.

I shuddered. The cup was covered with homoerotic art. Like ancient Greek urns, men straddling men on couches. Fondling, sucking, fucking.

I picked several pieces up, all the same, plus some of stylized hard penises.

162

"You find them interesting?" Selat asked. He was very close to me now too.

"Very interesting, yes," I replied. "But not really what I can sell in Atlanta—at least not in my shop. You have much more—out in the showroom—that I could use, though."

"But perhaps we have something you would want, could use, more privately," Selat said in a low voice. "We can give you a very good deal—a very good deal for someone who was a good friend of Uncle Karamat's—and, we hope, of Rafat and me too."

Rafat had his hands running up under my T-shirt, to my pecs.

"Let's see what kind of deal we can make," Selat said. He took the bowl I was looking at out of my hand and gently returned it to the shelf. Rafat was pulling me over into the center of the room.

"We fuck you now, yes?"

"Yes," I answered breathlessly.

"Both together?"

"If you want."

They sandwiched me, Selat in front and Rafat in back. They had already shucked their own Ts. Rafat pulled mine over my head as Selat unbuckled my belt, unzipped me, and let my shorts hit the floor. Rafat was embracing me from behind and moved a hand to cup my chin and turn my face to his for a deep kiss. Selat pulled my briefs down off my legs and he followed them down, going down on his knees and taking my cock in his mouth. Rafat went down on his knees too and he was working between my crack with his mouth and fingers.

I had to grab their heads, Selat's with one hand, and Rafat's with the other, to maintain my balance.

But I didn't have to do that long. The two stood, stripped off their own shorts and briefs, and began working me between them. I could feel both of their cocks between my thighs. For a brief moment, I thought they were going to take me, together, standing there. I had given permission for that, but I'd thought it would be something we'd work up to, if it happened. Selat had already raised one of my legs against his thigh with a hand under my knee. I felt he was on the cusp of

163

pulling the other one up and settling my channel on his cock—with Rafat's right there as well. I moaned, scared, but half wanting it. But when I was sure that was going to happen, they were moving me, toward the bed.

They had me on my back at the end of the bed and were tag-teaming me. Taking turns holding my legs spread and fucking me and feeding me their cocks while kneeling above my head. Every five minutes or so they would switch positions. They occasionally showed concern that maybe I had had enough. They didn't volunteer to stop altogether, but they assured me that they could finish me if I was growing weary. Fascinated by being taken by hunky twins, though, I encouraged them to fuck on.

One of them pulled out of me—I no longer remembered which was which—but rather than switching, the one at my head started working underneath me, until I was full on top of him and his hard cock was pushing up under my ball sack. The brothers worked together to get his cock inside me and then he crossed his arms tightly across my chest, right under my pits, which drew my arms up to where they were effectively trapped.

Then what I had both feared and hoped for before was happening. The other twin was working his cock inside me on top of his brother's. I panted and whimpered, surprised that I could take them as big as they'd both gotten.

"Can you manage?" a voice in my ear whispered. "I can tell Rafat—"

"No, please. Don't stop. I've never . . . but I want . . ." So the one on top was Rafat. The one under Selat.

And then Rafat began to pump, and I zipped right to heaven. I was spouting in no time and Rafat pulled out of me long enough to lean down and clean my cock with his mouth. And then he was inside me, pumping again. Selat was moaning now as well and the brothers kissed over my shoulder and then each, in turn, kissed me.

When I opened my eyes, there was another man in the room. A near duplicate of Karamat. He pulled his T over his head. The same hairy barrel chest.

"Our father, Kemal," Rafat said. "This is his shop. He can give you really, really good deal."

164

"Yes," I answered. I knew what he was asking.

Rafat's face and cock disappeared and now it was Kemal staring down in my eyes, Kemal entering me, Kemal—thicker than Rafat—pumping me on top of Selat's buried cock.

"Kemal says you are A number 1 good fuck," Selat said afterward, sitting beside me on the bed I was still laying on, panting and recovering. Selat was smiling broadly.

"The three of you were great too."

"Kemal, he doesn't speak English. So I ask for him. He says you can have two boxes—like that one over there—full of the pottery of your pick, for free—you just pay shipping and handling."

"That sounds good," I said. My mind was contemplating how much I had made on that marvelous fuck. I felt the need to close the deal before these guys figured out that I should be paying them for the cocking.

"You might want better deal—three boxes," Selat said rather haltingly.

"For what?" I asked.

"If you stay here, the night, with Kemal. And let him do whatever he wants with you."

Kemal was standing inside the door with the beaded curtain. His body was still beautiful to me. His smile was too. He was holding several lengths of nylon rope in one hand.

Ah, Avis, I thought, the deals I must make to keep your boutique shop profitable.

Hey, Good Buddy

The two had fought each other to exhaustion, each one trying to master the other, until finally they rolled away from each other in the bed of ferns. Joe was the first one to laugh.

"Yeah, but who woulda' known?" Al muttered. "You're such a cute little guy, and you've been eyeing me. I know you have."

"That's because you're such a big hunk—a real bear," Joe answered. "I can admire good muscle definition as well as the next guy." They were both laying on their backs, resting on their elbows, only in their unbuttoned green regulation shirts and their boots. The two were sprawled side by side under the low, protective branches of a tall fir tree. They were far enough off the trail leading up to Lower Mesa Falls that there was little chance of anyone stumbling on them—certainly not a park ranger. Joe and Al were the only two rangers in this section of Yellowstone Park.

"I think I had every reason to believe that this was the muscle you wanted to admire," Al, the big bear, said, as he fisted his still-hard cock with both hands—without overlap. Then he laughed too. Al always laughed at his own jokes. Sometimes others didn't—not just because they weren't as impressed with his jokes as he was, but also because of his intimidating size and the thick matting of black curly hair on his deeply tanned arms and spilling out of the neck of his shirt. He tried to keep the growth down on his chin, but his five-o'clock shadow had been building since 6:00 a.m.

"That's a very nice muscle, yes," Joe answered. "But as we both now know, we both like to be on the giving end of a 'hide the muscle' game, so this has all been very nice, but—" Joe reached for his gray trousers and started to rise from the ferns.

"Hey, wait. You aren't gonna leave me in this condition, are you?" Al was gesturing at his prodigious hard on.

"What do you propose?"

"Ever done a 69?"

Joe had, and they both therefore managed to come, but it wasn't easy going, and they had to apply more personal attention to their personal equipment than the project probably was worth.

"Kinda tame, wasn't it?"

"Yeah, for you too?" Al answered. "But better than nothing."

"But not better than what's possible," Joe answered after a few minutes as they lay there wishing it had been better.

"Meaning?"

"Maybe a bit of hunting would be rewarded."

"Out here? If you haven't noticed, you and I haven't seen much of anyone but each other for a couple of days—and we've both seen how much good that does. We could just go back to the station and put on a couple of DVDs. I guess I don't need to hide mine now or pretend like I don't know you've got 'em too."

"No, I mean hunting like in for real tail. You know what's down just outside the park near Ashton, don't you?"

"Sage brush and scrub pines?"

"There's a dude ranch down there too."

"Several of them, I think. So?"

"So, one of them—one of the ones closest to the park boundaries—is a gay dude ranch. And those guys come up into the park. I've seen them fucking inside the park."

"I'm not that much into just lookin'."

"Neither am I. I've seen them doing other things too. Interested in a little bit of fishing?"

"Fishing?"

"Fishing for pleasure. Oh, hell, get up and button up and come with me. We'll do a little bit of hunting and fishing."

Al had nothing better to do, so he just grunted, rose up out of the crushed ferns, pulled on his briefs and trousers, adjusted his shirt, and headed out in the direction Joe had already taken.

"Hey, wait up for me. Where we going?"

"Henry's Fork," Joe growled over his shoulder. "Upper branch. You comin' or not?"

* * * *

The two stood there, behind bushes and trees, watching the young guy for quite some time before they made a move. Joe had assured Al that it would only be a matter of time before they could make a move.

"See that pile of beer cans there? He can't last too much longer."

The guy was young, one of those blonds with spiked hair—too blond to naturally be his, although he probably wasn't too far off blond, they discovered when he took his T-shirt off and was just in shorts. The hair on his body was a light, blondish down.

He was thin, what you'd call willowy, with a nice body that was only lightly muscled, but muscled enough to say he wasn't too girlish. His face was sort of girlish, though, more pretty and sultry than manly handsome. His eyes were sort of broodish and his lips sensual and thick. He obviously liked jewelry, because he had multiple piercings with silver rings in them: an eyebrow, an ear, his lip—and when he finally rose up from where he was sitting and stretched and turned half facing Joe and Al, they could see he had a ring in his navel too. His shorts hung low on his slim hips. The curls of pubic hair from his groin peeking out from below his waistband showed light auburn tones.

169

"There, told you he wasn't a natural blond," Joe whispered.

"Sorta close, though. Looks kinda sissy to me," Al answered with a little snort.

"Out here beggars and choosers and such," Joe whispered back. "Besides, chances are good we won't be stuck with a third top with nowhere to go. I think he's kinda cute. You don't seem to be put off yourself. You've been workin' your yang for several minutes now."

"I'm so keyed up now, I could probably fuck a deer. I got a yin to use my yang."

"Shhh," Joe admonished. "I think we're about to be in business."

The young guy had been sitting beside a stream, where water was racing across rocks in the streambed. He had been sitting next to one of several deeper pools of water, lazily casting into the pool with a fishing line on a bamboo rod and frequently looking away from the pool and taking a swig of beer from the six-pack he'd brought. He looked like he was down to his last can. And he hadn't caught anything, even though the flash of light off of fish scales where the stream raced between the rocks promised that there were, indeed, fish to catch.

The young man stood and stretched. He pulled his pole back from the water and wedged the end of it between two rocks, leaving the line dangling in the water.

The shorts the guy was wearing were cut-off jeans, with practically no leg to them. A beam of sunlight caught his body as he grasped his fists behind his neck and stretched, working out the kinks, showing off his torso to the best effect. Al gave a little growl.

"Down, boy," Joe whispered. "You're going to get a piece of that."

"You sure?" Al answered. "He's going to get away."

"I don't think so. Wait for it. Just a couple of seconds more."

The young man was gingerly moving out into the stream, moving from one smooth-topped rock to another, being very careful because he was barefoot. His sandals were sitting by the side of the stream next to his T-shirt.

Reaching the middle of the stream, the young man turned toward where the water was rushing from.

Al moaned as the young man unbuttoned his fly, spread the sides of his skimpy denim shorts, and fished out his cock. Holding that in his hand, he arched his back and began to piss in a long, steady, golden arch—into the onrushing waters of the stream.

"Now," Joe growled. Not caring how much noise he was making, he strode out of the tree line and to the bank of the stream. Al stumbled out of the scrub too, in Joe's wake.

"Hey, good buddy. Watcha doin'?" Joe called out in a thunderous voice.

Startled, the young man nearly slipped off the rocks and into the stream. As fast as he could, he jammed his cock back into his shorts, but he left the fly unbuttoned, showing a cascade of curly light-brown hair in the gap.

"Fishing," he answered, although it sounded more like a croak. He could clearly see that he was facing two park rangers. He could also see that the big, scary, bear of the two had one of the biggest and thickest half-hard cocks he'd ever seen protruding out of this fly and being held in his fist. He'd sensed he hadn't mouthed the world "fishing" right and was about to say it again, but he swallowed the word the second time in the realization that he didn't have any sort of license to be fishing in a national park. He'd just slipped away from the dude ranch and come up into the park, following the bank of Henry's Fork. He'd come to the ranch for the fucking, but he'd been more of a sensation there than he had figured. He was fucked out for the moment—or at least had thought he was.

"Sorry, I don't have a license," he sheepishly admitted, not being able to keep his eyes off Al's club of a cock, "But I haven't caught anything. Maybe we can—"

"Fishing's the least of your problems, young man. What were you doing out there in the middle of the stream?"

"Just relieving myself."

"Relieving yourself, you say? Where did you come from? Did you come into the park from that all-men's dude ranch down outside of Ashton?"

"Yes, sir. I'm sorry, but I—"

"How old are you, son?" Joe was doing what he could to put on his official face and tone. It was hard for him to do and not laugh, though, with Al standing beside him and pulling on his meat. The young man was mesmerized by Al's cock. His own staff had come out of the gap in his shorts again and was standing up from his brown bush.

"Twenty."

"Yeah, right."

"I've got ID. There in my wallet, under my T-shirt."

"It's OK, I'll believe you. We can check the ID down at the sheriff's office."

"No, please," the young man moaned. "I didn't catch any fish."

"It isn't about the fish, son," Joe said with a mock sternness in his voice. "It's about that there pissing in the stream. Do you know where that water goes that you just pissed in?"

"Down the mountainside?" the young man answered. He sounded like he wasn't sure. And he sounded like he didn't know where this was going. He was licking his lips and staring at Al's cock, though, which had gone full hard in Al's hand.

"Yeah, down the mountainside. Past that dude ranch you're stayin' in. That water you just polluted is going into the water you'd be drinking in about a half an hour if you were down at that ranch. We take environmental protection very seriously in our national parks. We're gonna have to take you down to the sheriff's office in Ashton."

The young man moaned.

"Unless . . ." Al said.

"Unless what?" the young man whimpered.

"Unless you give it up for Ranger Al here and me. You come from that dude ranch, and I can see that you want it from Al. Open your legs for us both and we'll just overlook that pollution charge—even though we take environmental protection real seriously in this park."

* * * *

Joe and Al stood side by side, arms entwined, on the stream bank as the young man knelt before them and alternately

172

gave each of their cocks attention with his mouth. They groaned almost in unison as he tried to take both cocks together in his mouth at once. Al was particularly pleased when he found that the young man had a ball stud in his tongue—and knew full well what to do with it.

"Hey, lookee here. He's got a ring down here too," Al rang out with glee. The young man was stretched out on his side along a log, with Joe standing behind him, lifting his leg with one hand, and fucking him in a side split. The young man's head was arched over the end of the log and Joe was slow-pumping his throat with his cock. Al had just reached over to pay attention to the young man's cock and found the ring at the base of his penis, where the perineum began, and pulled gently on it.

"Look, it makes the cock bounce," he said.

Joe had claimed firsties, because it was his idea and his setup. Al good-naturedly acquiesced, with the comment, "You'd best go first. After I'd reamed him, he probably couldn't even feel you fuckin' him."

The young man came with Al stroking him and moaned and gagged as Al rubbed his tonsils with his cockhead.

For Al's turn, Al was sitting on the log, and the young man, was sitting in his lap, facing him and fucking himself on Al's staff by leveraging off the soft earth of the stream side with the balls of his feet. He was crouching more than sitting, though, so that he only had to take half of Al inside him. Joe was standing behind the young man, with his hands covering and worrying the young man's nipples. He was nuzzling the young man's neck with his face and trying to tease the young man to turn his face for a kiss. But the young man was more interested in exploring Al's hairy chest with his hands and lips.

"Enough of this shit," Al declared. He grabbed the young man by his waist, lifted his body and then jammed it down on his cock. The slight blond howled as Al started pumping his ass on his cock, slamming him up and down, burying the monster cock to the quick with each pull.

The young man's torso flopped back toward the ground, and Joe stifled his cries by pushing his cock between the young man's lips and beginning a slow pump.

173

Afterward the young man lay on his back between the log and the edge of the stream, his arm flung over his face, and moaned quietly.

Joe and Al sat next to each other on the log, both looking satiated and very satisfied with themselves.

"Hey, lookee there," Al sang out, "I think you've got a bite. Better pull in your line."

The young man moaned. He didn't move.

Joe went over and pulled in the line. "Yep. You got one. And it's a beauty. For another fuck, we'll let you take it home, no worries about a license. And no worry about pollution, either. It came from upstream. Your piss is down at the dude ranch now."

The young man moaned. Al leaned over and grabbed him by the waist.

The young man went home with his fish.

* * * *

"Hey, we're close to the stream," Joe said, as the two trudged along in the park the next day. "We might as well check it out."

They didn't bother to approach the spot of the previous day quietly. They just tromped in, laughing and joking with each other. They surely could be heard from a good distance.

As they entered the clearing, Joe and Al stopped in their tracks, both taking on big smiles.

"Hey, good buddies. Watcha doin'?" Joe sang out.

Their young man had brought a friend. The two twinks, each wearing just skimpy denim shorts, with their flies unbuttoned, turned from where they were standing in the middle of Henry's Fork stream, both still pissing in wide arcs into the center of the racing stream, both having broken into broad grins.

The eyes of both of them went to Al's fly, where he already had his monster cock out, ready to give them both a lesson in environmental protection—which Yellowstone Park takes very seriously.

uh-oh

Scott thought it was the whining that was getting to him—it certainly wasn't Chip's body. He leaned over that and ran his fingers along the rise of the little blond's butt cheek. Chip raised his buttocks in response, fully expecting Scott's fingers to move into the crevice.

Regardless of what Chip was preparing for, his attention was elsewhere. He was rattling on in that whiny little voice of his about the tension of the impending opening of the Broadway musical that he had a dancing role in.

How he was managing to segue that to his need for a car, Scott couldn't fathom. He almost found it amusing the many different ways Chip had been able to introduce the topic of cars since Scott hadn't given him that red Camaro convertible he'd said he wanted for Christmas. He'd gotten the topic introduced already now.

"The opening night party is at the producer's house out in the Hamptons, and I have no idea how I'm . . . uh, ohhh."

The fingers of one of Scott's hands had navigated the distance from the rise in Chip's firm buttocks to the hole in the crevice between the tight orbs, and he was rubbing the opening, making it bud for him. His other hand had gone underneath

Chip's raised pelvis and grasped the pert little cock it had found there. Chip jerked and moaned as Scott began to milk his cock and slipped a finger into his hole, but that didn't stop his litany of want.

"If this musical doesn't have legs, Tony told me of a dinner theater over in Jersey needing dancers. But I'd need a way of getting . . . emmufff."

Scott had taken his hand away from Chip's ass long enough to take hold of the mop of hair at the back of the blond dancer's head and maneuver his face to Scott's groin, where he forced the head of his cock between Chip's lips. This was the one sure way Scott had found to shut Chip's whining up.

In one sense Scott realized that his time with Chip had just about run its course. The sex was still good—Chip still made those little gurgling noises and cries of being stuffed that Scott liked to hear when he fucked the dancer, and Chip had the flexibility to handle the athletic fuck positions Scott enjoyed—but Chip was about to get on Scott's last nerve with his incessant whining for new toys.

Not that Scott couldn't afford them. His antique furniture reproduction business was going great guns, there was no end to the demand for what his carpenters turned out in New York City, and he was making money hand over fist. But what the hell was a Broadway dancer going to do with a sports car in the city anyway?

Scott wasn't blind. He could figure out what Chip and that stagehand, Tony, were doing behind his back. He knew it was Tony who wanted the car.

And, dammit, Scott had already gotten the car. He would have had it to give to Chip at Christmas, but red Camaro convertibles were pretty scarce and Chip would just continue to whine if he didn't get exactly what he ordered. So, it had taken longer than Scott figured it would to get the car.

Scott also was realistic enough that he hadn't had a name put on the title. He'd let Chip do that, and if Chip wanted to put Tony's name on the title, that would be OK with Scott. He'd try anything if he could get Chip back to just being the pleasant little, nonwhining, compliant fuck toy he'd been when Scott first found him.

Cruising bars for tail he liked—blond and boyish and flexible enough to take those enticing positions Scott had learned on a visit to India—was not something that Scott was prepared to do. He'd been lucky to have opened a bedroom door at a party to see Chip with his shoulders and knees to the carpet and his butt in the air and an Indian writer reverse fucking down into him. Scott hadn't seen anyone able to do that since he'd left South Asia, and later the Indian writer agreed with him that Chip was the most flexible fuck he'd been able to find in New York himself.

The writer had magnanimously put Scott in contact with Chip. Scott only later found out that the writer had also grown tired of Chip's whining and badgering him for expensive gifts.

But Scott had gotten Chip the red Camaro, just too late for Christmas. His backup plan to give it to him for Valentine's Day almost backfired too. He'd only just got the car parked in a garage off Madison Avenue, with the documents in the glove compartment, and a big white bow on top. Now he'd have to think of a clever way of giving the keys and directions to the garage parking place to Chip. He'd have to go out and maybe get flowers or a box of candy or something and have them delivered to the stage door tonight. But first . . .

"On the carpet, on your belly" he growled. Scott was no refined Manhattan Mogul. He'd come up through the construction and furniture-making business by way of the docks. He was a rough man underneath. When his sap was on the rise, he could take on the look and aspect of a gangster, and the positions he liked to put his fuck partners in were ones of control and dominance. He was not a man to deny or mess with when he was in high rut.

Chip dutifully rolled off the bed and onto the bedroom carpet, stretched out on his belly.

Scott came down on top of him, his head to Chip's feet. As Chip gurgled and groaned how big and filling Scott was, he forced his cock down inside Chip's channel in the reverse of most positions, moving his knees under Chip's armpits.

"Lock your ankles behind my neck, and your fists at my belly," he directed.

177

Chip did so, raising his legs with his extraordinary flexibility, arching his back so that Scott's torso was cradled inside Chip's bowed body. Then, with the leverage of his knees, Scott rocked them to a mutual ejaculation, digging deep inside Chip's gut, listening to Chip's declarations of being on the edge of not being able to handle it, while knowing that Chip would handle it. But with Scott realizing that there weren't many Chips around—not that many who could handle what put Scott into higher arousal heavens. And there was the rub.

Three hours later Scott was walking down Madison Avenue, still in a quandary about what to get to hold the Camaro keys and directions to the garage in when he was jostled on the street, and, in righting himself, looked up at the sign over a shop door and got his answer. "Leonidas Belgian Chocolates," the sign said.

The answer to Scott's question. He'd heard of those chocolates. They were world famous. And they had a shop right here on Madison Avenue. Somehow Scott thought you had to go to Belgium to get these chocolates, and he'd heard some of his clients say they did just that. That brand of chocolate must be enough to impress someone in the theater, like Chip. So, he decided he'd put the keys and directions inside the lid of a box of chocolates. And if the shop delivered, he was in business.

He went into the shop, which was bustling with activity. That was natural enough; it was the day before Valentine's Day. The shop was small, but a big store wasn't need to display what was only about a dozen different types and sizes of candy boxes. Scott was pleased to see there were three different sizes of red velvet heart-shaped boxes on display.

He went up to the counter, where there already was a man in a cashmere coat—looking very prosperous and well groomed—talking with the clerk. The clerk looked a little frazzled, no doubt because this must be one of the peak selling days at a shop like this, but he still was looking very good to Scott.

The young man wasn't tall, but he was slender—Scott would say he was willowy. He was a spiked-hair blond, with blonder tips, watery blue eyes, long, dark eyelashes (belying any claim of being a natural blond), and sensuous, unnaturally red lips. His hands were expressive, with fingers that were dexterously going about their complicated dance of moving this paper there and punching out this figure and that on the cash register.

He dropped his pencil, and when he bent over to retrieve it, the man in line ahead of Scott pointed out that the pencil was well behind him. Scott drew in his breath when he saw that the young man just widened the stance on his legs, reached through them, and retrieved the pencil.

Images of the young man, naked, in all sorts of compliant and subservient fuck positions raced through Scott's mind. Bent double like that, his hands grasping Scotts ankles, as Scott stood behind him and plowed his ass. Scott's blood began to boil.

The transaction before his seemed a bit complicated. Scott heard the gentleman saying he wanted the box of chocolates—he was buying the one named the "Velvet Heart Large" for $45—to be sent to the address given on one business card but the receipt to go to the address given on another business card, saying he had an assistant who took care of all of his financial affairs.

The clerk wasn't able to give the man in the cashmere coat his full attention because a customer had brushed a couple of boxes to the floor from a display across the room, and the clerk glanced over there to watch her put them back. But his hands were still busy moving this slip of paper to there, so Scott thought he must be in control of the transaction.

When Scott moved up to the counter, the young man's face flushed, and he gave Scott a brilliant smile. Scott wanted to think it was because of him—he found the smile to be downright luscious—but he was sure it was just because so much was going on in the busy store. Still, the images of the young guy and him together had made Scott hard, and he rubbed himself gently against the front of the counter as he spoke to the clerk.

Scott patiently explained that he'd take one of the Velvet Heart Large boxes of candy too, but he wanted this key and set of directions put in the lid and for the box to be delivered to the stage door of the Lunt-Fontanne Theatre for Chip Harden. The little blond clerk wagged his head and his fingers were busy moving bits of paper and ringing up the sale, but his attention was focused on Scott, still giving him an endearing, sloppy grin.

Scott had the sensation that the clerk knew he was hard and rubbing against the counter that separated them—in his mind not having that separation; in his mind standing with the complaint clerk draped on his torso, wrists locked behind Scott's neck and ankles locked behind his waist, and mining the smiling blond's ass deep—and that gave Scott an extra little charge of arousal. He hadn't felt this charged up in months.

"You do deliver, don't you?" Scott asked. He was sure they did. The man before him was having his box of candy delivered too. But Scott suddenly didn't want to end the conversation. The young clerk was giving him the biggest sex boost he'd had for some time. That didn't happen often. Scott wanted to savor the moment.

"Yes, we do. We have a delivery man."

When Scott got to the door, he turned, to see the clerk at the doorway to the back, covered by a beaded curtain, hand the two boxes of chocolate to another man standing just in the shadow of the doorway, beyond the beaded strands that were draped down the clerk's willowy body. Scott saw more than just the exchange of boxes, though, and what he saw made him regret slightly this whole Valentine's Day gift to Chip idea. But he just gave a sigh of resignation, opened his umbrella to the predicted and finally arrived rain, and started walking on up Madison toward his furniture shop.

* * * *

"There, that's done," Alex Clifton Dandridge, the 3rd, had muttered to himself as he left the Leonidas shop and headed off for his father's brokerage office. He saw a splatter hit the sleeve of his cashmere coat and he looked up, thinking "damned pigeons," but saw that it was only the beginning of the promised rain showers for the afternoon. He pulled up the collar of his coat, hunched over, and flagged down a taxi. It wasn't far, but it was too far to risk mussing himself up.

He hadn't really had time to come out and buy something last minute for Sarah for Valentine's Day. They were going out tomorrow evening, but he knew she would expect more than that. He'd take flowers tomorrow to add to the box of chocolates he was having sent over to her now. Then she'd expect a fuck after the play tomorrow night—they were going to a preview of that new musical opening next week at the Lunt-Fontanne Theatre—and he'd dutifully grit his teeth and give her what she wanted. They could taper off after the wedding. That's what most people in their class did anyway. She'd have a tennis pro or fitness instructor or something, and she'd assume he'd have a secretary or two. There she'd be wrong, though.

Alex had realized only at the last minute that Kyle, his assistant, wouldn't think of buying and sending a Valentine's Day gift to Sarah. Kyle did everything for Alex—and very efficiently too—including lying under him before Alex's father had said it was time for Alex to marry and settle down, and had hinted that his movement to the top of the firm depended on that.

Alex was sure that a Vandermeeden would satisfy his father. The old coot had been too preoccupied with business to realize that his son liked other men. He probably wouldn't notice—if he was still alive for it—if Alex and Sarah's first born looked like her tennis pro.

Kyle hadn't taken it well. He was still doing his job—and doing it well—but he wasn't at all pleased that Alex hadn't fucked him in the month since he'd gotten engaged. Well, Kyle didn't have anything to lose. But Alex knew the Vandermeedens well enough to know they'd have their eyes peeled and their ears plastered to the ground for any miscue on Alex's part. At least up to the wedding. The merger—and that was exactly what it was—was advantageous for both families, but it didn't matter much if the romance lasted. Very few marriages of any importance in this city were more than business.

Alex couldn't fault Kyle, though, for not buying Sarah's presents. He was faultless in every other way. He was even a good lay, although by the time Alex had disentangled himself from Sarah, he was sure that both he and Kyle would have moved on to other men.

As he rode the last few blocks in the taxi, Alex wondered if he should get something for Kyle too—just to string him along and keep him available. He was the best assistant Alex could imagine. And he was a great lay too.

* * * *

"Fuck him." Scott clicked off his cell phone. Chip hadn't even bothered to come home the previous night. And he hadn't called. Scott had had to call him.

And when Scott had mentioned the box of candy on the phone—asked Chip if he'd gotten it—he'd just gotten a snippy reply about it. And Scott had heard a snort in the background. Probably Tony, he thought. They probably were tooling around on Long Island now in the red Camaro convertible, playing Scott for a chump. Chip had gotten what he wanted and had gone off on a lark with Tony.

"Well, fuck them. I won't play the fool forever."

And now there was a glimmer of hope that he wouldn't have to. He hadn't moved on from Chip, because he didn't know how to—how to get what he wanted, what Chip gave him in spite of all the whining and the duplicity.

Scott kept thinking of the little blond trick with the spiked hair and the delicious smile behind that counter at the Leonidas chocolate shop—and how flexible he'd been when he bent over and was able to reach back between his legs for that dropped pencil.

And then what Scott had seen when he turned back as he was leaving the candy shop—the store clerk kissing the guy on the other side of the beaded curtain. Scott had seen enough of the guy in the black leather jacket to know that it was a guy—a hulking brute of a guy. And he knew the possessiveness of the hand with the studded leather wristband that the guy had at the clerk's waist as they kissed. The clerk took cock. Scott was sure of that. And he took it rough too.

Scott went to work, but all he could think about was the clerk in the Leonidas shop. His boyish blondness, his delicious smile, his flexibility in retrieving the pencil—and, most important, in now knowing he took cock, the steady smile he'd given Scott as he was serving him.

As he was serving him; as he was servicing him.

Scott couldn't take any more. He had his secretary call the Leonidas shop and find out when they closed. It would be late today, 8:00 p.m., she'd found out. Because it was Valentine's Day, a peak selling day for chocolatiers.

The furniture store was closing early. People didn't buy many antique furniture reproductions for last-minute Valentine's Day presents. But they—and Scott's employees—did tend to have someplace to go that evening. So Scott let them close early.

Then he sat there, in his darkening office, thinking of Chip and Tony tooling around Long Island in the red Camaro convertible Scott had bought and of that clerk in the Leonidas shop, with the delicious smile, the flexible body—and who took cock. Who took it rough.

At 7:45, Scott reached down and opened the bottom drawer of his desk. He'd bought himself a gift for Valentine's Day too. It was a black leather strap, a sling—a fairly long one, with double hoops at either end and a padded strip half way down the strap. He'd bought it to use with Chip tonight. But Scott didn't think Chip would be home tonight.

He put it into his briefcase, put on his coat, locked the front door of the store behind him, and started walking over to and down Madison Avenue.

"Uh, guess you're the last customer. We're about to close. Oh, it's you."

The words were almost choked off. The Leonidas candy shop clerk had worried about this all day. Something in the back of his mind had been bothering him about yesterday. Those two great-looking men who had come in—especially the second, dangerous-looking one. The guy who had sent a Valentine box to another man. And all of the bustling that had been going on in the shop at that time. Had he managed to get the candy and receipt to the right addresses on the first guy—and the second guy with what he'd wanted in the candy box. Was he sure he'd gotten that right? Was this guy here to complain. The clerk sure hoped not. He'd been fantasizing about that man all night. He'd come twice thinking about the guy—tying him up and then fucking him over and over again.

The man walked to him and put his hand on the clerk's arm, an aggressive, possessive motion that sent chills up the clerk's spine. The man had a hard-edged look to him. Like he could be demanding. That's what turned the clerk on. Stick, the delivery guy. He was cruel and demanding. Maybe a bit too much so. Maybe it was the exotic the clerk was after more than the cruel. The man was gripping his arm—tight, possessive, but not painfully tight.

The Leonidas candy store clerk's face turned into a broad smile and fluttering of his eyelashes.

Scott stood there, smiling back.

"Did you want another box of candy?"

"I'd like some candy, yes. But I brought a gift for you, if you might like it," Scott said. He opened his brief case and pulled out the leather sling. "Do you know what this is? Do you know what this is for?" he asked, keeping his eyes on the young clerk.

The look in the clerk's eyes told Scott that he, indeed, knew what could be done with that leather sling.

"I'll have to lock the door," he whispered.

"The other guy . . . the delivery guy . . ."

"He's making the last deliveries. He's going home from there. He's not coming back here. No one else is here."

Scott fucked the little blond clerk in the back room, beyond the doorway covered by the beaded curtain. The clerk lay on his spine on a low wood-topped counter where they filled the candy boxes. His thighs and ankles were bound in the hoops at either end of the black leather sling, holding his calves up, spread, and tight against his thighs. The sling was around his neck, with the padded section at the back of his neck. Scott was standing between his thighs, slow-pumping his ass channel with his cock.

Scott bent over and kissed the clerk on the lips. It was a sensuous, deep-tonguing, lingering kiss. The clerk was humming quietly, the vibrations of the kiss helping to thicken and lengthen Scott inside him. Scott moved his lips to the young man's nipples, one of them having a ring through it, while he began to increase the intensity of his pumping action. Scott got the nipple ring between his teeth and pulled gently. The clerk gasped and moaned. But he didn't ask Scott to stop.

Scott heard a drawer under the counter opening and he pulled away from teasing the clerk's nipples and raised his torso up to see what the clerk was doing. He had managed to open a drawer and he'd taken out a pear-shaped butt plug. Scott looked down into the clerk's eyes, with surprise, where he saw a saucy smile.

The clerk bent his torso up toward Scott's, and the older man looked on with awe and lust as the clerk managed to open his lips over the tip of his own cock and begin to suck. And even more surprising, his flexibility permitted him to move his hands around Scott's waist to Scott's butt cheeks, which were being separated. Scott gasped, moving to new heights of arousal, as he looked down the line of his torso and watched the young clerk sucking his own cock—and as he felt the butt plug entering his ass.

Cum burbled around the rim of the blond clerk's lips and he was butt fucking Scott with the plug when Scott arched his back, cried to the ceiling, and ejaculated.

That was it—the clerk was coming home with Scott tonight. Toss Chip out on his whiny little ass.

* * * *

When Alex Clifton Dandridge, the 3rd, got out of his BMW in the parking garage of his brokerage house on Valentine's Day morning, Kyle was standing there, all excited about something, and hopping back and forth on two feet. He was looking good, dressed in tight jeans and T-shirt and wearing loafers without socks. Kyle had a great body. It looked good in office clothes. It looked mighty fine dressed casual, as he was now. It looked terrific nude.

Now he was looking mighty fine and all smiles.

"What?" Alex said, only managing a half smile. Kyle hadn't been this happy to see him since the engagement. Had something happened to Sarah, he wondered.

"Thank-you, thank-you, thank-you," Kyle burbled. "I understand. I understand what you're saying."

"What?" Alex said again.

"Don't be coy," Kyle said. "Come, let me show you how grateful I am."

Kyle took Alex by the hand and pulled him down the row of cars, back to a dark corner of the garage—where Alex saw a new red Camaro convertible with a gigantic white bow on top of it. Engraved along a side of the ribbon that showed was the phrase "Be Mine."

"I don't . . ." Alex started to say. But his attention was arrested by the realization that Kyle had already stripped off his T-shirt and jeans and hadn't been wearing any briefs.

"In the backseat," Kyle muttered. "Here. Your trousers first."

Somehow Kyle managed to get his mouth between Alex's legs and onto his cock in the cramped backseat of the Camaro. And in short order the red sports car was rocking back and forth without any forward motion as Kyle, facing Alex, bounced his ass channel up and down on Alex's cock, while holding his boss's face into his nipples.

Alex had been a month without Kyle's exuberant fucking. He only now realized how much he'd missed him. He had no idea what this beribboned sports car crap was all about, but now he realized that Sarah or no Sarah, father's approval or no approval, he wasn't going to go more than two days anymore without fucking Kyle. Best fucking Valentine's Day present he'd ever gotten.

Uncle Carl

"My name is Nario. You are Mr. Armstead?"

"Yes. I was expecting my uncle."

"He could not come. I'm am his boy."

Yes, I'll just bet you are, I thought. But then he clarified, if not enough to make a difference to me.

"I am his houseboy. Welcome to Naples, Mr. Armstead."

"Call me Harry, Please. Is it far from here to Positano?"

"No, not too far. The worst part will be getting through the airport traffic. Then it is a very pleasant ride, a scenic ride down the Amalfi coast. Your uncle has picked a very beautiful spot to live in."

And a very beautiful houseboy, I thought. But then I knew he would. Some things never change. I certainly didn't think Uncle Carl would change for anyone. He always expected the world to change for him. Not in this respect, of course—him being here in Italy rather than back in England with the rest of the family—well, most of the rest of the family. That's what I had been sent here to do. I had come to try to get Gordon to come home.

Nario was certainly a cute little trick. Small and deeply tanned—the olive Mediterranean complexion. Curly black hair, a beautiful androgynous face, with a winsome smile. His mincing steps as he preceded me to the baggage claim gave him away. Just like my uncle liked them. Didn't do a thing for me, though. Better here than in England, of course. We'd been well through that. But this was one of the reasons why I was here. I was charged to tell Carl he could come home now—if he had given up the ways that had gotten him exiled. Seeing who he'd hired as a houseboy, though, made me think that part of the mission was a lost cause.

I wondered if Nario too was some important person's favorite son—someone who could dismember Carl at will if he found out what was happening to his precious child. Not that Carl picked them underage, mind you. He just went for the danger of a powerful backlash.

I was on edge and disgruntled. I hadn't told anyone the whole of why I was here. I had only told Uncle Carl that the family wanted me to talk to him—and then only through telegrams. He had said that my plane would be met. He didn't say he wasn't meeting it, though.

As we left the airport, I briefly had the fearful thought that Uncle Carl wasn't even at his exile villa in Positano. He flitted all over the world. He was a portrait photographer of choice by the rich, famous, royal, and, when he needed the money, the want-to-bes. He could go anywhere but England. And, if our circle of friends could be trusted to have their collective ears to the ground, he was even wanted back in England. Despite everything. In fact, I wouldn't be surprised to find that the well-heeled in London had greased the skids to just make his trouble go away so that he could return.

And return he could, my family had discerned. And it was one of the two legs of mission I'd been sent here to accomplish. But whereas I hadn't defined these to Carl, I also hadn't told my family all of the reasons I was willing to be the messenger.

If they knew what I knew—indeed, all that Uncle Carl knew—they wouldn't have sent me. Not in a million years. They also wouldn't welcome Uncle Carl home in a million years.

The drive in the Fiat down the coast of Italy from Naples did quite a bit to assuage my nervousness and pique. And when we crossed the mountains surrounding the sea side town of Positano, west along the rugged coast from Salerno, and descended into the semicircle of old dwellings holding onto the mountainside for dear life, I was completely captivated.

I could understand why Uncle Carl had chosen this escape hatch. And I could understand why he might not want to leave here to return to England.

The Fiat wound its way down a few levels through narrow streets and hair-pin curves until he came to a white stuccoed villa wedged between two ochre ones. It appeared to be mainly only one story, with a large, fully windowed room at one side on the top, opening out onto an open veranda, with a bougainvillea-covered loggia as a buffer between the room and the open air.

This would be a perfect art studio for painting, I thought. And then the dread hit me that perhaps it was. There was a semicircular drive tucked into the narrow stretch of front courtyard between the front of the villa and the cobblestoned road. The courtyard was ringed by a high stuccoed wall, with just an opening at one end into the vehicle turnaround, an identical one at the other end for the vehicle exit, and a iron-gated pedestrian entrance between.

Nario pulled into the turnabout and moved all the way around so that the nose of the car almost spilled out onto the roadway again.

Uncle Carl was at the door, beaming at me and rubbing his hands. He hadn't aged hardly any in the four years since I'd last seen him. Still looking disingenuously benign and almost grandfatherly—he was my father's older brother. A happy smile on his face. He may have put on a bit of weight, but he always had been the stalwart, solid-body type. I knew that he was deceptively strong and that most of what looked like the beginnings of fat was actually muscle. I trusted that he still took his long morning walks and had a weight room tucked around the villa somewhere. Although where it might be was a mystery to me. The villa didn't look very large.

When he ushered me into the main room, however, while Nario struggled getting my luggage out of the boot of the car and carrying it in, I begin to learn that the exterior presentation of the villa was deceiving.

We were on only one of five floors of the villa, he told me, as I walked straight to the large windows at the back of the room and marveled at the panoramic sight down the slope of the town, to the harbor below, and out into the Golfo di Salerno. This view alone was worth the trip.

This floor was largely one room, with a square section in the front corner for the kitchen. On the town side of that room was the dining L. To my right was a spiral staircase leading up and down. The room was richly appointed with old English furniture and oriental rugs purloined from the family estates in England. Contrast to this, however, was the artwork covering the three walls not covered with glass and overlooking the harbor.

All of the celebrities who Uncle Carl had photographed over the years—indeed, was still photographing—and the blown up art photos on his walls were all of meltingly beautiful and androgynous youths—in the nude. The photographs were provocative and just this side of pornographic—and edge that I had known Uncle Carl to cross but, in this, at least, he had shown a bit of discretion in his life. I was to find that on the next level down, Carl's photograph studio, and the one below it, housing four bedrooms and two baths, he had not held back on the photographs.

I was to be shocked—although I told myself that I shouldn't be—to see that he still displayed some photographs I remembered well. Ones the authorities must have found quite damning when they had come for Uncle Carl in his wing of Armstead Rest just outside Cambridge. How Carl was able to get the sons and daughters of some of the richer and more powerful to pose for him like this was beyond me. But, then, who was I to question his powers and his infatuation with danger?

The floor at the bottom of the house contained a laundry, a dark room, storage, a well-stocked wine cellar, and Nario's small bedroom and bath. Both this level and the bedroom level had no view, being blocked by the back wall of the villa immediate down the steep slope from Carl's villa

"You didn't show me the roof," I said to Carl as we sat out on the full-width balcony between the house and the harbor view on the living-room level—which made the floors below it deeper than the two upper levels. Nario had served us drinks and disappeared, after Carl told him he'd be down in the studio shortly.

"That's Edward's domain," Carl said. "I rarely go up there, and he rarely comes down in my studio."

"You still meet in the bedroom?"

"Yes, we're still together."

"I thought Edward was in the gaol," I said. "He didn't have the connections you do."

"He was for a while, but I made your father get him out. Edward shouldn't fare worse than I did just because I came from position and money and he didn't. Now, if you can take care of yourself for a while—"

"Where is Edward, Uncle Carl? For that matter, where is Gordon? I came to try to convince him to come back to England. The family is worried. Nationals are coming up. He needs to prepare for them."

"Gordon is of age. He can make his own decisions where he goes."

"Only barely. And mentally he's still a child. You know that. His entire life is figure skating. If he can't go to nationals or doesn't do well there, it will crush him. You know that. And I know he's of age. That's why I'm not asking you to return him. I want to talk to him."

"He's in Milan. Edward has taken him there."

"You . . . let . . . Edward take Gordon anywhere?" I was close to hyperventilating. Gordon was my younger brother. He was a vision on ice, but he didn't have a clue what to do with himself.

"I'm sure the family knew what Gordon was doing here. On his nineteenth birthday, he made a beeline for Italy." Carl raised his hand, staving off what he knew would be a scathing reply from me. It was all tied up with what had sent Carl scurrying for an Italian exile. The scandals had involved our

191

family as much as anyone else's. "Gordon has been keeping up with his practice," Carl said. "He's skating at the Milan Skating Club. That's where Edward took him. There are only four facilities good enough for his preparation. They are all in the Milan region. He and Edward should be back tomorrow. I cabled that you were coming. I surmised that it was to take Gordon back to England. Both he and I know the nationals are looming."

"Seeing that Gordon makes the nationals in London is only one of my family missions, Carl. The other one involves you directly."

"Me?"

"Yes. Father believes it's safe for you to come home now. The two young men . . . their families have emigrated to Australia. They are no longer a problem."

"Good lord, how much did that cost Adrian? That MP was quite the news hound at the time. And to have left his future in politics—"

"He is ambitious enough to stake his future in Australia. You made sure that his family name would always be linked to a sordid scandal if he'd remained in London."

"Well, I must say, your father must love his older brother dearly to arrange for me to come home. It's quite a noble gesture after he robbed me of the barony and—"

"We could hardly have the head of household guiding the family from prison, Uncle. You fucked your own way out of the barony, I do believe."

Carl laughed. "What a bald—and appropriate—way to refer to it, Nephew. You always were good with your tongue."

I winced. "Well, the family can tolerate your return. And England seems to be clamoring for it. I do believe even the queen is ready to sit for you."

"Return? Why in heaven's name would I return? Look around. Why would I leave this paradise and go back to an ungrateful England?"

"You didn't leave much room for England to be grateful. And, yes, now that I'm here, I can see why you'd want to stay. Nario is quite a pretty little trick. Some Italian count's son, I assume?"

"He's Sicilian."

"Sicily. You mean Mafia? And his family doesn't know he's here?"

Carl just smiled.

"So, you haven't changed," I said. I swept my arm toward the room behind us. "And he seems to be staring at us from various places on three walls in your living room. This, I suppose is what his uncles will see when they come in, guns blazing."

"You should see the ones in the bedroom," Carl said with a little cackle of self-congratulation. "In fact, Nario is waiting for me now. Downstairs in my studio. If you are interested, by all means come downstairs and watch me work. If not, I see you have brought a book. Stay up here and read. There is no finer backdrop for reading on a balcony anywhere to be found in the world. Oh, mercy me. Why should I want to leave Positano?"

With a bit of effort that provided me the first evidence of the passage of four years in my uncle's later middle age, Carl hoisted himself from his chair and descended the spiral staircase. I gave reading a chance to grip me, but it was no use. I had to know if Carl had changed at all. I rose from the chair and quietly descended the staircase and went to the beaded curtain that separated the landing of the floor below from Carl's huge photography studio.

Carl was finishing up positioning the lights so that they shone on Nario, naked, and sitting provocatively in an antique, red velvet-upholstered slipper chair on a damask-draped platform.

I dug my nails into the palm of my hands and shivered as I saw Carl disrobe, pick up a camera, and move around the chair, taking photos of Nario from various positions. Nario knew how to pose, and he had a beautiful, if diminutive, body. The gazes he gave for the camera under long, fluttering eyelashes were sensual while still having an edge of youthful innocence. How old was Nario, I wondered? Was Carl pushing his usual modus operande and skating on thin ice even here in Italy? Thus far, as far as I knew, he hadn't breached the age divide. But he certainly liked them young looking—and with powerful relatives with short tempers.

I decided, with bitter remembrances, that this really was Carl's problem. And Edward's as well. I presumed that Nario was old enough to know what he was doing—and that he knew enough not to be bragging on the streets of Sicily about what he was doing.

I watched Carl's dangling cock become less dangly and more upright as he moved around Nario. I should have moved away from the beaded curtain when, as I knew would be the case, I saw Carl moving in on Nario. I wanted to look away, but I couldn't, as Carl put the camera down, moved Nario to where his chest lay on the top of the back of the slipper chair, with his arms swaying down toward the floor on the other side, nudged Nario's thigh in a wider stance, and began to fuck him slowly and languidly from behind. Carl had picked up the camera again and directed Nario to turn his head to him, and Carl took close-ups of Nario's face as he was being fucked.

Carl was long and thick and Nario was small—just as Carl liked them—and Nario's expressions were an emotional mix of pain and passion and longing.

Carl had amazing stamina for a man his age. Nario was clearly exhausted before Carl was done with him. After ejaculation, Carl turned Nario around in the chair so that he was slumped in a sitting position, with his legs splayed wide and his arms artfully arranged in an seemingly natural askew position behind his head, one arm behind his neck, showing his hairless armpit and pulling his pecs tight and the other arm draped behind the back of the chair.

Nario's facial expression in post-total fuck was priceless, although Carl was sure to put a big price tag on it. These were Carl's most infamous studies in the art underground—the photos that brought him the most money—the splayed out body of a completely fucked young man, showing facial expressions of mixed satisfaction, violation, and exhaustion—and evoking the reaction of "Isn't that?" Carl reveled in the viewer's revelation of what young celebrity or well-connected youth that was. There was never a question of what had happened to the subject of these photographs right before they were taken.

"You can return to your reading now, Harry," Carl called out to me when he had taken the photographs he wanted to take. "I'm finished now. As you can see, I haven't changed, and I have no reason to leave this paradise—or the beauties they provide me."

Carl wasn't finished with Nario. I knew he wouldn't be if he had remained true to form. Going down on his knees between Nario's thighs in the chair, recharged, and a new postcoital pose in mind, Carl grasped Nario's legs and lifted and spread them, and thrust his cock inside Nario's rolled up buttocks again. Nario moaned and clasped his hands around Carl's neck. Carl kissed him on the mouth. I turned and left as Nario began to burble in Italian.

I went to the room where Nario had taken my luggage, one floor down. It was on the front of the house and only had a couple of half windows opening to the side. The view was of an ochre stuccoed wall of the adjacent villa, not more than eight feet away. There were other curtained areas around the walls of the shape of windows, giving an illusion that the room would be airy if they were open. I pulled aside one of the curtains and then another, and then I quickly closed both, my stomach threatening to give dry heaves. The photographs were some of the very explicit nudes Carl photograph—none of them of a single subject. I recognized the model for most of them, and I was shocked in the recognition. I fled the room and went back to the balcony two flights up and forced myself to read from my book.

Dinner was late, with just the two of us, Carl and me, at the table and Nario buzzing around us, giving full service, but not giving any hint at the full service he'd given earlier in the day. The food was gourmet. I heard activity in the kitchen, so I surmised there was a cook out there. She was humming, so I surmised that she lived out. I had never known Carl to allow a woman to spend a night under his roof, nor had I ever encountered a woman who would want to. The wine also was first rate. And there were at least three bottles of it served and emptied before I voiced my weariness from short flights and interminable waits in lounges and passenger check lines between London and Naples, and declared my intent to go to bed and read a bit before going to sleep.

I did not mention the photographs in my room. I believed that more than once Carl was on the edge of bringing them up. I could tell that by that mischievous little smile he had. But he said nothing. There was more silence than discussion, but what discussion there was was of the art world. I had started my professional life in an art auction house. I was surprised to find that Carl was well versed in what was being sold and for how much.

"For Edward's sake," he said. "Someday he will be discovered."

Not likely, I thought. But I didn't say as much. Edward's art was insipid. That had always surprised me because I had found Edward to be intense and forceful. I would have expected broad, telling strokes in oil from him, rather than the washed-out watercolors of sailboats. Of course there was Edward's private collection. His rendering of the same theme that drove Carl's life—the search for the perfect depiction of the face of a handsome young man right after being fucked by the artist. That art of Edward's was, technically, excellent. And it sold well. But it wasn't going to be sold in the reputable, high-stakes auction houses, and it wasn't going to make his public reputation.

Both Carl and Edward had overextended themselves in those months in England before the authorities got on to them. Both moaned of having found the perfect subject and rendered their individual modes of art perfectly—but only with one youth, the son of a duke. In search of regaining this, they had been sloppy in their techniques of developing subjects, and it had caught up with them.

I had trouble sleeping, and part of that was because of my curiosity of what Edward was up to, painting wise. I eventually realized I wasn't going to be able to sleep until I satisfied that question. I quietly got out of bed and padded up the two flights to Edward's studio at the top of the house.

He had never been a neat person in his studio. Chaos reigned here and it took me a few minutes to focus on what was where. I wanted to see canvases, the sheets of rice paper he liked to use for his water colors. There were plenty of the latter around. The harbor below was the subject of many of those, and Positano obviously had been a good influence on his work. His

196

technique had improved significantly. Many of these were vibrant and the strokes bold and sure. Several, I thought were good enough for the auction houses. I didn't know if I would say anything about that, though. I found Edward foreboding and overwhelming. The distance between us these last four years had been perfectly fine with me.

Edward was a ruggedly handsome man of towering height and muscular build. He was a good ten years younger than Uncle Carl. Carl had taught him in art school. He'd taught him art and then he had taught him how to fuck, and, finally, he had taught him how to share. Of the two, though, I had always thought of Edward as the more cruel and dangerous lover of men.

I found a couple of canvases, with cloths over them. I uncovered one, and my hand began to tremble. I quickly uncovered two more.

I, of course, knew it. I knew it before I had come. The whole family had known it. They were just pretending it wasn't so. I pretended too, but of all of them, I had the most reason to accept reality.

The paintings were all of Gordon—my younger brother—and they were all nudes of his splayed body and various positions of surrender. And the faces of all revealed without a doubt, that his visage had been captured right after he'd been fucked.

I didn't want to look at them. I covered them and quickly left the studio and descended the spiral staircase. As I reached the bedroom level, I heard the sounds. I knew what they were, of course. They hadn't even bothered to close the door. The door led into the master bedroom, which was dominated by a king-sized poster bed. Carl and Edward's bed, I knew. Nario was lying in the center of the bed, legs running up either side of Carl's chest, as Carl, buttocks pistoning, fucked Nario deeply. There was a camera on the bed beside them. I was sure that Carl knew enough about the working of light and shadows even to be able to collect excellent photographs this late at night.

Edward dropped off Gordon at the entrance the next day and then drove on to somewhere else. I didn't ask where he had gone or how long he would be gone. And Carl didn't volunteer the information. I thought perhaps that Edward was staying down in the town for as long as I was there. If so, he was being thoughtful—and perhaps he was changing, that his months in the goal had changed him somehow. But then I thought of those paintings of Gordon in his studios, and I realized that Edward had not changed a bit. And this had gone on under the observation of Uncle Carl. My father was violent man. If he knew for sure . . . even though he and Carl were brothers . . .

For the first time I began to wonder what my father's real motives were for wanting Uncle Carl to return to England as well as Gordon.

Gordon seemed relieved to see me. I think he only needed someone in the family to come to him and tell him that he needed to return to England and pick up his quest for the figure skating gold again.

He assured me that he had been diligent in practicing on the ice—and had spent more time in Milan than here. I believed him, but then I knew how fast Edward could paint. I wanted to ask him if our uncle, Carl, had also photographed him as Edward had painted him. But I really didn't want to know the answer to that—and it wouldn't have changed anything if he had.

I showed Gordon his return air ticket to London the next day, and he didn't argue. He just went off to pack.

"I assume we'll be sitting together," he said as he stood from the patio table on the balcony and prepared to leave.

"No, we won't be travel together," I answered. "I have family business in Naples, as well. I'll be following on the weekend. But I will be at the airport to see you off safely."

That seemed to satisfy him. And I knew I'd have to be there to see him off. He was still such a child in mind. Large airports confused him. There would be a family car and chauffeur on the London end to meet him. To meet us both, as a matter of fact, but the family business in Naples was something I hadn't actually told the family about.

I had trouble sleeping that night too. The sounds of sex from the master bedroom were louder, more insistent that night. And I heard more than two voices. Curious, I left my bed and padded out into the corridor. As the night before, the master bedroom door had been left ajar. It was almost as if Carl was taunting me, teasing me.

I went into the shadow cast by the door, to a place where I could see the bed. The light in the room was glaring. Spots were directed to the bed. Nario, naked, was moving around the bed with both a video and a still camera in his hands. I nonsensically wondered if Carl was teaching him photography—and, if so, how good he was.

Carl was lying on his back in the center of the bed. I could hardly see him, because my view was obstructed by the broad back of a somewhat younger man, who was facing Carl and straddling his legs. Edward, I suddenly realized. But that wasn't what had me mesmerized. There, sandwiched between them, back to Edward and hunched over the chest of Carl, his eyes squinched up in a mix of agony and ecstasy. My brother, Gordon.

All three men were naked. Both Carl's and Edward's cocks were inside Gordon.

I nearly burst in on them. But I didn't. Gordon was of age now, and I had known, truthfully, what I'd find when I got here. Tomorrow. I'd put Gordon on a plane tomorrow. And then no more would be said about it. The family need know nothing about. I had protected them from this earlier—or so I argued myself into believing now, rationalizing away all thoughts that my father already knew. I would protect the family from the truth now, if I could. Gordon wouldn't talk. He would probably go on to be with men, but that was his choice. I had known for some time that he would do that.

I went back to my room, closed the door, climbed into bed, and buried my head under the pillows. Mercifully, in an hour or two—or three—I managed to drift off to a restless sleep.

* * * *

I got home from the airport in Naples after dark the next day. The planes had all been late and the airport was chaos.

Gordon walked around at my side, glassy eyed, and acting like a frightened rabbit.

I said nothing to him about what I had seen the previous night. He said nothing either to indicate what had happened, but I got the impression that Carl and Edward had gone farther with him in the night than ever before, because he was quiet and somewhat distant, and obviously was anxious to get out of the villa and on his way back to England.

Neither Carl nor Edward saw us off—or appeared at breakfast or lunch. They were both in their separate studios. No doubt, I reasoned each working hard to capture the previous night's work in their art. I heard humming from both studios when I passed, so I gathered they were very pleased with themselves.

Nario served me a solitary dinner at the dining room table. Again the food was excellent and the wine was flowing. Neither Carl nor Edward appeared.

I went to bed early. I left the door open to my room, and before I stripped down and climbed up onto the bed, I went around and opened the drapes that had been covering all of the photographs. I laid down on the bed and moved my gaze around the room, taking in all of the photographs in turn, remembering. Waiting.

Carl was the first to appear. Naked. Smiling.

"The photographs were a nice touch, don't you think?" he asked. He laughed, walked over to the foot of the bed, grasped my ankles, and pulled me down to him. I had become hard looking at the photographs. He came to me hard as well. While waiting, I had lubed my channel well, so without preliminaries, Uncle Carl splayed my legs, moved between my thighs, and began fucking me.

"Just like our early days," he murmured. "You are still as beautiful as you were then, when those photos were taken."

I raised my hands to his gray-haired, hairy chest and let my fingers play in the silkiness of him. Searching for and find his nipples and rubbing them to hear him groan—just as he had all those years ago.

My eyes went to each photograph on the wall that I could see. Me, a young me—the son of a duke. A younger Carl and Edward as well. Fucking—or immediately after being fucked.

"You were always perfection, my little bird," Carl was murmuring as he plowed me deep. "Never since have we been able to capture the perfection—the released innocence and awakening to the cock of men—of that summer of photos of you."

Edward was in the room now. And Nario as well. Nario had a video camera at the ready and a still camera in his other hand. Carl pulled out of me and reached for the camera. Edward put his hand behind the edge of the curtain of one of the photographs and strong lights came on, focused on the bed.

I knew then that Carl had started to prepare for me as soon as I'd sent him the telegram that it was me who was coming to fetch Gordon. He had known why it was me—why I would have volunteered to do that.

There was, of course, no family business in Naples. And I had no idea whether I would be returning to the weekend or not. Now, after having Carl's cock inside me again after so many years, I rather thought not—that I wouldn't be catching a plane back to London on the weekend.

Edward took up the position Carl had vacated. I cried out as he thrust inside me. He was younger, longer, thicker, more vigorous—crueler—then Carl was. No—pant, pant, moan—I would not be returning to London on the weekend.

Edward was digging into my chest, twisting my nipples, and I was howling. He slapped me on the face and told me to be quiet. I whimpered, but I didn't really want him to stop punishing me. I deserved punishment. I had come to Carl. So, so young. I had seen him fuck young men in his studio—my friends, sons of famous people. I wanted that too. I was the son of a duke. Surely he'd want me too. He hadn't refused me. He told me that I was just the beautiful, androgynous body that he wanted for his art. Edward had agreed.

I had wanted Carl, not Edward. but Edward had taken me first, repeatedly, cruelly, gloriously, while Carl had fired off those shots on the wall. And then an assistant had taken the camera and both Edward and Carl . . .

"Oh, god, oh holy shit. Fuck me, Edward. It's been so long." I rose up to his chest, reaching down for his buttocks, holding him deep inside me. I bit him on the nipple and he screamed, pushed me down onto the bed and backhanded me across the face, whipping my head to the side. I felt blood in my mouth.

"Get that dazed look," Edward cried out.

"Got it," Carl answered, his voice excited.

Carl moved around us, snapping off photographs. Nario was beside and behind him, holding the whirring video camera.

I lurched up to Edward's chest again. He was pumping, pumping, pumping. God, he was virile. And so big.

I grabbed his head between my hands and brought his lips to mine, letting him taste the blood he had released. He shuddered and lifted me up off the bed, roughly, turned me, and slammed me down into a club chair. I was draped over the back of the chair, totally spent and exhausted after he had finally finished pumping me from behind.

"Yes! That's the look. Perfection," Carl cried out, full of exhilaration, as he moved around me, in post-fuck exhaustion, snapping off shots of my face. Edward reached over and turned me in the chair, and my body just slid down the chair and onto the floor, Carl firing off stills the entire time.

"Both of us now," Carl said with an excited voice.

I knew what was coming. It's how they always ended their sessions with me—even that first one—the one where I thought I was going to die. And didn't care if I did as long as they kept fucking me. It's how they ended their session with Gordon the previous night.

Carl was on his back on the bed. His cock was standing at full attention. Edward pulled me up from the floor and carried me over to the bed, and laid me stretched out on top of Carl, my shoulder blades on his chest. I whimpered, as Edward took hold of Carl's cock and moved it to my channel and helped guide it in. Carl was embracing my torso in his arms and kissing my neck and nibbling on my ear.

Nario was taking all of the photographs now.

Edward knelt between thighs, working my cock with a hand and cupping and squeezing my balls, as Carl fucked up into

202

me from underneath. When I had come for Edward, he moved in between my thighs, positioned his cock with his hand, and slowly entered me, the underside of his cock on top of Carl's already encased cock.

I panted and huffed and cried out for the fuck. Remembering how good it had been. Both of them. Making love to me, making love to each other. I had never risen to such heights since.

Edward began to pump me seriously.

Oh, God! No, I wasn't going to be returning to London on the weekend. Thank god I hadn't aged so much in the past years that they no longer wanted me.

"If father saw you doing this, he's kill you!" I cried out as I ejaculated.

"Yes, I know he would," Carl answered with a cackle. "Isn't it delicious?"

Nuclear Meltdown

It was all happening so fast. I didn't even have time to feel panic. I just felt a dullness and a foreboding—and a creeping sense of being trapped in a web of some sort. No, more like a cocoon, the sticky thread winding around and around me. Smothering me.

"Just a few minutes, Dr. Winthrop, and you can go back to your room. I know this has been a shock to you. We have just a few more questions tonight, but most can wait until tomorrow. I suggest that you try to get some rest tonight."

"I have a lecture . . . a lecture to give tomorrow afternoon," I replied, looking at the police detective, Adolf Stander. He had been very efficient and solicitous—and respectful. He obviously was very good at this. The Swiss, I am sure, have high-level international situations well in hand and quickly, and with the highest level of discretion. The special Einsatzgruppe Tigris arm of the Swiss Federal Criminal Police arrived at the Lucerne Radisson Blu hotel and conference center and took over the investigation within a half hour of the murder.

"You did say that this isn't your room, didn't you? That it was that of the victim, Dr. Pak Jong-hee?"

"Yes, yes, of course. We were conferring on some notes, here in Dr. Pak's room . . . in preparation for delegation talks tomorrow morning before the afternoon lecture sessions. And . . . and . . . the assailant . . . just burst in. He went right for Pak. It was over in seconds."

I had to concentrate, try not to hyperventilate. I had to be careful not to say too much. I felt like I was spiraling down already—being sucked down into a vortex.

"And Dr. Pak is North Korean, right, not South Korean? And you're American?"

"Yes, yes, that's right. Nuclear physicists. Advisers both. We had met before. We leave the political negotiations to the principals. We just advise on technical issues."

Oh, god, if that only were true, I thought. How did I let myself get involved in this? Where was Frank? Shouldn't he just be sweeping in here and handling everything? They'd told me that it was just about over. That Pak wanted to defect.

"Perhaps I should speak with the respective delegation head," Standler said. "After," he continued, "after they've come for the . . . ah, yes, here they come now."

I'd been sitting, quaking, on the bed all of the time that the detective was hovering around me. And the body was there, right there on the floor. I could have turned away. I should have turned away. But I couldn't. The knife was still inside him, in his gut, the handle protruding, his eyes open, looking at me. With such a look of surprise. Accusing me.

But I'd done nothing. This wasn't anything like I did. I don't know why I'd even been caught up in this. Frank hadn't told me that anything like this could happen. But, yes, I did know why.

It was my damning weakness.

* * * *

It had been those years in the Air Force in Thailand. The Thai men were so nubile, brown as a berry, and willing. Always the winning smile, the readiness to please.

I'd thought I had put all of that behind me. I'd returned to the university when I'd left the Air Force and continued my studies in nuclear physics. A good professorship had led to government contracts, work that went ever deeper into government scientific and defense projects. And as the work had deepened, it had grown more secret, requiring ever higher security clearances.

The bubble had burst one evening in the sauna of a Georgetown men's gym.

I had seen him when I was working out on the exercise floor. All smiles, just like those young men years ago in Bangkok. He was Thai, of course, and small, and brown, bordering on effeminate, but perfectly formed. And he moved like a dancer. He was doing some sort of Oriental slow-movement exercises, showing a fantastically flexible body. And he had his eyes on me, giving me saucy looks. Gazes that took me back to the Patpong tenderloin district of Bangkok—and to all those talented and willing young men.

I left the gym floor and took a long shower. I was aroused. I couldn't deny that. And I was remembering those earlier days. But times had moved on. I even was married now. Although when it came to arousal, my desires went back to earlier days.

I wrapped a towel around my waist and went into the sauna room. A young, muscle-bound man in the club's signature shorts and T-shirt was standing by the door of the sauna when I went in. I hadn't seen him there before, but he gave me a friendly smile as if we had met.

"We were closing early tonight, professor," he said. "But the front desk said you could stay as long as you wanted. Just close the outer door when you leave."

I thought that was nice of them—and trusting, which later gave me a bitter laugh. And I did want the session in the sauna.

He handed me another, large and high-pile towel, and I went into the sauna and laid that out on the top bench, opposite the door, and stretched out full length on my back. The heat of the sauna was soothing, and I was drifting between feeling the tension draining from my body and semiconsciousness.

I didn't hear him enter the sauna. The first indication I had that I wasn't alone was when I felt his hands on my calves, below my knees, gently spreading my legs. I looked down in surprise. It was the berry-brown, nubile Thai, and he was looking up between my legs, under the towel, and he was smiling.

"Umm, so big," he said, fluttering his eyelashes. "Me like. Me like a lot."

He was moving his hands on my legs, gently massaging. I was frozen there, in shock. All, of course, except for my cock, which was engorging.

"I saw you in the exercise room," he whispered. "And I tell myself that one handsome man. I bet he has big cock. I bet I like to fuck with that man. And the look you gave me. I knew you want to fuck with me too. You fuck Thai men before, I bet."

I moaned.

"So I stay behind when they close up up front. I know you still back here. We fuck fuck, OK?"

"Sorry, I think I'd better . . ." I started to say, and I sat up, ready to leave—or at least try to. But he already had the big toe of one of my feet in his mouth, and the palm of a hand high up and inside my thigh.

I tried to gather my strength, knowing I needed to leave. But the hand was tantalizing. My brain was screaming its want, its need for the hand to rise higher. And then it did, encircling my cock, and I laid back with a groan, letting every sensation point inside me race to my penis. His hand worked me for a few minutes while I closed my eyes and covered my face with an arm and fought with my desires. When I felt the wetness of his lips and mouth pull me inside him, I groaned and gave up any struggle, giving myself fully over to the pleasure of the suck.

When I opened my eyes, he had reversed himself on me and his sweet little buttocks and a pert cock and balls were right there at my face, ready for my attention and preparation. I ran a hand between his legs, pulled his cock back through, and moved between licking and sucking on his pulsing hole and on his cock.

He wound up on his tailbone on the top step, legs splayed, and me between those legs and rising and falling on the balls of my feet on the lower bench as I fucked him in a slow, slow, fast, slow, slow rhythm that had him murmuring "fuck me, fuck me, fuck me," in a singsong little voice.

They let me cum before the two men—one of them the young man who handed me the towel when I entered the sauna—burst into the room and flashed their federal government badges in my face.

The young Thai man at least had the decency to tell me he was sorry and that he'd thoroughly enjoyed the fucking. He said I had the biggest cock of anyone who had plowed him.

They sweated me for two days on the dire consequences on my career and private life of what I had been caught doing. On the third day, they informed me that there was an out. I was scheduled to attend U.S.-North Korean nuclear proliferation talks in Beijing as a scientific adviser later in the year. I could save my career by helping them convince a North Korean nuclear physicist who had a proclivity for men of my age and physique—and an extra big cock, as I had—to defect to the United States.

"When we approached him, he asked for you by name," one of the interrogators said.

They would arrange the encounters. I wouldn't even have to seduce him. All I would have to do is service his sexual needs and act as a go-between. He would know that I was there to service him when we first met. A piece of cake. Very little to do to save my career. And I'd even enjoy it. He was a well-turned-out small-stature Oriental. And I had already proven my weakness for such men.

I wracked my brain trying to figure out who this might be. I had been at a few meetings with the North Koreans—and the last time we'd met in Beijing, any of the men who wanted to could go to a traditional Turkish bath, where we were naked, and there were some North Koreans there. But, again, I don't remember any of them showing particular interest in me—other than that I did get attention for the size of my equipment whenever I was in a communal shower or locker room. I had grown accustomed to that, though.

When we next met in Beijing, I had no trouble picking him out. His name was Pak Jong-hee, and although he was a senior scientist and was shown extra deference by his North Korean delegation during the meetings, he was young and small, lithe, and brown—and he made my cock harden knowing that I was meant to fuck him.

I don't remember having seen him at an earlier conference—especially at the Beijing session where several of the men were naked together in the Turkish bath. This was surprising, because he was strikingly attractive to me. Of course, until my handlers had forced an encounter in the sauna in Georgetown, I had pretty successfully suppressed my desire for men—even small, boyish ones like Pak.

He obviously had noticed me. As Frank, my handler had promised, it was fairly obvious that arrangements had already been made with him—and most likely that he had picked me. He frequently looked at me and lowered his eyes demurely in a signal from young Oriental men indicating that they wanted to be mastered.

On the third day of the negotiations, which weren't going well and from which the North Korean delegation had absented itself, Frank told me to prepare myself well, which I did. I was conducted to the same steamy, decorative tile-covered Turkish bath chamber that I had been entertained in during a previous Beijing conference.

When I got to the door of the bath, Frank and another U.S. delegation member who was there purely for security purposes were waiting for me. I was wearing only a silk robe and sandals. As I was ushered through the door, my robe was taken off my back.

"Remember, we want him to be very happy and satisfied," Frank murmured as I passed him. "We will handle the discussions with him on where it goes from here. If he wishes to take our offer, you will be assigned together and you will be servicing him as often as he wants it. Remember, your career is on the line here too."

"Protection or not?" I asked. When I had been suborned, there had been no protection; it had been completely impromptu—and frenzied.

"Packets, already slit, on the side of the pool."

Packets, I thought. More than one. Oh, god. Could I stand up to the challenge? I was quite a bit older than I had been in Thailand—when I could take three sweet young men in quick succession.

At first I thought I was the first of several to arrive. But that was not so. I was the second and last to arrive. Pak Jong-hee was already sitting on a subterranean tiled bench in the octagon-shaped pool. He was staring at me—or rather, at what was swinging between my legs—and he was giving me a sultry smile.

I saw the pile of condom packets and a bottle of lubricant in a tray on the pool side beside where he was sitting.

I slipped my sandals off and slowly walked to the pool and down the steps into the pool at the opposite side from where he sat, eyes glued to my midsection and a sloppy grin on his mouth.

I had my balls and the root of my cock cupped in one of my hands as I walked. I was filling out as I saw him lift his hips to the surface of the water and show that he was in full, curved erection.

When I had approached him in the water, which came up to above my knees and would be where the tip of my cock would touch if I was not in erection myself, Pak smiled, placed the palms of his hands on my buttocks, and pulled me on to his swallowing mouth. He was a master of the suck, and I groaned and moaned as he deep-throated me and worried my piss slit with his tongue.

After fifteen minutes or so of his expert attention to my cock, I reached down and lifted him out of the water, laid him on his back, hooked his legs on my hips, and moved my mouth to his cock, balls, and hole.

He was begging for it in nearly flawless English—with a fine grasp of the crudities of gay male sex—when he took the initiative to crown my cock with a condom and stroke that and his entrance with lubricant.

That was as much control as I allowed him, though. I knew the looks he had given me during the conference. He wanted to be mastered.

Still standing, I lifted him up and set him down on my cock. He clung to me—small and lithe and flexible—as I grabbed his buttocks, spread the cheeks, and pulled him up and down on my cock. I was fucking only at half depth, but Pak was moaning to beat the band.

I laid him back down on the side of the pool and started plowing him deep and fast and hard. He writhed under me and cried out—but he was crying for it, not asking for mercy—and dug his fingernails into my shoulders and my chest. He came quickly after that. I pulled the condom off and came on his belly.

We held there for several minutes as he worked my cock back up with his hands. He whimpered for it and I turned him belly down to the tiles, crouched over him, and reached for a condom packet.

"No rubber," he whispered. "I'm clean. I want it all the way."

OK, I thought. I remembered what Frank said: whatever he wants. Pak got it all the way in one long, deep, skin-on-skin thrust. He wailed like a stuck pig for the next twenty minutes, but each time I offered to let up or stop, he commanded me to fuck him harder. I complied as best I could. And from the way he was stretched out, not moving, just moaning, when I put my sandals on and left the bath, I could report to Frank that his pigeon must be well satisfied.

Over the next year, we found ourselves sitting behind the same negotiations table three times. And each time Frank and his crew managed to get us alone for a "negotiations" session of our own.

This is what brought us to the fifth floor room at the Lucerne Radisson Blu conference center. Not Pak's room, really—or mine—but one that Pak had managed to book separately. Frank had made arrangements in the shower of the men's gym in the hotel—where indeed, I entered a shower where Pak already was and fucked him from behind against the wet tiles of the shower. But afterward, Pak had said he had made arrangements of his own.

Only when I got to the room did I realize Frank probably didn't even know about it. Always before he and another member of his team or two was lurking somewhere in the vicinity. He wasn't there this time. But Frank had clearly told me to give Pak what he wanted—saying they were very close to defection day. So, I met Pak in the room.

212

And I was giving him what he wanted on the bed, when the assailant—another Korean, I don't know whether a South Korean wanting to neutralize a North Korean nuclear expert or a North Korean realizing Pak was about to defect—burst into the room.

Both men had knifes. I don't know how Pak had gotten his so quickly.

Within seconds, I was alone, with one dead Korean on the floor and the other giving me explicit directions and then gone as well.

* * * *

The body was gone. Detective Standler was gone—consulting, no doubt with the heads of both the North Korean and American delegations, working on smoothing this over, making as much of it go away as possible. The lab technicians were gone—for a coffee break. They'd be back.

I had stopped trembling enough to be able to rise up off the bed, dressed but quickly and sloppily so—I'm sure Detective Standler had tuned into that.

I started for the door to leave and go back to my room. But the door to the adjoining room was open. A naked Pak Jong-hee was lounging against the door frame and giving me a shy smile.

"They will find out quickly it isn't you," I mumbled, still in shock.

"We have time. Come into this room. They'll never know. You can go back to your room in a while and pack."

"Pack?" I asked, as I permitted him to reach out and take me by the arm and guide me into an identical room next to the murder room.

"Who was that you killed? We can't just . . . they think it's you." I was burbling, but I'd just seen a man killed. This was way out of my frame of reference.

"This is perfect for the defection," Pak said. "By the time they realize it isn't me, we'll be over the Italian border."

"The Italian border?" I said weakly. This was all moving too fast. But I seemed to be the only one without a program.

213

"Come over here," Pak said in the seductive voice that my dick had been programmed to jerk erect at.

He pushed me down into a seated position on the side of the bed. His hands went to the waistband of my trousers, and he jerked them off in one long pull. My cock jumped erect, hitting him in the cheek.

"To Italy? Who, what?" I asked, as he pushed my legs apart and knelt between my thighs.

"Oh, gawd. Oh holy, shit," I exclaimed as his mouth lowered over my cock. He was embracing my waist in his arms. I wasn't going anywhere for a while.

But he said we were going to Italy. He must have a car at his disposal. What kind of defection was this? Frank? The Americans? Or . . . "Oh shit, the North Koreans?"

Who fuckin' was defecting here—to whom?

I thought I had cried it out. Challenged Pak with the question.

But I hadn't. I'd fallen back on the bed, my back arched, my hands clawing at the bedspread. He was working my cock and swallowing my balls. All I could do was moan.

I heard the door open, and two men entered the room. They were still in the shadow of the doorway and I was watching closely to see them come into the light. Were they Koreans or Americans?

Into the Dark

Momma, please. I won't talk back anymore. Let me out of the closet, Momma. Or turn on a light. You know how scared I am of the dark. Don't leave me here in the dark, Momma. Please. Please Momma. Momma? Momma?

* * * *

Brandon leaned over the low, padded cubicle wall and winked at Colleen and told her she was looking mighty fine today. Then, as he turned and moved down the corridor between the cubicles, a large, apparently heavy file box under his arm, he barely missed running into Rhonda, and gave her a cheery hello and a big smile before going on his way.

Rhonda stopped by Colleen's cubicle as well. "Brandon's been very chipper today."

"Yes, isn't he a dreamboat," Colleen answered. "He's been so 'up' for a couple of weeks now. And it suits him. He always was a hunk, but it seemed like he was afraid of something—of his own shadow."

"I heard that Norris wants to push him ahead," Rhonda said. "He wanted him to be more outgoing, so Brandon's been going to a specialist. Someone who is helping him."

"A specialist? Do you mean a shrink?"

"Something like that, I think. I've heard he's using hypnosis or something. Anyway, it's put me all a flutter with Brandon. He's strutting around now like he's getting it good. He could have gotten it from me even before—but he's really something now. I melt whenever he looks at me."

"Rhonda!" Colleen exclaimed. But her cheeks were burning.

"Don't tell me you wouldn't go into the break room alone with him, Colleen Thomas. I've heard you talking about him."

"He's married," Colleen said with a forced gasp.

"Yeah, well, we both can dream, can't we? Besides now he always looks like he's just been with a woman. And I'm not going to lie and say I didn't wish that woman was me. I can tell you I wouldn't turn him down either."

Both young women giggled then, and Rhonda turned and went on her way down the corridor.

Brandon had already reached the door of the file room. He went in and walked to the back of the room and returned the file carton he'd carried in into its niche on the metal rack. The overhead light went out, the door closed behind him, and he heard the click of a lock.

He was in total darkness, and, from the heavy breathing near the door, he knew he wasn't alone.

Already beginning to pant, Brandon turned and leaned back on a worktable beside the rack where he'd stowed the file on the shelves. He moaned and spread his legs as a heavy-breathing figure moved between his thighs. A hand was buried in the hair at the back of his head and he was arched backward. He opened his lips as the lips of another took possession of them, opening them to a searching tongue. With one hand the figure held Brandon's head arched back and with the other the buttons on Brandon's shirt were being released. The lips went to his nipples.

Brandon moaned. He reached down and fumbled with the belt of the figure pressed into his pelvis, lowered a zipper, pulled out a hardening and already-sheathed and slick cock, and began to stroke it. The man pressed into him was unbuckling Brandon's belt as well and pushing his trousers off his legs.

With a groan, Brandon hooked his legs around the phantom of the dark's very real waist and whispered in a hoarse and insistent voice, "Oh, god, yes. Now. Fuck me, fuck me." He made pained, whimpering sounds as the cock invaded his channel. Stiff-armed, Brandon was arched back on the surface of the work table, his ankles crossed at the small of the man's heavily muscled back, trembling and urging the cocking on. The man buried his face in the hollow of Brandon's neck and sucked hard. Six, seven, eight deep strokes.

Then he pulled out of Brandon and turned him to where Brandon was standing on the floor but bent over the table. The man grabbed Brandon's tie, pulled it around to the back, and used it as reins to arch Brandon's torso up and back with every stroke of the renewed attack of his cock inside the young man's channel. The underside of Brandon's hard cock was stroking across the surface of the work table, and his assaulter moved his free hand around Brandon's waist and cupped the top of Brandon's cock with his palm, giving Brandon the friction of his own cock between skin and work table surface.

Twenty-five, twenty-six, twenty-seven strokes inside Brandon and he jerked and lurched, gave a little cry, and shot cum across the surface of the table. Three more strokes, and the man enjoyed his own ejaculation deep inside Brandon's channel.

They hunched there, panting in stereo—Brandon's tenor to the man's bass—until the man softened inside Brandon. He pulled out, reached around and buttoned Brandon's dress shirt again, and then reached down and pulled Brandon's trousers back up his legs, zipped him, and rebuckled his belt.

Brandon was alone, hunched over the table, when the light went back on and the door opened and shut quickly after that. He stood up from the table, looked around with only a slightly confused look, moved his head to one side to take a crick out of his neck. He looked at the rack beside him. The box he had put into place was where it belonged. He smiled slightly to himself and turned and left the file room.

As he walked back along the corridor between the cubicles, he paused once more to give Colleen a smile and a slightly saucy look.

Colleen did a bit of a double take. His eyes looked dreamy and he certainly did, as Rhonda had mentioned twenty minutes earlier, look like he'd been "getting some." She even got the heady hint of a musky smell in the air that she'd have to admit she found arousing.

It'd been nearly a half hour since he'd passed by. Had she seen Rhonda in that half hour? She'd have to think. Maybe Rhonda was getting something she wasn't. True, he was married, but she'd been giving it to Mr. Watson in accounting and he was married too—and Brandon was a whole lot hunkier than Mr. Watson was.

* * * *

"I think that was a very good session, Brandon," Dr. Milton said at the door of his treatment room. "I think we're coming along very nicely. Very nicely indeed."

"Thank you, Doctor. I do feel quite refreshed. I was a little nervous when I came in today, but feel like I'm walking on clouds now."

Brandon smiled at the man who was sitting in the waiting room as he left to walk uptown to the apartment he shared with his wife, Cindy. They'd been married for a year, and it really was her problems that had sent Brandon looking for help. His fear of the dark was ruining her sleep. The tossing and turning had sent them to separate twin beds already, something they both knew was unusual for near newlyweds, but it was the light that had really gotten to her. Brandon hadn't been able to sleep—or do anything—in the dark. And Cindy couldn't sleep with the lights on. After Dr. Milton had started treating Brandon, now the dark of night, in his own bed, didn't cause Brandon to toss and turn and cry out in fear. They were thinking of exchanging the twins for a king already, and Cindy now only wore the night mask and had the sound machine on out of habit.

The man, not at all bad looking for his age, but probably pushing forty, smiled back at Brandon. He stood as Brandon was leaving. He was a professional type—probably a lawyer. But he hadn't gone to pot. He had kept himself in good shape. Brandon was wondering what the man could be seeing Milton for as he got out of the elevator and walked out onto the street.

The man had been taking a wallet out of his pocket as he stood. Brandon's office paid for his visits without Brandon having to pay anything. Norris had told him that they'd cover it as part of his executive training. They obviously liked his work, and it had only been the effects of his insomnia that had been holding Brandon back from promotion.

Brandon had stopped on the street. He had no idea why he was stopped, but when he saw that he was standing by the cashier's booth to a movie theater, he had the sudden urge to go in. He had no idea what the movie was even, but it didn't seem to matter.

The movie hadn't started when he entered the theater. He moved to the top row of the balcony. Very few patrons were attending the showing, and all of them were much farther down, nearer the screen.

The lights went out and the movie started, one of the dark-atmosphere movies—and rather racy—all sorts of meaningful, longing looks and hoarse talking and grasping fumbling.

Brandon wasn't alone. A man sat down next to him, in the dark. He put his arm around Brandon's shoulders, and Brandon raised his arm, permitting the man's hand to go under his pit and to clutch his chest on top of one of his pecs. The man's other hand was in Brandon's lap, unzipping him and pulling out his cock. Brandon turned his face to the other man, not being able to discern the man's features, although they looked slightly familiar, and the two kissed.

Brandon reached over, unzipped the man, brought his cock out, and started stroking it.

After the man had leaned over and sucked Brandon hard, Brandon did the same for him. The man pulled Brandon's trousers off his legs, and sat Brandon on his cock, facing the screen.

In a dark bedroom scene on the screen, a couple languidly fucked, all legs and entwining arms and sighs and groans.

Brandon watched the scene, not really seeing it, as, with his hands gripping the back of the seat in front of him, he fucked himself on the man's cock, using the balls of his feet for leverage in his rising and falling. The man groaned behind him, ejaculated, and pulled Brandon into his lap. He snaked his hands around Brandon's waist and placed one hand on Brandon's belly to hold him close, still skewered on a softening cock, and stroked Brandon to his own coming with the other hand.

Brandon moaned to his finish, his unseeing eyes glued to the movie screen.

On the way home from the movie, he stopped and bought Cindy a bouquet of flowers. He was feeling randy. They'd have quite a session tonight. Cindy seemed to enjoy the fucking—a lot—but he tried to bring her something like flowers to warn her when he felt particularly hot, so she could think of a reason to hold him off that particular night if she wasn't in the mood as well.

* * * *

The doorbell rang after dinner, and when Brandon answered it, he saw Dr. Milton—and another man, younger and in an UPS delivery uniform, standing in the outer hallway in front of the door.

"I left my office and saw that you had left your briefcase, Brandon," Dr. Milton said. "I pass by here on the way home anyway, so I thought I'd drop it off to you."

"Thanks, Doctor. I hadn't even realized I'd left it there," Brandon said.

"Umm. This is my son, Jim, Brandon. Sorry, I should have introduced him immediately."

"Quite all right. Hello, Jim."

"Hello. Umm, would you mind if I used your bathroom?"

"Sure. Go ahead. The guest bathroom is right over there, by the door to the patio."

While Jim was gone, Cindy appeared and she and Brandon engaged in some chit-chat with Dr. Milton.

Later that night, Brandon was on top of Cindy in her twin bed, her legs open to him, writhing under him, as he plowed her hard and deep for the second time that evening. He had no idea why he was so randy—and she showed no evidence of caring as long as he was.

He rolled off of her with a groan and padded off to the bathroom to take a leak and a shower. When he came back, she appeared to be in a deep sleep already. Her sound machine was on, her night mask was covering her eyes, and she'd even taken a couple of sleeping pills. The sleeping pills was another thing Brandon hoped Cindy could wean herself away from once his problem with the dark was fully sorted out.

Brandon laid down on his own bed, on top of the covers. He didn't get under the covers until the middle of the night, and he slept in the nude. He reached over and turned out the light. He laid there, eyes open, slightly panting, feeling his arousal returning. His hand went to his cock.

The hand was brushed away. There was another hand on his cock. And then a mouth came down over it, and Brandon stretched and raised his arms over his head and purred. He no longer was being sucked. Someone was sitting on his belly. It was a man. His cock was slapping against Brandon's belly. Hands were taking Brandon's wrists, one after the other, and tying them off on the brass rails of the twin headboard.

Brandon sighed and moaned as the man lowered his lips on Brandon's. The lips were soon replaced by a plump cock, and Brandon's mouth was as open to that as he had been to the tongue that preceded it.

At length, the probing, hard cock was replaced by a ball gag and Brandon's hips were being raised with broad hands palming and spreading his buttocks. The cock slowly entered his channel, the going being tough because it was so thick. It entered and entered and entered, Brandon's hips being further raised on top of strong thighs as knees moved under the small of his back.

Brandon moaned and groaned. He dug his heels into the mattress, and when the deep, long-stroking started, he started a counter rhythm all his own against the stroking of the cock, using his feet for leverage.

When Cindy woke in the morning's light and pulled off her sleeping mask, she looked down to watch the bobbing of Brandon's head as he sucked on her nipples. She moved her hands to the small of his back and held him to her, enjoying the coordination of the bunching of the muscles at the base of his back, running onto his buttocks, with the rhythm of the fuck deep inside her.

She didn't know what was making Brandon so randy of late. But she certainly was benefiting from it. She reached over and took the thick, slickened dildo off her nightstand, and Brandon lurched and groaned as she reached around and worked it into his ass.

This was a fetish of his that had started even before they were married. She was long past trying to figure out why ass play with a dildo made Brandon extra horny during their sex. All that mattered to her was that it did.

* * * *

"Now, remember, Brandon," Dr. Milton was saying as he sat next to where Brandon was stretched out on a backless and armless couch, "As you drift into that world of pleasure and security, you will forget the dark as being a place of fear and confinement. You will think of it as a world of pleasure and freedom—freedom to express yourself and take your full pleasures."

Brandon's body was relaxing. He was drifting off as Dr. Milton's singsong voice helped him to move to that other world—a world of dark, but a world without fear, without inhibitions, of pure pleasure.

Milton continued droning on for a few minutes, listening for the shallow breathing, the slight pant—the pant of arousal that Milton himself had created in this luscious, young, hard-bodied man lolling on his couch.

"It's dark and getting darker, much darker." This wasn't so, the room was in full light. But Milton was making it so in

Brandon's mind. "You are moving to that fully free pleasure world."

Brandon was laying on his belly, fully stretched on the couch, totally relaxed, a sensuous smile on his face and a bit of drool. He had raised his hips a bit and was slowing rubbing his basket against the leather of the couch.

Milton smiled, stood up from his chair, and moved around the room, turning off lights. He went to the windows and closed the blinds. It was almost pitch black in the room. He stripped off his trousers and briefs and then returned to the couch and pulled Brandon's trousers off his legs.

He stood there beside the couch, working up his cock. Brandon turned his head toward him and sighed, and Milton slipped the cock between the young man's lips.

Ten minutes later he was straddling Brandon's pelvis with his knees, riding his ass, while Brandon gripped the legs of the couch and moaned and pumped his pelvis back onto the doctor's cock. Fifteen minutes later, the doctor let out a little grunt and came. He rose off Brandon, let Brandon clean his cock with his mouth. Then he pulled his briefs and trousers back on and went to the door to the waiting room.

The same man who had been there the previous day and who had since heard—if not really paid attention to—an art movie in a nearby movie house came in, handed the doctor a tidy sum of money.

He removed and carefully folded his business suit and laid it on a chair. He walked over to the couch and reached for Brandon's ankles and turned the young man on his back. Brandon looked up at him—in the darkness—with a dreamy smile and hooded eyes of already being satiated, but ready for more.

The man was already hard, having let his mind go over this scene all the time he was in the waiting room and listening to Dr. Milton's grunts and groans and Brandon's little cries of the taking.

He spread-eagled Brandon's legs and thrust inside him. Brandon arched his back, clawed at the leather of the sofa, and moaned his new acceptance—his embracing—of the dark.

Remembering Miles

I hadn't seen Cousin Miles for nearly twenty years, and he looked more like it had been thirty. He looked so defeated and withdrawn into himself. And my memories were of a vibrant athlete. He wasn't really a cousin in the blood-relative sense. Uncle John and Aunt Frieda had adopted both him and his sister, Mandy, because they couldn't have any of their own. You could have told he wasn't really related to us. We are Mediterranean, not so tall, with olive skin and dark hair and eyes, and Miles was a Nordic blond giant. Mandy was Korean, so that was another slice altogether.

We were at a family reunion in a small town in Missouri southwest of Springfield—where my mother's ancestors somehow landed from "the old country" right before the Civil War. We'd picked this time and place to meet in the first real reunion of one aging generation and my not-so-young cousins and all of our children because the family house—where Uncle John and Aunt Frieda had lived—was soon to be knocked down in favor of an access road to a new elementary school. No one in my family had lived in the old white, boxy Victorian house for a couple of decades. It had been a B&B most of that time. But being a B&B now made it an ideal place for us to meet and steep ourselves in fleeting family nostalgia.

Uncle John was nearly ten years older than my mother. Both of them were gone now. Frieda was still with us; she handled logistics because she had just moved across town, whereas the rest of her generation had moved away as quickly as possible. My family had bounced from West Coast to East Coast, without a stop in between in Missouri. My father didn't think there was much worth seeing other than tornadoes in the middle of the country.

That doesn't mean we never stopped in Missouri on our moves between the coasts, however. Before I was twelve, we probably stopped there three or four times. And after the first time, I always looked forward to a weekend or week in that old white Victorian house. It wasn't because of the house or even that I was that tired of driving by the time we hit Missouri. It was because of Miles.

Miles was eight years older than I was, but he was always home when we visited his parents, even the last time when he was close to graduating college. And to me he was a god. He was always smiling and willing to play with my brother and sisters and me—active games like volleyball and kickball and touch football out on the extensive, green-grass side yard of my uncle's house. He was tall and athletic, and when I was introduced to Greek mythology, I equated him with Apollo. He could play football and basketball and did so for his high school team—and then basketball for the University of Missouri, where he studied music and trained to become a high school band director himself.

Sometime during the second visit, I discovered that I was in love with him. I was only about ten, so I had no idea what that meant. I just knew that there was no one else in the world who made me more happy than he did and that I wanted to somehow zip up in height and dye my hair blond—which I did in high school—and not just be with Miles, but to *be* Miles.

On the third visit, when I was twelve and he was in college, I got the obsession that he loved me too. Not like he loved the other cousins—simply because they were related to him, but because I was someone special to him. Later in life when I overheard my parents talking about Miles—and seeming to be worried about something—I heard my mother say that he treated each and every one of his students like they were special. My father had snorted and said something under his breath, which led to a chill between my parents that lasted two days. But I was affronted by that remark. I didn't want a Miles who treated all of his students like they were special. I wanted a Miles who treated just me as special. And that last summer we visited Missouri while Miles was still there he did, indeed, make me feel special.

In volleyball or kickball he was always there, backing me up, making sure I was in place to return the ball. He didn't show that he could outshine me—which of course he could—but it was more like he was enabling me. I'd feel the touch of his hand on my arm, guiding me toward where he instinctively knew the ball was coming, and I'd move there. But I would be more thrilled that he touched me than that I got the ball returned.

Once while we were playing kickball, the ball went off into a copse of trees at the edge of the lot, where a town-owned wooded area started, and we found ourselves facing each other, panting, around behind a tree, where the ball had rolled. We were both hidden from the field, and just standing there, breathing hard, and looking at each other. And just for a second, I thought that something was going to happen. I didn't know at the time what that was, but I built on that in my dreams. And as I became older, I began to make something sexual out of— something I intellectually accepted wasn't there but something that, emotionally, I wanted to have been there.

I think that's why when I myself was in college, I permitted myself to be seduced by Sam Strickler. He was a tall, Nordic blond football player. I was smaller and more wiry, swifter of foot really, so my sport was soccer. But we'd often be in the locker room together, showering, after practice, and Sam showed special interest in me. I was attracted to him too. Not because I thought of myself as gay at the time or even that there was any special attraction to Sam himself. He was really the arrogant type, and I was to find that it was all about the hunt with him. I was just what he wanted as long as he didn't yet have me. But not long after I'd let him seduce me, he was looking beyond me to his next conquest. I'm convinced that I went with him because he was a substitute for my memories of Miles. He was tall, blond, blue-eyed, and well built.

I didn't have any serious gay experiences after that, not counting a bit of groping, and an unfortunate spring break weekend in Florida that I blame on alcohol, but I always kept in the back of my mind what experience I'd had—which I always tagged with an image of Miles—and I intellectually accepted that everyone probably was basically bisexual and that I just chose for now not to practice anything but the heterosexual element of it.

I married Barbara out of college, and we had our allotted older boy and younger girl and drifted into normal suburban existence.

And then we started to get e-mails about the old family home in Missouri being taken down and wouldn't it be nice if the whole family could convene there in the summer for a reunion? I didn't think we could get away or that it would be a good vacation for the kids, just sitting in an old house in a nowhere town and listening to old folks reminisce. Barbara, however, said it was a great opportunity for the kids to meet family members they'd never known before and that I'd always regret not having been there to see the old homestead for a last time. So we went.

I didn't recognize who Miles was for the first two days. There simply were too many people there and he had simply changed too much. The group was too large to all stay in the B&B. This situation was partially addressed by tents erected in the side yard—Frieda's idea—where the kids of the family camped out, most of them loving the idea, and the adults taking turns staying out there with them. And then some of the adults, those without children, stayed in one of two motels nearby. Barbara and I had a room in the B&B. Since Frieda declared that men and women would stay in the tents with the kids on alternate nights, though, Barbara and I didn't occupy our B&B room together when either of us had kiddy patrol duty.

During the day we all just sort of milled around the old Victorian house or went off on excursions in small groups. The family had originally lived outside the town, so there was an excursion to the acreage that had been the original family farm.

And to the old schoolhouse, the walls of which were still there, even if the roof had caved in. And, of course to the graveyard. There even were feints toward the town's old, dying center, for tours on what once was open and what building was what a hundred years ago. Barbara and the kids went on some of these jaunts. I didn't go on many. The town had been robust when I had visited here as a child. The roof had still been on the old two-room schoolhouse my great grandfather and his ten siblings had all sat in, together, in an amalgamation of class years. I didn't really want to see the town in decline. I think I had dragged my feet about coming to the reunion at all because I didn't want to know the old Victorian house was coming down.

A gaggle of older generation women took up squatters rights in the B&B front room and chattered incessantly about family lore, and I found it comforting to go in there occasionally, sit on the periphery, and let anecdotes that I had usually only half remembered roll over me.

One afternoon, with my family off with some others from the younger generation in search of a McDonalds—they had to go all the way into Springfield to find one—I wandered into the parlor. I'd been upstairs taking a nap to recover from tent duty the previous night and the impossibility of getting one tent quiet before another one erupted. I had been dumb to think the kids would be bored coming to this reunion; they were having a ball with their second cousins. The nap was the reason I wasn't on the McDonald's search. I could have used a Big Mac right about then myself.

As I sat in the corner of the parlor, looking through an old, yellowed *Saturday Evening Post*, I noticed that the chatter between my aunts Peggy and Helen and a couple of older women cousins and a few in-laws and out-laws I'd have trouble dredging up names for had become quite hushed. Only Helen's fleeting looks beyond the parlor door and the front hall toward the dining room drew my attention there too.

A sad-looking man who appeared to be in his forties, gaunt and trembly of hands, was sitting at one of the tables in the dining room, playing solitaire. I'd seen him a couple of times earlier in the two days we'd been there, but he always seemed to be detached from the group, standing a bit aside, eyes cast down, and a bit hunched over. He was tall, but he looked like his clothes were a couple of sizes too big for him.

"It's such a pity," I heard Peggy say in hushed tones. "He really does look ill. Frieda had mentioned something about it—but you know how she just brushes by the subject."

"I'm surprised he came." That was Helen speaking, again in a stage whisper that reached me but probably not across the hall into the dining room.

"He comes to see Frieda," an unidentified younger woman said. She had been introduced to me as the wife of a distant cousin who I think lived on a farm nearby. It certainly seemed she was a local. She was one of the women who was taking charge of the arrangements and activities. "She's in the home now, you know, and her house is sold. But Miles comes from Springfield at least once a month to see her."

The name "Miles" hit me hard. My eyes darted to the other room, and after considerable reconstruction effort, I was able to recognize Miles emerging somehow, forlornly, from inside the body hunched over the card table.

"That has got to have been recent," Helen murmured. "You know what Frieda thought about the man he was living with."

"He was probably a very nice man, Helen," Aunt Peggy said. Her lips were pursed in such a way to covey that she could go either way on whether that was true depending on where the conversation went from there. "Times were just different in those days. I know John and Frieda's hearts were broken that Miles never married. But . . . well, times were much different fifteen years ago. That's all I can say."

"He started coming after his partner died," the local relative said. "And Frieda seems to get a lot of comfort from him now. It's really too bad about him, though. I'm not sure who will go first now, Frieda or him. I've always said that the worst tragedy for a parent is to outlive your children. What with Mandy and that tornado. That was such a terrible thing. Now all Frieda has is Miles. But for how long, one must wonder."

"That's so true, Susan," Peggy said. "Frieda really started going downhill when Mandy was killed in that tornado."

So, the local relative's name was Susan. I'd have to try to remember that. And, yes, there was quite a to do when Mandy got tossed across town inside that single-wide trailer by a tornado. That, of course, had just given substance to my dad's aversion to ever living in the Midwest. I remember him saying more than once that tornados were the only entertainment going in the center of the country and that there wasn't a thing fun about them. Much more was made of Mandy's death than of Miles's partner's death, I now remember, and they'd happened at about the same time.

Over the years, I had gradually gleaned from my parents' guarded conversations that Miles was living with a man in Springfield. Miles was a band teacher in a high school there and taught private lessons. And he was living with an older businessman. The situation was whispered around the family and, because Uncle John and Aunt Frieda obviously were devastated by it, no one openly spoke of it. Miles had been a golden boy. His adoptive parents would have done anything for him and had such high expectations for him. Obviously teaching in high school and living with an older man wasn't anywhere to be found on their expectations list.

When Miles's partner died, the buzz in the family hit a new level, but it was composed mainly of innuendo and, truth be known, relief.

I wasn't relieved, though. The death brought back into my mind and emotions feelings for Miles—and what they had led to in my own life. I was embarrassed and felt guilty, without even fully intellectualizing what I should be feeling guilty about. And I felt a profound sadness for Miles. While initially shocked that he was gay and wondering if he had been actively gay when I had come in contact with him, I had secretly saluted his decision to live his life as he wished. I thought he was being true to himself, which was more than what I saw going on in my extended family—and was what, I'm sure, goes on in most extended families—the two-faced treatment of each other. The sweet talk to the faces of others and the gossip, criticism, and twittering behind their backs.

At the time of his partner's death, I found out what Miles's address was—which wasn't easy without revealing why I wanted it—and sent Miles a condolence card and a brief note that I hoped read as genuinely sympathetic as I felt. Miles wrote back, telling me that my card meant a lot to him—that I was the only one in the family who had mentioned the death to him at all. No one from his family had come to the funeral.

We exchanged letters for a few months, but I got wrapped up in courting Barbara where we both worked and I'm afraid I let the contact down at my end.

And there he was, sitting in the dining room, playing solitaire. I knew I would set the family women to buzzing if I got up and went in to talk to him.

But I did just that.

He looked up, startled, when I approached the table.

"Is it OK for me to sit . . . Miles? It is Miles, isn't it?"

"Yes, of course," he said in almost a whisper. He looked into the living room, as did I. The women were watching us intently—without looking directly at us, of course. "But maybe you don't really want to, David."

"You know who I am?"

"Yes, of course. You're on Facebook. I've followed you and your family through recent years."

"But you didn't ask to be friends."

"No. I didn't. I didn't know how you would respond . . . the family situation being what it is."

"I'm sorry you felt that way, Miles. I wouldn't for the world have wanted you to feel that way. I'd like to talk with you—become acquainted again. But maybe you'd be more comfortable if we took a walk."

"Yes, I think so. You can wait for me out on the front porch and I'll come out in a moment."

"No, let's leave together. Give them something to talk about."

He gave me a surprised look laced with gratitude. But he stood up from the table, with a look of pain at the movement shooting briefly across his face, and we walked out of the house and toward the woods beyond the field of tents, side by side.

* * * *

"Are you living alone, or have you—?"

"Yes, I'm still alone," Miles answered. "After Paul, there didn't seem to be anything else for me. I'd lost all ability to find someone, and scrutiny in the school system made any looking dangerous."

We had walked into the woods on a path that I hadn't remembered as being there in my youth. But we hadn't been able to go too far into the forest before Miles was winded and had to stop. Where we stopped seemed to be at the same tree where we'd paused briefly to pick up the kickball so many years ago. But I was probably just being overdramatic in thinking that.

"You do know what it meant that I was living with Paul, don't you?" Miles asked. "That we were lovers."

"Yes, of course," I answered.

"And you're still talking with me? You walked into the woods with me?"

"Yes. It doesn't matter to me."

"It seems to matter to the rest of the family."

"Well bully for them then. But I'm surprised you came to the reunion. I know you've been cut off from the family. I'm just sorry I stopped exchanging letters with you. I didn't mean to. Life just caught up with me."

"I understand perfectly. You had a normal life to establish. I've seen photos of your wife and children. I envy you your normal life. I would have liked to have had children. But, as a teacher, I guess I managed to do that anyway. I didn't really want to come to the reunion, but my mother wanted me to come. I've been such a disappointment to her that I owed bringing her over here every day. It's the least I could do." He smiled wanly at me. He was sitting on a log and I was standing near him, my foot raised and resting farther down on the log.

"You envy me? That's funny. I've always envied you."

"Me?"

"Yes. You know we all thought you were a god when we were growing up. You were so handsome and capable and always smiling. And you were a cousin, but you were older than we were, able to do all of those things we wouldn't be able to do for years."

"And then I shocked and disappointed you."

233

"Not a bit of it. I continued to envy you. You were making choices and following them, come what may. You were being brave and living life on your own terms."

"My, you were idealistic."

"No. I was in love. Would it shock you to know that I wanted that sort of attention from you—or that I tried it out when I was in college?"

"Yes, of course," Miles said after a long pause. And I could tell from the expression on his face that indeed it did. "And you acted on it?"

"Yes, with someone who looked just like you. But he wasn't as nice as you." I was touching his knee with my hand.

"I think you are just feeling sorry for me, David. I know I must look like a sad wreck now. That's very kind of you . . . but I think we should be going back to the house now. Mother will be tired and wanting to go home."

He struggled to get up from the log and I reached down to help him. But he shrank away from me.

"I'm sorry that I said anything, Miles. I went beyond bounds. But it's such a surprise to see you, and I've held that in for so long."

"It's OK . . . it's OK. But let's go back now."

We didn't say anything on the way back, and he walked, stooped over a few paces ahead of me. I didn't try to come up to his level. All of my life I'd tried to come up to his level, but I knew that it wasn't to be.

As we emerged from the woods, we saw his mother, Frieda, standing on the porch, looking very concerned. And the curtains in the parlor window were shaking enough for me to know that there were several sets of eyes lurking just beyond them. I almost laughed out loud.

Sensing the attention as well, Miles leaned away from me. But I locked my arm in his and pulled him closer as we walked back to civilization.

* * * *

Miles lay there on his back on the bed in his motel room, moaning and looking up into my face with an expression of wonder, arousal, and, slightly of concern, as if he just couldn't believe that I was crouched over him, my fists buried in the mattress at either side of his shoulders, gazing intently down into his eyes, and slowly riding his cock.

He was longer and thicker than I had imagined he'd be—certainly bigger than Sam Strickler had been—and I felt totally liberated in being able to do what I knew I'd wanted to do with Miles for decades.

There had been no problem being absent from the B&B this evening; Barbara was spending the night with the kids in the tent. And if she'd asked, I already had an excuse ready of not being in the mood to be with the family for supper and having gone to a local diner. It had been harder to wheedle the list of accommodations out of Susan without revealing I wanted to know the motel and room number where I could find Miles—but I managed.

After a quick meal at the diner, I was at Miles's motel room door. He dropped his jaw when he answered the door. He already was in his sleeping bottoms, and his body was still in good condition despite how gaunt his wasting disease had made him. He stood there, momentarily, not knowing what to do or say.

"Hadn't we better go in?" I said. "I think some other members of the family are staying here too."

That set him in motion. He drew me into the room and then, in shock, I think, let me lead him to the bed and push him down on his back. He moaned and started to cry softly as I knelt over him on the bed and took his cock in my mouth.

I stayed the night and we fucked over and over again, with him eventually taking charge and huddling over me, embracing me into his body, and plowing me hard and deep.

* * * *

Eight months after the reunion, the news shot around the family that Miles had died of a heart attack. I mourned him, but having had that one night with him had released guilt and tensions within me. He had wanted to apologize, thinking he had seduced me, but I assured him that we had just taken care of what was unfinished business for both of us. We resumed our letter exchanges—by e-mail now—for the remainder of the time we had, although we never reached for the level of passion in them that we had attained in fact. They were very cousinly exchanges. But I can only hope that they meant as much to him as they did to me.

My biggest regret was that I had no one to send condolences to when he died, because Aunt Frieda had died the month before Miles did. I'm sure, though, that she died happy that she went before Miles did. I had talked to her the last day of the reunion, and I was heartened to know that, in her last months, she loved her son as much as she ever had. I think Miles was comforted when I assured him in my next e-mail to him that she did so. I'm not sure she ever felt comfortable enough to tell him that directly herself, though.

The Compassionate Reporter

"Lou is chasing another story down, Gavin, and this one doesn't look like more than a short paragraph in the local news section. So if you've got an hour or two, could you check this out? And if you don't have an hour or two, I'd like to know what you're doing; what you're working on now was due on my desk an hour ago."

The city editor handed Gavin a telephone message form.

"OK, boss. I'll catch lunch while I'm out if that's OK with you."

"Yeah, sure. Just don't get too involved in this one, Gavin. It's not worth more than a paragraph, even if that. A short paragraph. No going after a feature series."

"Sure, boss."

"I mean it, Gavin. You're a good writer, but what you need to learn beyond the universal getting your copy in on deadline is in determining what a story can be milked for. You tend to get too wrapped up in it. That's one reason I'm giving you this one—to see how well you can stay within the bounds of what the story is worth. This one probably isn't worth anything. That's a hint for you. If you come back and don't even have a paragraph, I'll know you're learning."

Gavin waited for the city editor to waltz off to shake some other reporter's tree before he scowled and read the telephone message. He knew that the editor was just doing his job. But how long did they need to dwell on the feature series he'd proposed to do over in the Deer Haven subdevelopment about toxic groundwater before someone pointed out that a car wash had been put in at the strip mall just up the creek from the housing area?

He read the message. It was from some guy saying the Proctor Street area was unsafe because he'd gotten robbed and assaulted there. Yeah, that's what the Proctor area is good for, Gavin thought, as he unfolded himself from behind his desk and headed for the stairs. He didn't think he'd have trouble keeping this to a paragraph, if that. And then maybe the city editor would get off his back about the botched feature idea.

* * * *

"Hi, I'm from *The Sentinel*. Name's Gavin Grimes. You called and said you wanted to report something about an assault and robbery?" Gavin was swinging the telephone form in front of the face of what looked like a frightened little rabbit, in human form, at the door of the third floor walkup. From the bruising on the young man's face and arms, Gavin was assured he was at the right apartment door.

The young man, at least partially Hispanic, Gavin thought, but quite good-looking and well proportioned, even if small of stature, stood there for another moment, a deer-in-the-headlights look about him. On his almost beautiful face, with the lock of curly black hair hanging down over an eyebrow, the bruises perhaps looked like more of an outrage than they really were. Gavin's sense of compassion—along with a much baser instinct—flipped in, and, despite everything his editor had told him, both Gavin's parenting instincts and his nose for a story began to twitch.

238

"Could I come in?" he said when the young man didn't answer. "You did want to talk to someone on the paper about your problem, didn't you?"

Gavin wondered if the young man could speak English. He started to see how much of his high school Spanish he could dredge up. But then the young man saved him.

"Yes, I'm Diego Kent. I don't know if this is a good—"

"Yeah, talk to him. And remember to tell him like I told you." The voice was deep and gruff and the big bruiser of a guy in a brown UPS uniform who materialized from the shadows of the interior matched the voice.

Gavin stood aside as the big guy pushed past Diego and into the hallway and then clattered down the stairs.

Diego looked shyly at Gavin and then stood aside, the gesture pulling Gavin into a small living room with a mismatched collection of grimy, overstuffed sofa and chairs that looked like cats had had a ball clawing and pulling stuffing out. Adjacent to the living room was a dining el, with a set of steel-legged table and chairs with red laminate and vinyl upholstery that immediately made Gavin think of the 1950s. Sharp assessor that he was, Gavin immediately noted—helped by dust marks that made a large square on a drab wall—that there probably had once been a gigantic flat-screen TV on one wall of the living room that now was completely bare.

Diego motioned to the sofa, which dipped at one end, but not too precariously. Gavin sat there and took out his notebook. Diego went to an upholstered chair and dropped more than sank into it. He gave a little moan as he did so. Gavin snapped his notebook shut.

"You're in pain. What have you done for that?"

Diego looked at him with a stupid expression on his face. "Done?"

"Did you put ice on the bruises or take any sort of pain reliever or use any ointment to deaden the pain?"

"No. Germane said I should sleep it off and then call you guys this morning. He's pissed about the TV and computer being taken."

"OK, just a few minutes. I'm going out to get something for that bruising. I'll be right back."

Gavin had seen a mom and pop convenience store on the corner of Proctor and 10th Street as he had driven up. He clumped down the stairs and across the street. They had Tylenol and Bengay. He didn't know how much good either would do, but they were better than nothing. And he got a pack of frozen peas out of a freezer. It was a little late for that too, but, again, it was better than not doing anything. In less than twenty minutes, he was back in the apartment.

"Where's the worst bruising?"

"My ribs I think," Diego answered.

"Well, take the T off and come over to the dining room table. Get a glass of water from the kitchen on your way. Take the Tylenol first."

Gavin watched Diego walk to the kitchen, which was just a space off the dining area separated by an eating counter, and then into the dining area. Gavin was concerned about the young man's health, yes, but he was quite aware that he was finding Diego very attractive—and arousing—as well. Something about a young, beautiful man suffering brought out conflicting instincts in Gavin.

"Here are two Tylenol," Gavin said. "Take a couple of these every four hours or so. And slip that T off . . . oh, god, that is a bad bruise on your side. Here sit in this chair and put this bag of frozen peas against that bruise under your eye. I'll rub some Bengay on the chest bruise and then you can hold the cold pack against that for a while too."

Gavin's hand trembled as he gently rubbed the Bengay into a large bruise below Diego's right pectoral.

"How did you get this bruise?"

"He . . . they punched me in the face and I fell against the coffee table in there."

"And then they took the TV and the computer?"

"Yes."

"How many were there?"

"Two. Maybe three."

"How did they get in? Was the door locked?"

"I don't know how they got in. The door, I suppose." There was a pause. "But maybe someplace else. Germane says it's important to say the door was locked. I was asleep on the sofa."

"Did you recognize them?"

"Uhh, no."

"And then they were gone. They just knocked you aside, took the TV and computer, and left?"

There was a pause.

"They just left, Diego?" Gavin could feel Diego trembling under his gliding fingers. He was trembling too. He didn't know why Diego started trembling at that question. But Gavin was all too aware why he was trembling. The young man was perfection itself. Gavin had a weakness for small, dark men.

"Germane wants me to say more than one did it. He says three. I did say there were three, didn't I?"

"Did what, Diego? Did they do more than beat and rob you?"

"They took me into the bedroom."

Oh, my god, Gavin thought. "It must have been—"

"Germane takes me into the bedroom," Diego said in a small voice. He had raised a hand and put it over Gavin's on top of his bruise.

"I don't mind being taken into the bedroom." Diego said. "You're being very nice to me. And you are very nice. Nobody did anything else for me. You went out and got medicine."

"Diego."

"Would you take me into the bedroom? But be good to me? Germane, he . . . I so wish someone would be good to me."

Gavin couldn't help himself. He moved behind Diego and moved his free hand over Diego's shoulder and laid it over the young man's nipple. Diego raised his face to Gavin and Gavin leaned over and they kissed.

* * * *

Diego was laying on his good side on the double bed in the bedroom. Gavin didn't know the last time the sheets had been changed on the bed and he didn't particularly care. His eyes were held by Diego's, watching how expressive the young man was in showing how Gavin's cock was pleasuring him.

Gavin was being as careful as he could be. Diego had requested that they be able to maintain eye contact, so the young man was on his side, with his torso bent so that his head and shoulders were flat on the surface of the bed. Gavin had one of Diego's legs running up his torso and the other one was bent, with Diego leveraging off the floor with his toes. Gavin was slowly pumping the young man, being careful not to worry his bruises any more than necessary.

The moaning from the young Hispanic was very arousing to Gavin. He ejaculated much faster than he had wanted too. Then, while still inside Diego, he encased the young man's hard cock in with a fist and brought him to a spouting as well. All the time Diego maintained eye contact, telling Gavin how much he was enjoying this slow, sensual fuck.

"Tell me what you told the police about the robbery and assault, Diego. I'll write it up for the newspaper. But I need more information."

The two were entwined on the bed, Diego still sighing from the encounter. Gavin felt the young man stiffen when he asked that question.

"We haven't gone to the police yet," he said. "Germane says we need to have something to push them. That the police will just say we shouldn't be living in this neighborhood. Or . . . or that Germane did it. He said we need to have something in the newspaper."

"Them? Not the police. Ah . . . do you mean the insurance company?"

"Uh."

"Ah, I see."

"Diego." The voice was deep, commanding.

Both Gavin and Diego looked up. Diego was trembling again, and Gavin couldn't claim he wasn't.

Germane was standing in the doorway, scowling.

"I think you'd better leave, Mr. Reporter."

Gavin didn't wait for another invitation. He rose from the bed, gathered up his clothes, and brushed through the doorway past Germane. He quickly dressed in the living room, and stumbled out of the apartment and down the stairs. Not until he hit the bottom of the stairs did he gather enough wits about himself to worry about Diego. He climbed half way back up the stairs and called out. "I'll write it up. Just like Diego said it. It'll be in the paper. It's OK. It's not Diego's fault."

Then, knowing full well why Diego had those bruises, he ran out into the street and looked wildly about, not, at that instant, remembering where he'd left his car.

* * * *

Gavin was sitting at his desk, trying to decide what he could write up on the robbery and theft that would meet Germane's need but still get past the city editor. He was sweating, almost to the edge of tears. He had left Diego there to face the music alone. He felt like a worm, like the lowest of the low. He could have gone back, but he didn't. He had reasoned that the newspaper coverage was what Germane wanted, so that not going back but coming here instead was the right thing to do.

He'd gotten all the way back to *The Sentinel*'s office before he realized what he'd seen leaning up against the wall in the bedroom. At the time, he'd been too excited about getting inside Diego that it hadn't registered. But now he realized that he'd seen a large flat-screen TV and a computer leaning up against the bedroom wall.

He was taken out of his misery on what to write fairly quickly—but only to be dropped into a larger misery.

"Is that the man who beat and sexually assaulted you— and then stole your TV set and computer?" The sound of the voice cut all the way across the city room from the door to the hallway. The hubbub in the room died immediately, and all faces, including Gavin's turned toward the doorway.

Gavin had difficulty focusing, but the softly spoken, "Yes, sir," galvanized his attention. He knew the voice.

The policemen in the doorway was pointing at Gavin. Standing next to him, his face even more battered than the last time Gavin had seen him, stood Diego. He was crying.

Gavin pushed the delete button on his computer. Was it all in the plan even for Diego to get him into the bedroom and the bed, Gavin wondered. For some reason, he felt more hurt that that might be the case than that he'd been played to support the theft and beating story.

Germane was going to get a bigger story published now than Gavin had been writing, he knew. But it wouldn't be Gavin who wrote the story.

Back Where . . .

I rolled over in the bed, reaching for Esteban, but he wasn't there, setting off in me a mild zing of irritation. He'd gone to sleep last night while I was fucking him and now he wasn't there at all in the morning. This brought the decision I had to make back to mind and was, perhaps, yet another nail in the decision—two decisions actually. I had an opportunity to head up the Radio y Televisión Martí radio transmission operations from Marathon Key targeting to Cuba what we called information and the Cuban government called American propaganda. So that was one decision. But another decision was whether to ask Esteban to go with me or to encourage him to stay in Miami. It's unlikely the *Miami Herald* would have anything for him to do on Marathon Key.

I smelled the coffee brewing out in the kitchen. That might have been what woke me up to begin with. Groaning, I crawled out of bed and stumbled toward the shower. I had a full day's work to wedge into a half day in the office before I started out driving from Miami down to Marathon Key and then on, the next day, down to Key West to check out our Cuban radio-monitoring activity down there. And I hadn't even packed yet.

I'd needed a good fuck last night or this morning. I was strung out, and I needed something to siphon off some of the tension. Esteban had let me down. Esteban had been letting me down a lot lately—not least by letting himself go. We'd been together, what, fifteen years now? And it had only been of late that he'd slowed down. And it was showing in his waistline and the effect of gravity on his face.

This was all bringing my decision to a head. Maybe I was in a rut. Maybe Esteban was getting too old and slow and uninteresting for me. Something to think about. This had a great deal to do with going down to see the operation at Marathon Key. I didn't really have to see that operation for a decision on whether I wanted the job there. It was the further trip down to Key West that was motivating me to take this exploratory journey. Key West was less than fifty miles from Marathon. I could live there and just do with the overnight facilities at the Marathon office when I couldn't be more than an hour from work. Sometimes it took me more than an hour through traffic just to drive to work across Miami from my apartment.

Key West was where it was at; Key West was where it was happening. Life was short, and I had a lot of delicious young men to go through yet.

I started to include that I wasn't getting any younger, but that gave me a twinge. I looked into the mirror over the bathroom sink and then at myself full length in the tall mirror on the bathroom side of the door, and I choked down those words. I looked damn good. And I worked hard to stay that way— unlike what Esteban had been doing of late, whenever he took the time to try to keep in shape.

Esteban was just pouring the OJ and coffee and setting out an omelet and toast when I got to the kitchen.

"Gotta gobble fast," I said as I sat down to it. "Gotta pack. I'll be leaving from the office."

"You're all packed," Esteban said, as he sat down in a chair across from me and looked at me. I hadn't told him anything about the Marathon Key operation offer, but I could tell that he sensed there was something going on. "I did that last evening while you were on the computer—you'd left most of what you'll need out on the chair in the bedroom. I packed after I got the Jag gassed up for your trip."

"I'm packed? I wanted the glen plaid suit—"

"I'd taken it to the cleaners," Esteban said. "You somehow struggled with some marinara sauce at the paper's annual banquet last weekend, so I took it out to have it cleaned. Got it back yesterday afternoon, though, and it's packed with all of that other stuff you put out. You're taking an awful lot of party clothes for a business trip, I must say."

"Have you seen the radio script I brought home last night for editing? I thought I left it by the computer, but when I looked for it—"

"It's in your briefcase. I edited it for you. It's a good piece, but you really should read those aloud more when you write them, Carlos. It's not like written essays. Certain words don't come out right in spoken form when they are put together."

"You're always saying that."

"Because it's always true. I've been editing your radio copy for what? More than fifteen years now. I edited your copy before we hooked up—before I left the station and went to the paper."

"Yeah, yeah. I picked you because of your editing abilities."

The kitchen went silent. Esteban gave me a hurt look and went to the kitchen stove, turning away from me, and moved pots around in meaningless patterns on the stove top.

Embarrassed at having said that, and not meaning it, of course—we'd really had something going, at least until late—I swallowed my coffee in big gulps and stood to gather everything I needed and hit the road. He was so sensitive, getting to be high maintenance.

He wasn't at the door when I left; he was still puttering and pouting at the stove, facing away from me. I was relieved, really. We had a rule that when either of us left the apartment, the other one would be at the door for a kiss. Esteban was pretty adamant about that ritual. The man he'd been living with before he had hooked up with me had left one morning without a kiss, was run over by a hit-and-run driver, and died without ever

247

returning. Esteban always said we needed to treat even the most temporary good-bye as if it was our last. But I wasn't in the mood for that sort of contact this morning; I thought that maybe all he had to do was look into my eyes and he'd know where I really was going—and why.

At the door, not wanting to leave in silence, I called out. "I think we're out of red wine."

"I'll stop and get some more on the way home tonight," he answered without turning.

"Well, I'm off."

"Have a good trip."

It was almost as if he knew what I was thinking about our relationship and how this trip might end it.

There was no kiss at the door.

* * * *

It had been a good decision to drive my own car down— well, Esteban's and my Jaguar convertible. This was an encumbrance I guessed I might have to face—who got the Jaguar. But I was the one who had wanted to buy the Jag. I had the top down all the way down the key-hopping Route 1 from Marathon down to Key West, and every cute guy I passed coming into Key West was attracted by the Jag and then gave me the eye. I loved getting the eye; it told me I still had what it took. I'd have a ball here, I just knew I would if I could keep Ramon Famosa off the scent.

Ramon was the sole employee of our Key West outpost office. Its facilities included an office and a house on the government's Truman Annex at the very southeast tip of Key West—and thus also of the United States. He recorded and translated radio broadcasts from Havana and sent the transcripts up to Miami to our studios there, where we composed radio content that responded to what Havana was saying. He also somehow managed to get some regional Cuban newspapers down there that we didn't always get up in Miami.

I had been glad when the office sent Ramon down here. Otherwise I might have gotten into trouble. Ramon was quite the looker, and if he'd shown the slightest bit of interest in me, I think I would have gone off the deep end. Office romances were the kiss of death in Radio Martí, however—and there was Esteban. I don't know how it came about that Ramon was sent down here; it had seemed to have been an overnight "now you see him/now you don't" move at the time.

But as good looking as he was, he would be in the way of what I wanted to do in Key West. I wanted to party and to share all of this goodness I had in me—which included, I've always been told, a cock to die for. Key West was just the playground for this sort of death. And if—I was thinking more in terms of when now—I moved to the Marathon operation, I could Key West myself away. The more serious and conventional Ramon was sort of a waste down here, I thought. Although I had overshot the Key West position some time ago, there was a time when this would have been the perfect assignment for me. Key West was one of the gay male magnets of the world.

That evening, after pretending to be fascinated by Ramon's briefing on his operations—at least as fascinated as I was with seeing him, as two years away from Miami had just made him more attractive and arousing than I'd remembered him to be—I had the hardest time breaking away from him so that I could cruise the gay bars on and off Duval Street. Ramon said he wanted to show me the night life here. I assumed he was talking sedate jazz bars, as he seemed to be crazy for that music, and this wasn't how I wanted to spend my time.

So, I told him I was tired and wanted to go back to my hotel off Mallory Square, and, eventually, he'd reluctantly let me go. He'd offered to let me stay with him in the small house we provided for him on the Truman Annex, but I wanted to wake up in someone sweet's bed, and he surely would have been shocked if I'd brought a little honey back to his place for the night.

I was driving the Jag, so I took it out to Duval and parked it on the street in front of a gay bar I'd already researched as someplace I wanted to visit.

The Bourbon Street Pub was right on Duval, and the crowd around its entrance left no doubt that it was a gay bar. I got enough cat calls when I pulled myself out of the Jag before pushing through the crowd and entering the dimly lit bar area that I knew I wouldn't be lonely tonight unless I wanted to be. It was noisy and crowded. Soft-core porn films were flashing on screens on all four walls, and the shadows on three sides of the room enveloped booths offering some semblance of privacy, although I could see from the undulating bodies there that all forms of pleasure were being explored from smoking weed to blowing cocks and even more intimate pursuits.

This was what I was looking for and this is what I loved about Key West. Anything goes there; no need for inhibitions. One of the deep-side walls was fronted its entire length with a long bar, and along this at intervals rose shiny metal poles running up from the bar top to the high ceiling. Barely legal young men in thong bikinis were playing the poles to something close to the beat of the loud, heavy-metal music.

I saddled up to a bar stool and ordered a scotch on the rocks. It had barely arrived when a young blond, with a curl hanging down over a blue eye topped by long lashes and sparkly gold shadow paint on his eyelids, insinuated himself in beside me. He was dressed in white cotton trousers and shirt, which was opened to the waist, and had a filmy blue scarf around his neck that matched the shade of his eyes.

"Buy a girl a drink?" he asked.

"Sure," I said. He was very young. Just what I was in the mood for. Esteban no longer was any sort of young.

That done, he took a sip, primping like he thought he'd learned from Bette Davis, and pulled my face down to where he could whisper in my ear.

"If you take me someplace, I'll make you a very happy man," he whispered.

"Take you someplace, huh? But I just got here, and I understand there's something called The Pile downstairs."

"You drove up in the Jaguar convertible, didn't you?"

"You noticed."

"Drive me down to the beach in your car and I'll take you to heaven."

He gave me an expert and efficient blow job in the front seat of the Jag in the parking lot of a beach at the northeast end of the key not far from the airport. Esteban actually gave better—and longer-lasting—head, but the novelty of a new, young man doing it did, indeed, take me to heaven.

"I have a room at a hotel," I said when he was done.

"Maybe I'm interested," he said. "Maybe if you do something nice for me."

"What would that be?"

"Let my friends and me borrow your Jag for a day."

I paused for several seconds. There was no way I was going to let a stranger drive off in my car. "I'll take you back to the Bourbon Street Pub," I answered. "And we'll see what is what."

Well, what was what was that the young man disappeared into the crowd when he couldn't wheedle the keys to the Jag from me. And in his wake, I looked around the room. No one else even close to my age was in there, and I was suddenly feeling out of place. The music also was so loud I couldn't think. I hit the street.

Just down the block from there, I stopped in front of a bar called KWest. I remembered the name from my research and I went in. The music was more subdued, and the place wasn't as crowded as the Bourbon Street Pub had been. The clientele looked a little older too, and the bartender, who was mouthing off to a guy at the bar, looked like he was as old as I was.

As old as I was. I thought back to the blond trick I'd just left. Jaguars are nice, but back when I was cruising the scene, no guy would look at a flash car when I was in view. There it was again. "In my day." How many years had it been since I'd even cruised a bar? Maybe five. Esteban and I had done that together for several years after we moved in together, but then we just fell out of the habit. He was a great fuck; we'd just stay home and do it when we had the time. We both had demanding careers. At some point it had just been simpler to stay home and fuck than to do all of the preliminary shopping.

Once more I went up to the bar.

"What'll it be, Pops?" the rude bartender said when I finally got his attention and he'd come over.

"Pops." The old guy had called me Pops. The guy who must be at least as old as I was.

"I don't got all day," he said. "Order a drink or take a hike."

That was my second scotch on the rocks of the evening.

There were some nice-looking guys in here. Still, I wouldn't have to worry about anyone not being of age with this crowd.

It wasn't long, though, before an Italian-looking dark-haired beauty, with an androgynous look and brilliant red lipstick, slid down the bar to perch on the stool next to mine.

"Lonely?" he asked. He had a smooth, deep baritone of a voice.

"I've been lonelier," I answered.

"Sort of quiet in here tonight."

"Yep, but I like the music here better than the last bar I was in," I responded. "That gave me a headache."

"It's a little livelier upstairs."

"Upstairs?"

"Yes, they have rooms. Would you be interested in making a little music up there tonight, darling?" He added, "Just you and me?" so I wouldn't miss the implication.

I looked him up and down. He had a good body. A lot better shape than Esteban. He was maybe in his mid twenties. I'm not sure I would have been interested at the height of my cruising days, but . . .

He leaned into me and whispered, "I'll blow you for twenty-five; we can go all the way, either of us top, for a hundred."

He wanted me to pay! God, I'd never paid for sex in my life. He was OK, but no Apollo, and he wanted me to pay him a hundred bucks for sex.

I must have been displaying a shocked expression, because he gave me a slightly irritated look and said, "It's the going rate on Duval Street, honey. It's not like you're a prime stud or anything. I see some friends at a table over there. You make up your mind while I'm still here, you let me know, ya hear?"

He pulled himself off the barstool next to me, and clumped over toward a line of tables in shadows. It was only then that I realized that he was wearing a skirt and high heels.

My emotions were mixed. He was kinkier than anything I'd ever considered before, so, on the one hand, I felt relief he'd backed off. But on the other hand, I'd never paid for sex in my life—and he'd said I wasn't a prime stud.

In front of me there was a ceiling-high mirror running behind the bar for its whole length. I looked hard at myself in the mirror. I hardly recognized the man staring back at me. That wasn't the same face I'd seen in my bathroom mirror just that morning. This was the face of that face's father.

As I stared into the mirror, though, I saw movement at the tables across the room, and, with a sense of horror, I recognized Ramon Formosa, our man in Key West. He had seen me too, and he rose and walked toward me.

He was smiling. "Hi, Carlos," he said. Then he laughed. "If you'd let me show you around the key this evening, I'd eventually have brought you here."

"Here?" I said.

"Yes, of course." There was a pause and then he laughed. "You didn't know I was gay, did you?"

"No," I murmured, still in shock.

"I'm sorry. I thought you knew. That's why I was transferred from Miami so quickly. A bit too friendly with Renata's husband. You, know, the chief Spanish linguist, Renata. But I knew you were gay too. I guess you didn't know I knew that."

"No, I didn't," I said weakly.

"Sort of too bad," he said. "You know I had a crush on you then. I would have done anything you asked of me."

"I . . . I didn't know that."

"I think I might still have a crush on you."

We fucked in his bed in the company-supplied little house on the Truman Annex. Ramon liked twisted positions— me sidesplitting him or jack hammering down into him from above with him supported on the floor on his shoulders—and he wanted it again and again, being obviously pleased at the size of me. He exhausted me, and, with him, it was I who first cried uncle and drifted off into a spent sleep. He wanted it again in the morning, and I did what I could, although my back was in pain from the calisthenics of the previous evening.

As we lay there, panting—me panting more heavily then he was—my cock still inside him as he lay cupped into my lap, he whispered something to me. I had to have him repeat it because there was a pounding in my ears still from the exertion of the fuck.

"Was I good for you?"

"Yes, of course," I said. I realized I might have been lying, though. As vigorous as the fucks had been and how insistently he asked for them to start again after we had both come, I wasn't sure I would survive a week with him. With Esteban, it was slower, more sensual. Not nearly as athletic. And after the time we had been together, we fit perfectly, each knowing what the other wanted—and when he wanted it.

"If I was in Miami, we could fuck more often," he whispered. "And isn't it true that you are on the promotion board? I sure could use a higher salary."

So.

I made my retreat as diplomatically as I could. I had planned to stay two more days in Key West, but suddenly I felt so old and out of the game. I had found out what I needed to know in Key West, but it certainly wasn't what I had thought I'd learn.

With each mile north on the Overseas Highway up the spine of the keys to Miami, I remembered yet another trait of Esteban's that was laudable and that I should have appreciated better.

"You're home early," he remarked when I came through the apartment door.

"I missed you," I said. "I found that I missed you too much."

"And the job in Marathon?" he asked.

"You knew about that? You knew I was considering taking a position in the keys?"

"Yes. Jorge at your office told me you had that opportunity."

"I can't take that job," I answered. "You're here. I can't—and won't—ask you to give up your position at the paper."

254

Estaban's face took on several expressions at once, running from shock to relief to the look of love. It took him a moment to get control of his voice because he said, "So, you're back?"

"Yes, back where I belong." I turned away from him so he couldn't see the tears of my realization of what I had almost lost swell in my eyes.

"Do you have to go into the office this afternoon?"

"No. Is the bed made?"

"Yes, of course."

"Can we muss it up?"

"Yes, of course."

About the Author

Habu is one of the pen names of a former supersonic spy jet pilot, intelligence agent, male model, movie actor, and diplomat. A wild youth in South East Asia was spent enjoying whatever sexual opportunities came his way, and much of his gay male writing is about recalling incidents from those days and inventing ones he'd perhaps have liked to experience. He now leads a very quiet and ordinary happily married family life.

An American, he is a published mainstream novelist and short story writer under another name and in another dimension of his life. He has written or cowritten (with Sabb) over 500 published short stories and nearly 100 published erotica e-books, primarily of gay fiction but also memoir, straight fiction and ménage fiction. His hand and creative writing can be seen in stories and books by habu, sr71plt, Dirk Hessian, Shabbu, and Stephen Kessel—among unrevealed others that might surprise readers. The fictionalized GM memoir *Flying High, Diving Deep* is loosely based on his life experiences. He can be found at the adults only gay male site www.BarbarianSpy.com, which he shares with Sabb and Dirk Hessian.

Our authors always like to receive feedback, and appreciate it when readers post reviews at Goodreads, and other sites.

BarbarianSpy
FOR LITERARY HEAT

Not all books listed below may currently be on release.

BOOKS BY DIRK HESSIAN
Xtreme Erotica
The King's Men
Shores of Tripoli
Prophecy of Noto
Pretender's Fate
General Erotica/Romance
Constantinople
The Beautiful Way
Blue and Gray
Colonel's Treasure
Beginning of Time
Labyrinth
BOOKS BY HABU
Gay Erotica
Memoir Faction
Flying High, Diving Deep
Xtreme Erotica
Second Coming
Vortex: Sacrificed by Curiosity
Dark Angel Sounding
General Erotica
Romance
Gotta Keep Trying
Finding Amnad
Platres Conclave
Other
Beyond the Beaded Curtain
Hard Knocks U
Habu's Christmas Balls
My Neighbour's Spa

Man's Man
Trip Money
Clint Folsom Mysteries Compendium Volume 1
Death to Blonds - Stolen Judgment (Clint Folsom Mystery)
Clint Folsom Mysteries Compendium Volume 2
Grab Bag 1
Grab Bag 2
Grab Bag 3
The Indian Doctor
Sailorboy
Home to Fire Island
The Sporting Life
Brambleton
Fetish Galore!
Choke Hold
Literary Gay Erotica
Cairo Surrender
The Handyman
Homeward Bound
Journey to Mirage
Menage Erotica
13 Ways for Halloween
Luther
The Indian Prince
BOOKS BY SHABBU
Finding Jason
Dirty Pool
Operation Black Jade
Cigars!
Angel in the Barn
Gayly Complicated
Despoiling David
The Tree of Idleness
I Met a Man
The Interview
Rough Road to Happiness

www.ingramcontent.com/pod-product-compliance
Lightning Source LLC
Chambersburg PA
CBHW020747250626
47155CB00003B/953